ALABASTER ALIBI

A ROCK SHOP MYSTERY

S. D. BROWN

ANYTIME BOOKS

ISBN 13: 978-1981467235

ISBN 10: 1981467288

Any Time Books

For Lyle

CHAPTER ONE

J asper gripped the steering wheel hard when the hitchhiker in the passenger seat pulled a Derringer Snake Eye pistol from a battered canvas bag.

This is not a good day to die, thought Jasper. *I have plans for this evening—an appointment with the Captain James Tiberius Kirk and the Reverend Jack Daniels.*

The old 1962, turquoise-colored Chevy veered into a deep rut and jerked to the right. Jasper fought the wheel. The truck swerved. Red dust swirled into the cab and with it came the dry wracking coughs of his passenger.

Jasper eyed the man half hidden under a matted mass of iron-gray dreadlocks and thought, *don't let that gun go off.* The man's clothes were so worn they matched the bleak gray of his hair in the fading light. By comparison, Jasper felt almost dapper in his blue jeans, red plaid shirt and brown herringbone Baker Boy cap.

"You know I don't like guns, Ralph," Jasper said. "Put it away."

"You'll need the protection when they come for you." Ralph's unsteady fingers fumbled with the glove box. The gun slipped and for a quarter of a second it was in free fall. Jasper stared down its barrel and hoped the safety was engaged. It clattered onto the floorboard. Nothing happened. No explosion.

Jasper breathed out.

After three attempts Ralph got the little door open, retrieved the pistol and stashed it under a map. He slid a box of bullets under the seat. "Safety first. Keep 'em separate."

"I don't need . . ." Jasper started to say, but stopped before delivering his usual anti-gun sermon. Jasper knew Ralph wanted to be helpful. But the old vet was the last person who should be packing a gun. He had enough problems without a concealed weapon charge. "Thanks," Jasper said. When he got back to town, he'd turn the firearm over to Chief Stone for disposal.

"You were the smart one," Ralph said. "I should've joined you in Canada."

Silently Jasper agreed. It was a damn shame Ralph had been drafted into the war. Now with the gun out of sight, he shifted into a higher gear as the road smoothed out.

"They came again last night," Ralph said.

"Who?" Jasper asked, anticipating the answer.

"You know. The men from the sky."

"What did they want this time?"

"Said I should remember my oath. Said I could disappear and no one would notice. But I outsmarted them because I still have some marbles left in this here noggin." He tapped his left temple. "I lit up, took a hit and played the drugged-out, brain-burned vet." He started to cough again. "Aliens don't like the sweet smoke."

"Maybe if you smoked less of the stuff, you'd quit seeing them."

"I didn't imagine them." Ralph suddenly sounded belligerent. "They're as real as you and me sitting in this here truck. And they asked about you and that thing."

"How about some jazz?" Jasper flipped on the radio, hoping Benny Goodman would bring down Ralph's agitation. Ralph loved music.

Didn't work. Ralph kept up his rant. "You should forget that thing. Act as if you never saw it. If they think you know, your life is as worthless as a burnt slice of rye."

Jasper pulled up to a rundown shack next to an ancient cedar grove, the only building left standing on the old Shoemaker Homestead. Originally it had been a tool shed. Not much of a place but it kept the rain, snow, wind and scorching sun at bay.

"Brought you some of those chili beans you like," Jasper said. "Plus some other stuff." Both men got out. Jasper opened the back of his camper and pulled out a large cardboard box.

"You're a real friend," Ralph said and took the box from Jasper. "I appreciate all you do for me. That's why I got you the gun."

Jasper nodded. "Thanks. The meds from Doc Shore are in there, too. You're taking them regularly, aren't you?"

"Yeah, yeah, yeah. But I'm serious. You've got to forget you ever saw it. If anyone asks, play dumb."

"I will. Just remember to take your meds." Jasper climbed back into the truck. "I could use a couple hundred pounds of alabaster when you get the time."

"Roger Wilco," Ralph said and saluted.

The sun dropped below the horizon leaving a fiery red blaze in its wake. By the time Jasper reached town the only light in the sky came from the streetlights of East Sedona. He drove to the long three-door garage across the alley from the rear of *THE ALABASTER* and shut off his engine. It was good to be home.

He walked across the dirt path to the rear entrance and let himself into the over-large storage room between the store and his living quarters. He knew he should check to see if Jacob had locked up properly, but it'd been a long day. Besides, the boy had proved himself to be reliable even if he was just sixteen. The receipts could wait until morning. He had Star Trek to watch.

Just as he reached the door to the apartment, an odd sounding clang came from the store. It sounded like something had bumped into the filing cabinet behind the counter. A rat? Not likely.

A muffled curse followed.

Jasper froze. Someone was in the store. Someone, who didn't sound the least bit like Jacob.

Taking stealthy steps, Jasper picked his way across the creaky floorboards and put his ear to the door. The intruder made no effort to be quiet. Items were picked up and plunked down, each with a curse.

It sounded like a systematic search. A single searcher? Or was there an accomplice? More puzzling, what was the intruder searching for? Maybe Ralph's ramblings weren't the paranoid words of a man who'd self-medicated with booze and dope for too many years.

Jasper eased the door open a crack and peered in. A silhouetted form in a bulky coat crouched over a lower shelf across from the cash register. Shadows obscured the intruder's face. All Jasper could see clearly was a flashlight's beam focused on a gloved hand and in it a carved, white alabaster sphere.

"Crap." The carved stone ball dropped. It clipped the edge of the shelf and bounced onto the floor. It rolled toward the front of the store and the trespasser followed its path.

Jasper used the moment to push open the door wide enough to slip through. The phone sat alongside the register. Next to it was a large hunting knife he'd purchased to split selenite crystals into smaller chunks. Behind the counter was a baseball bat. He grabbed the metal bat, snuck up behind the burglar and said, "What do you think you're doing?"

The intruder snapped upright, but Jasper still couldn't make out the face. They scuffled and Jasper felt himself being slammed into the counter. The bat wrenched from his hand. He stumbled, his arms windmilling.

Jasper felt a fist slam into the soft bones of his nose. Tasted the hot gush of metallic blood in his mouth. Felt its slick trail run down his chin. He fell back. Grappled for purchase on the counter. The phone crashed to the floor with a ding. His fingers brushed the hilt of the knife, but only for a second.

The assailant grabbed Jasper. Spun him. Both lost their footing. They went down hard. A searing pain pierced Jasper's side.

That's when he recognized his assailant.

"You?" Jasper struggled for breath.

Dust motes shimmered in the streaks of light from the windowpanes. Outside came the mournful cry of a lone coyote.

"I'm sorry, Jasper. You're not supposed to be here. It ruins everything."

THE KILLER BENT over Jasper and pried the gold lapel pin from the man's dying grasp. At least now the crime scene appeared to be just another senseless robbery gone bad. An empty cash register with a discarded body slumped on the floor under it. The murder weapon, an anonymous cheap WalMart hunting knife, glinted in the puddle of blood. The viscous liquid had already formed a satin skin that looked midnight black in the moonlight.

It was a regrettable kill. Jasper Marlon had been a friend.

At least the bleed-out had been quick. Merciful even. Unexpected. The corpse still wore the shocked expression of betrayal. Eyes open wide. A careless brush of red dust on his cheek. His hat askew. Disbelief lingering on parted lips that seemed to whisper over and over the telltale echo of Jasper's last gasped word.

"Why?"

CHAPTER TWO

F ired. Disbarred. Divorced.

By the end of the legal proceedings, I just wanted to slip into an existence where no one knew me or who I'd been. I moved south and found work. Two jobs—both part- time.

Tuesday afternoon I was at job number one dressed in a dark blue T-shirt and slacks to match my fellow minimum wage drones. It was three days before Halloween and Southern California was gripped in an unseasonable heat wave. I wiped my forehead with the back of my hand and forced a smile.

"Welcome to *Burgers: Fast and Friendly*. May I take your order please?"

The man at the front of the lunch rush-hour line had no business in this part of East L.A. A real suit type, who should be dining at *Mauricio's* on Hollywood and Vine. At one time he was just the kind of guy I'd have found appealing, but I'd learned my lesson. He looked too much like a lawyer or worse, a real estate agent and I was done with that whole scene.

He squinted at my name tag. It read, Rosinda. I'd borrowed it when I got to work. Mine had been mangled two weeks earlier by a rogue washing machine. Since then I'd been Rosinda, Monica, Ellie and Marvin.

"Rosinda," the man said as if he knew me, his low-pitched voice friendly. Combined with a ready smile his dark eyes exuded warmth. The fact that he was tall, dark, and handsome didn't hurt. Most women caught in his spell wouldn't try to escape. Why would they want to?

A red warning flare blasted. What was I thinking? My face flushed with heat and I hoped he couldn't read minds. Such thoughts were both risky and foolish. Besides, he wasn't my type. Not anymore.

"Hey man, hit on her later," the teen behind him said and rattled his chain belt.

Mr. Suit didn't break a sweat. In spite of the heat, he looked cool in his charcoal gray ensemble and red power tie. "I'm looking for a Ms. Alabaster Marie Renault."

At his use of my maiden name, I stiffened. My instincts were right. This man was dangerous.

"If you don't want to order, get out of the line," the chain-belt kid said.

Silently I agreed with the punk.

"I understand Ms. Renault works here?"

"Cut the questions. If I don't get my burger and fries soon, I won't be responsible for what happens." Then the kid did a really stupid thing. He body-bumped into the back of Mr. Suit with two raised fists.

The man swiveled, his black leather briefcase clipping the kid's knee.

Chain-belt glared. "What? You got a problem?"

During the exchange, I'd slipped into panic mode.

Mr. Suit returned his attention to me. Couldn't tell if he was brave or stupid to turn his back on the kid.

"Is she here today?"

My smile brightened, I shook my head and in an accent that almost matched the real Rosinda's, said, "I'm sorry. I cannot help you."

He raised one brow, his eyes not letting me go.

Suddenly I felt like I had to get out of there before I confessed I was who he was looking for. "Would you like to place your order now?"

"No, thank you. I'd like to speak to the manager."

"Si, senor." I turned to the high school girl scooping hash brown bites into little white paper bags. "Take over here, I need to find Jose."

I rushed into the kitchen, untying and flinging my apron in the laundry basket. My fingers fumbled with the combination on my locker. After three tries I snatched my purse, dug for car keys and fled to the rear emergency exit. I didn't hesitate even though Jose had made it clear that any employee using it as a shortcut to the parking lot could kiss their job good-bye. Oh well, a long-term career in fast food wasn't my dream.

Using both hands, I shoved the release bar.

The alarm blasted as the heavy metal door clanged against the brick wall. Sprinting like an Olympian, I headed for my battered red Ford Escort in the employee parking lot. My lungs felt like they were about to explode.

Deep down I knew my knee-jerk fear was irrational, but I didn't feel safe until I was driving out of the lot. Then, just my luck, the stoplight at the corner turned red. My fingers tapped the steering wheel, urging the light to turn green.

Adjusting the rear-view mirror, I could see Mr. Suit in a face-off with Jose in front of the restaurant.

"Don't let them see me," I whispered over and over as if reciting a Buddhist mantra on my path to enlightenment.

Neither man looked happy. Jose's hands flailed in the air and I could tell he was shouting a colorful litany of the man's ancestry. He stabbed the air with his right index finger just inches from the Suit's nose.

I slunk lower in my seat. The light turned green. I took off in the surge of traffic, suppressing unladylike giggles. It felt like I'd won a race. Or a court battle. My first win in a long time. Not that you could call it a total victory when I was acting like a fugitive from justice. A totally crazy reaction since I hadn't committed any crime. The truth is that I just didn't have the energy to rehash the past. Plus I'd dealt with enough smug lawyers for a lifetime of misery. It's hard to believe I'd been one.

My ex-husband had sent guys like Mr. Suit after me twice before. Once to sign papers. The other time he demanded the return of his grandmother's engagement ring. Like I really wanted it. What did George want this time? There was nothing left for him to loot. He already had it all.

I frowned.

Wallowing in self-pity was both counter-productive and clouded my judgment. So what if I was the clichéd victim of a cheating husband? Hundreds of thousands of women go through divorce every year and like the majority of them, *I was better off without him.*

I pinched my earlobe hard. It was a silly new age reflexology thing I'd read about in *The Magazine*. The crazy thing is that it works. The pain cleared my mind and pulled me to the present. It allowed me to focus and focus was what I needed at the moment. Where to start?

One, someone had hired a suit to track me down.

Two, if it was George, I wasn't playing his games anymore.

Three, I couldn't imagine who else would be interested in my whereabouts. That sent me back to two.

I'd be damned if I'd let my sneaky ex-husband screw me again, figuratively or literally. The divorce was final which legally meant I didn't have to deal with him ever again. Or listen to his advice.

Four. Whoever he'd hired was good. How else had Mr. Suit tracked me to the burger joint? The guy couldn't be a P.I. He looked too much like a lawyer. Whatever he wanted with me, I had no interest in his latest take on bad news.

It was time to think about relocating. Again.

I headed for home. There was a fifty-fifty chance he didn't have the address or he would have hit me there, first thing in the A.M.

Still, just to be on the safe side I drove by my apartment twice before parking a block away to make my approach on foot. Scanned the street and parking lot of the NO-TEL MOTEL, a two-story low-budget dump. The hand-painted sign out front boasted of hourly, weekly, or monthly rates. As a monthly, my room sat in the rear.

Safe inside, I flipped on the radio from habit. The walls were thin and I'm not into voyeurism. I took a quick survey to see that no one had been snooping around, but everything looked the same as when I'd left for work. My rental didn't come with maid service and I'd been in a hurry that morning. The bed was still unmade, trash can full, and my breakfast dishes squatted in the tiny sink. I'm pretty neat most of the time, but this morning I'd overslept.

I grabbed a notebook, sat on the edge of the bed and began scribbling. It helped me think. Okay. No contact with my family since the indictment. No credit card. No land line. No bank accounts. I'd paid my rent every two weeks with a money order. Since I'd registered my car, I'd moved twice. My driver's license wasn't up for renewal for another three years, two addresses ago.

My thoughts finally zeroed in on the only possibility left.

I let out the breath I'd been holding and flexed my fingers. It was clear. Mr. Suit must have tracked me through my social security number to the burger joint. Well good for him. That was the end of my legal trail.

Tension drained from my rigid shoulders. My second job paid cash under the table. My current address hadn't been listed on either job application. All I had to do was dodge him until he got tired of looking.

I'd give Jose a ring and say I'd been called out of town on an emergency and wouldn't be back for three weeks. I doubted whoever hired Mr. Tall-Dark-and-Handsome had unlimited cash reserves to have the guy hang around waiting for my return. In the meantime, I'd try to find another job to cover my expenses.

It felt good to have a plan.

I glanced at the clock. My next work shift started in twenty-five minutes. Enough time to change out of the snappy burger joint corporate uniform and into presentable street clothes. A mere fifteen minutes to strip, speed shower, and head out. It's a good thing I'd mastered the natural look. I was back in my car in record time.

One perk of my second job is that I got to park right in front. No walking half a block to an employee parking lot. I locked the car, went inside and came back out with two magnetic signs to stick on my front doors.

Angel's Pizza
A taste of heaven in every bite!
FREE DELIVERY

Business was slow. By eight there were only three pizza deliveries. The fourth and last delivery of the night was called in at 8:45 PM. We closed at nine. I hoped the late diner tipped big. I could use the money.

Angel sang out in a rich tenor as he slid a large pepperoni and olive pizza into a red checked box. "Carson Inn, room 212. On Seventh. It's Angel time. Suit up."

The occasional free pizza almost compensated for the ridiculous delivery costume I had to wear. For the fourth time that night I slipped on the *sassy* hot pink Lycra wig and switched on its battery-operated halo. The bright orange gauzy angel wings were already in the car.

I zipped the hot cardboard box into a stay-warm delivery bag and drove the five minutes to the Carson Inn. Parked. Shrugged on the angel wings. Two minutes to find the room.

When I knocked, the door shifted inward a few inches. Through the crack in the door, I could see that the lights were on, but the room looked empty.

A weird premonition skittered down my spine, and I never get premonitions. Why was the door unlocked? This wasn't good. No normal person would leave their door open in this part of town. Not if they were sane. My sense of self-preservation went on alert as I tensed, ready to flee at the slightest threat of danger.

"Pizza delivery!" I hollered.

"Come on in, door's open," a man's voice called over the sound of a bathroom fan.

He sounded normal enough.

I used the pizza box to push open the door, stopping on the threshold, not sure if I wanted to enter. A battle of strong competing odors surged from the room. Pepperoni, anchovies, Italian sausage, spices, and cheese. On the bed were at least eight boxes of take-out pizzas from *Angel's* competitors stacked in three neat piles. The man must have ordered a pizza from every delivery place in a twenty-mile radius.

So the guy probably wasn't a homicidal crazy, he just had a serious pizza addiction.

The bathroom door opened.

"Damn it to hell," he said. "What a waste of time."

I turned, but only caught a flash of brown hair before the door slammed shut again.

Okay, now that was strange. That weird premonition shiver raced down my neck again. Something about this guy gave me the creeps. Had he been checking me out? I just wanted to get paid and out of there quick.

"Where do you want the pizza?"

"Leave it. Money's on the table," he said over the sound of water splashing in the sink.

I crossed the room to the little Formica topped table, plunked down the pizza carrier, unzipped it, and slid out the pizza. Even though I'd eaten four slices earlier, it smelled wonderful. Two bills lay on the table, a twenty and a five.

"It's only $16.95," I called.

"That's okay," he said. "Keep the change."

Did he mean from the twenty or the twenty-five? The extra five would put me closer to the cash I needed to move, but taking it felt like stealing. I picked up both bills and stared into the eyes of Honest Abe. *Do the right thing*, they urged.

I glanced back at the bathroom door.

It was wide open. The guy stood on the threshold like a calendar pin-up in his white sleeveless ribbed tank. To say he had a nice physique would be a major understatement. His dark eyes stared at me like lasers trying to strip away the pink wig and the sparkle stars from my face.

Maybe it was the room or the setting, but it took me a few seconds longer than it should have to place him. Another contributing factor was his sculpted biceps. I gulped, shoved both bills in my pocket and bolted for the exit.

Mr. Suit must have seen the panic in my eyes and rushed toward the door. I slammed into him and we both went down. I landed on my knees, momentarily blinded. The wig had slid over my eyes. I shoved it back with the heel of my hand and scrambled to my feet. He was lightning fast and beat me to the room's only way out.

"What do you want with me?" I blurted out, panting from the scuffle.

He grinned, a predatory gleam sparkled in his eyes.

If I could have reached one, I would have grabbed a pizza box and thrown it at his smug handsome face.

CHAPTER THREE

M r. Suit blocked the motel room's only exit. My survival nerves went on high alert as I considered alternate possibilities of escape.

One: talk my way out. Two: go for the window. Three: retreat to the bathroom and lock myself in. Or four: scream like a pig at the slaughter.

His hand snaked out and snatched the pink wig from my head.

"Four!" I screamed and scrambled back, tripped and fell onto the bed. My angel wings crumpled but didn't offer any protection from the sharp corner of a pizza box that jabbed into my back. "Ouch."

He reached into his pants pocket. My god, did he have a knife?

Panting, I reverse-crab-walked like a drunken crustacean on unstable sand, scattering the pizza boxes as I tried to put distance between us. My wings snagged on the bedspread and I was trapped. This couldn't be happening. I was too young to die— the victim of a homicidal pizza-eating maniac.

He removed a business card from a small leather holder and handed it to me.

What could I do? I read it in my high-pitched squeaky about-to-lose-control voice. "Alex Farmer, attorney at law. From Sedona, Arizona."

He went to the closet, pulled a white shirt from a hanger and slipped it on. I got off the bed and watched him warily as he slowly buttoned it from top to bottom in a reverse strip tease.

My face blushed. Where had that thought come from? His tracking me down was where my focus should be centered, not on his buff physique.

So focus. I'd been right about him being a lawyer. Which made him even more dangerous, but I had to give him points for tenacity. Jose must have told him I was moonlighting as a pizza delivery person. Still, I wasn't out of the woods.

"What do you want?" I repeated and frowned, expecting him to maybe whip out a subpoena.

"Please have a seat while I get the documents."

I ran nervous fingers through my wig-matted hair with my left hand and flipped at the edge of his business card with my right thumb. Even if he was legit, having a little get-together in a motel room didn't seem like the smartest move. Not when the main piece of furniture was a bed. Even lawyers could be rapist or murderers. Especially the good-looking ones.

"I don't need to sit, just tell me what this is about."

He sank into one of the two vinyl chairs at the tiny table under the window. "I am from Sedona and represent the estate of Jasper Marlon."

I blew out a sigh. At least he wasn't a messenger of doom from my ex. "And that has what, to do with me?"

"You are Alabaster Marie Renault, the daughter of Jade Marie Jamison, aren't you?"

"What if I am?"

"You're named as a co-heir of your uncle Jasper's estate."

"A co-heir?" I said, processing the information. A long-lost rich uncle who'd left me millions sounded fantastic. Too bad I didn't have one. I shook my head. "You have me confused with someone else. My uncle died in Vietnam before I was born. And his name was Flint."

My stomach growled.

Mr. Farmer set his briefcase next to the pizza on the table and flipped open the box. In a voice that sounded a lot like a dog trainer's, he said, "Sit. Have some pizza."

I didn't budge.

Pride is a wonderful thing, but then my stomach roared like a wild animal caged behind unyielding ribs, proving adrenaline stress is more powerful than starvation to pique one's appetite.

He lifted a piece, took a bite and chewed slowly, not once letting his gaze slip from my face. His dark eyes intense. Measuring. He took another bite.

Suddenly I was starved. What harm would there be in eating one little piece of pizza? My mouth washed with anticipatory saliva. The odds of him attacking me, with a full mouth of olives, pepperoni and cheese, were low.

"It's good. Best I've tasted tonight." He took another bite and seductively wiped a stray string of cheese from his lips with his middle finger, all the while gazing at me. "Like the ad says, it's heavenly. Join me. Have a slice."

Danger alert! "I'm sorry, but I don't know you from Adam." I flipped his business card onto the table. "Anyone can print up a business card."

"Listen. Just hear me out. Give me one hour of your time. It'll be worth your while."

My glance slid to the king-size bed. "I'm sorry, but I'm not interested in spending an hour in a motel room with a strange man."

A momentary flash of anger, or maybe it was annoyance, flared in his eyes. "Denny's is next door. It'll be less private, but you can rest assured your virtue will remain intact. FYI . . . Angels aren't my type."

That's when I remembered my wings and my face went to 500 degrees Fahrenheit. I shrugged out of them and clutched the crumpled wire and gauze in front of me like a shield.

He grinned. "It's your call."

Walking out would have given me great satisfaction, but the practical part of me nagged, could I afford to? What if I did have an uncle Jasper?

He seemed to sense my indecision. "The reason you may not know about your uncle Jasper, is that he became estranged from your family in December of 1968." Mr. Farmer's voice hardened. "They disowned him when he chose Canada over the draft."

He made it sound like it was my fault, which was entirely unfair. Besides, if Jasper Marlon was a relative, I think I would have heard about it from someone in the family. Plus this stranger looked more like a movie actor than a lawyer.

"Where's the hidden camera?" I asked. "How much is my ex paying you to do a Candid Camera on me?"

Instead of answering my question, he pulled out a manila folder and dropped it on the table.

The file was about a half-inch thick. Someone had done a thorough job researching my past. On top was a faded copy of my senior picture. If you didn't look too close, I still resembled the girl in the photo. The same dirty blond hair and slightly crooked nose, but my blue eyes had lost their innocence. Mr. Farmer should have recognized me at the burger joint. Maybe the hairnet and baseball cap had thrown him off. "I need to make a phone call."

"Be my guest."

I stepped out of the room into the warm night air and dialed.

The phone rang four times before it was picked up.

"Hello," came a sleepy, but annoyed female voice.

"Mom, it's me. Allie."

I tried not to grip the phone too hard as I heard the familiar contempt in my mother's voice. It seeped from the handset like electrically charged attack ions.

"Do you know what time it is?" Mom demanded.

I looked at the clock. It was nine fifteen. That meant it was after midnight in Florida. I heard my stepfather Hank's voice in the background. "Who's calling at this time of night?"

"Allie." My mother didn't bother to cover the receiver. "She probably wants money."

"I'm sorry to wake you, Mom, but it's important. I need to ask— "

"We're not your personal ATM," she said, interrupting me.

When had she ever been? I'd never borrowed a cent from her. Taking a big breath to keep from saying something a daughter should never say to her mother regardless of provocation, I said, "I don't want money."

"Well, what is it, then?"

"I want to know about Uncle Jasper."

Silence.

"Mom, do I have an Uncle Jasper?"

"I thought he'd be dead by now."

"He is."

"Good," my mother said and hung up.

I took a deep breath and digested my mother's harsh words before stepping back into the room. In my absence, he'd made a single stack of the pizza boxes.

"Okay," I said. "It seems that I do have an Uncle Jasper in my lineage. "I'll meet you at Denny's." I'd stop by my car to dump the wings, the wig and the stay-hot carrying case.

"Can you get the door?" he asked. His briefcase dangled in one hand under the tower of pizza boxes. The lower half of his face was blocked.

"You do realize restaurants don't allow outside food to be brought in," I said.

His dreamy eyes looked up and he gave a slight shake of his head. "Don't you ever give up?"

"It's been a long day," I shot back.

We shared an intense stare down, his resolute eyes boring into mine. "If it's not too much trouble, will you see that the door's locked?"

Okay, I'd been a little harsh, as in L.A. bitchy. He was just doing his job, and if I was about to inherit a fortune and he was the officer of the court handling the estate, I should cut him some slack. "Sorry. Do you need me to carry a few boxes?"

"I'm good. Just get the door."

I followed him out and along the second floor walk to the stairs. At the bottom, I headed for my car. He crossed the parking lot in the opposite direction of the restaurant. Where was he going?

I unlocked my car, but couldn't stop watching him. After tossing my stuff in and grabbing my purse from under the driver's seat, I slid in behind the wheel. The car had to be moved. It was parked in a fifteen-minute delivery zone. Experience had taught me that most motel receptionists had tow-truck delivery services on speed dial.

I adjusted the rear view mirror for a better view of the handsome Alex Farmer, attorney at law from Sedona, Arizona.

He crossed the street to a little park and stopped by a double swing set. Bathed in the glow of a streetlight, he set the pizza boxes on the ground and waited. Out of the shadows emerged a grizzled man wrapped in a ragged blanket. The lawyer handed him a pizza.

My eyebrows went up. "Hmmmmm." Maybe there was more to him than good looks and a law degree.

Soon a second street derelict arrived and then another. Once the boxes were dispersed, he spun and headed toward Denny's. That's when I caught sight of my reflection. The matted hair. One cheek covered in purple sparkle stars, the other streaked with iridescent pink glitter.

I looked like crap. It's not that I wanted to impress Mr. Alex Farmer. I just wanted to erase this first impression—to look like a competent normal-type person. I picked off the stars with a fingernail, grabbed a tissue from the glove box and attempted to rub the sheen from my skin. With or without the wig, my hair was a lost cause even after a quick finger-fluff.

He'd reached the front door to the diner and sauntered inside.

I grimaced at my reflection, started the car, backed out and drove the sixty feet to a legal parking spot curbside.

Before entering Denny's I took a deep cleansing breath.

The wonderful fragrance of bacon, hamburgers, fries, and sausage, greeted me like a long-lost friend. I paused to savor the scents. He'd settled at a dark green vinyl booth close to the restrooms. Not the most desirable location, but the most private. I slid in across from him.

"Okay, Mr. Farmer, shoot."

"Call me, Alex. Sedona's a small town. We'll be seeing a lot of each other."

"Okay, Alex," I said, deciding to let that one pass. I wasn't sure what point he was making. It's not like I was moving to Sedona.

The waitress appeared with a flirtatious smile, filled his coffee and grudgingly poured me a cup. Which was pretty rude. How did she know we weren't a couple? Him, a big-time corporate-type taking me out after a Hollywood shoot. I doctored my coffee with three creams and sugar while she took my order. Rare steak and eggs followed by apple pie, for me. Nothing for Alex.

We waited for the waitress to move out of earshot before either of us spoke. I was first to break the silence.

"Okay, Alex. You have my undivided attention for the next hour."

"This should explain." He handed me a cream-colored envelope with my name printed on the front. On the back, three blobs of red wax stamped with an ornate "JM" double sealed the missive. To complete the security overkill, it'd been officially notarized.

Alex watched as I tore open the envelope and read.

Dear Allie,

If you're reading this letter, it means I'm dead and that Alex has finally found you. Forgive me for not contacting you sooner. Now it's too late for us to become acquainted. I'm sorry.

Over the years I wanted to meet you, but I knew it would cause friction for you in the family.

I've watched your accomplishments, and have been proud to call you kin. But it is the dignity you showed as you faced your dreadful ordeal that impressed me most. As friends and family abandoned you, you showed the courage to accept the consequences of life's choices.

You notice that I did not use the word, *crime*, for I am sure in my heart that you did not knowingly commit a real crime. Yes, you broke the law, but without malice or for personal gain, harming no one, and faced punishment that far outweighed your indiscretion.

It's difficult to start over with nothing. Therefore, I'm leaving you and Colin Phelps joint partnership in *The Alabaster*. Colin's father was a dear friend. The business has the potential to provide you both with comfortable livings and a chance to start over.

Take it with my blessing. May you live long and prosper.

Fondly,

Jasper

This man who could easily pass for a young Cary Grant studied me and I found myself saying the first inane thing that popped into my head. "So Uncle Jasper was a Star Trek fan?"

"More like an obsessed Trekkie," he said and smiled.

The smile took me off guard. Minus the scowl he was hot. "How did he die?" I asked.

His mouth transformed into a grim line. "Stabbed during a break-in two months ago. From the evidence, it looks like a vagrant killed Jasper for a lousy hundred-and-fifty bucks."

"A vagrant? So they caught the guy?"

Alex grunted. "Not yet."

"Do they have any concrete leads?"

He shrugged. "The police aren't exactly forthcoming."

"Does Sedona even have a competent investigative unit to handle a murder case? After two months, I'd say the case is cold. Maybe they should call in outside help."

"I don't think Chief Stone would take kindly to the suggestion."

"Why not?"

"Let's just say, he's kind of a lone wolf."

"Maybe that's the problem."

"No. He's more than competent. He worked a stint in New York City's homicide division for five years. Returned last year when his father had a stroke. After coming home, he stayed."

I gave him a skeptical look. "You're saying, he gave up a successful career in New York to become a small-time police chief?" Even as the words slipped from my lips, they shamed me. I was as hypocritical as the rest.

His eyes narrowed like a Peregrine falcon ready for the kill. "Hard to believe you and Jasper fell from the same family tree."

"What do you mean?"

"Given the way you were raised, I don't know if you can understand." He ran a hand through his short, cropped hair. "To Jasper. To Chief Stone. To me. Family comes first. Even if you have to sacrifice your own personal desires, reputation or goals to protect them. That's why Jasper named you as one of his heirs and used your name for the business. He considered it his duty to provide for you. To give you a new lease on life."

Incredible. He'd named his business after me in spite of how the family, my mother in particular, had treated him. It both humbled and honored me. Jasper must have been some guy. "I wish I could have met him."

The waitress arrived with more coffee and my trucker's feast served on a platter. She plunked it in front of me along with two

20

smaller dishes for the toast and pie. Alex watched while I carved off the excess fat with a steak knife and slid it onto the toast under the eggs. I dug in.

"You always eat like that?" he asked.

"Only when I'm hungry," I said. I didn't tell him that this was the first steak I'd had in over a year. It wasn't exactly filet mignon, but it tasted pretty good. "So tell me why the police think a vagrant killed him?"

"The five thousand dollars still in his safe."

"And that's significant, because?" I bit into a morsel of steak.

"Locals knew Jasper kept cash on the premises. They would have taken it, too."

"But why keep that much money around?" I started on the eggs.

"He bought from the miners who'd wander in from the desert."

"Wouldn't checks be smarter for bookkeeping purposes?"

He shrugged. "Probably, but Jasper did things his way."

I digested the information. I might not be a P.I., but I had a good track record investigating crime during my stint as an assistant DA. I had a talent for spotting details the police overlooked. Maybe I could give this Stone a hand. I owed Jasper that much. "Describe to me the best you can, what you know of the crime scene."

He looked taken aback. "Based on what?"

"Based on what you've heard from the cops, gossip and the news."

While he talked, I cleaned my plate and tried to envision the crime scene. It was like I was on rewind and had returned to my life as a prosecutor. Pretend you are there in the space where the murder was committed. The visualization technique almost always worked for me. I closed my eyes. Pictured a man on the floor. Stabbed to death. An empty cash register, but that was as far as I could get. It was too much like a movie scene, unreal and sanitized. I'd need real crime scene photos. But from what Alex had said about the police chief, I doubted they would be forthcoming.

I opened my eyes and reached for the pie as a thought popped into my head.

"Maybe the killer didn't want cash," I said. "Maybe the killer had a different motive and staged it to look like a theft. "

"Possible, but I don't see it. Everyone liked Jasper."

"Obviously, not everyone," I said. "You're sure the police don't have other potential leads?"

"None, but the obvious. Motive, means and opportunity." He stared at me for a moment and then added, "Like who stands to benefit from Jasper's death."

I dropped my fork at the implication. It clipped the edge of the table, spun like a whirly-gig and disappeared. Suddenly I'd lost my appetite. I sat straighter, raised my chin and said in a flat, emotionless voice, "The night Jasper died, I was delivering pizzas."

Alex gave me a quizzical look that made me feel uneasy. "How can you be sure? I haven't told you the date of the murder."

CHAPTER FOUR

I pushed the dirty dishes to the outer edge of the faux wood laminate table and used my napkin to brush away invisible crumbs from its surface. Planting my elbows and leaning forward to rest my chin in my hand, I smiled. "I've delivered pizzas every night for the last six months. Does the co-heir have an alibi for the night in question?"

Alex nodded. "Signed. Sealed. And delivered to the police chief two weeks ago."

"I'm sure my boss will be happy to sign an affidavit as well."

He nodded. "That ties up another loose end for Chief Stone."

"Great."

My face flushed for the umpteenth time when I realized I'd been staring into his gorgeous eyes too intently. "Hey, it's late. Just give me a run down. When will the estate be settled?" Maybe I could survive on the pizza delivery job without begging Jose to keep my day job. Rent was due in two weeks.

"It already is. If you and Colin accept the terms of Jasper's will."

"Don't I have to have my name officially cleared, first?"

"You were a prosecutor for too long."

"What do you mean?"

"You've forgotten that a man, or in your case, a woman is presumed innocent until proven guilty."

"Only on paper." I frowned, thinking of my indictment. At the first hint of a rumor, I'd been fired.

His face lightened up and I realized he'd been toying with me. He hadn't really thought I was guilty.

"You'll be a nice addition to Sedona. Wouldn't surprise me, if you turned more than a few heads, with or without the sparkles."

Was he flirting with me? Must be my over-stimulated imagination. Even so, the compliment caressed my bruised ego. It'd been a long time since I'd been attracted to anyone. Not that I could afford to be side-tracked by the sexy twinkle in his dark eyes. Best not to go there.

I was single and doing just fine. Better than fine. I was an heiress.

He handed me a document typed on legal sized paper. "This is your copy. Once the papers are signed and you agree to the terms, it's all but settled."

I skimmed the details and tried to ignore him watching me. "Seems pretty straightforward. Sedona, here I come."

He laughed. "One more thing. When Jasper couldn't locate you, he had me draw up a codicil."

My shoulders slumped. There would be another condition. Why couldn't life just be easy? I plastered on a fake smile. It was fine. If I couldn't meet it, at least Uncle Jasper's largess had given me something that couldn't be rescinded. Pride and hope for a better life. At that moment, I vowed to stop being a victim. No more minimum-wage jobs. I had three college degrees. Even if I couldn't return to the law, having been disbarred for life, I could find something else less degrading than fast food obscurity.

Alex handed me the second document.

I couldn't bring myself to look at it.

"Just tell me."

He took a moment to study the document like he didn't know what was in it. "You and Colin must run THE ALABASTER as equal partners for two years. You'll both receive a generous salary and all profits over a hundred thousand are to be split fifty-fifty."

I mentally gave myself a shake. Obviously I was over-tired or over-eager. I'd neglected to ask the most important question.

"What kind of a business is *The Alabaster*?" A vision of an old hotel popped into my head. Next flashed a hazy picture of this Colin guy happily sitting at the front desk schmoozing with the customers, while I slaved away cleaning rooms and washing piles of dirty sheets and towels.

"A rock shop," Alex said.

"A rock shop," I repeated, trying to process this new bit of information. "That sells rocks?"

He nodded, looking amused.

"Building rocks? Or landscape rocks?"

The hint of a smile expanded, warming his features. "Collecting rocks."

"People collect rocks," I said, totally confused. "And he made a living at it?"

"It's a good business. Jasper was closed half the time and did pretty well. He sold a little of everything. Carvings. Jewelry. Bookends. Crystals. Minerals."

"So the rock business is lucrative?"

"It has potential." He took a sip of coffee. "If at the end of the two year probation period either of you wishes to liquidate, you must offer your share to the other before selling to an outsider."

"What if one of us bails before the two years are up?"

"All assets go to the remaining heir."

"What if neither of us wants to run a rock shop?"

"You'll make the Sedona Foundation, a nonprofit, very happy."

"I see. Tell me about Colin. What kind of a business partner will he make?"

The waitress came over to the table. "Anything else I can get you?"

"Please, I'd like a glass of milk to go with my pie and a clean fork," I said.

"And you, sir?" she asked as she picked up the empty plates. "Sure you wouldn't like some dessert?"

"I'm good," Alex said. Once she left, he asked, "Now where were we?"

"You were going to tell me about Colin."

A shadow flitted across his face. "I think you should draw your own conclusions."

That didn't sound very promising. "So he's difficult to deal with."

"I didn't say that." His voice made it clear that the subject was closed.

I tried a different track. "How old is he?"

"A few years older than me," he said.

Alex looked to be in his early forties. Hopefully Colin's being ten years or so my senior wouldn't make him think he was the boss and I the junior partner.

The waitress appeared with my milk, a clean fork and the bill. She rested her hand on Alex's shoulder. "Anything else I can offer you, honey?" she asked as though she was offering him more than another cup of coffee.

I stiffened and dismissed her with a, "Thanks, we're just fine." I reached across the table as if to touch his hand.

"You heard the lady. We're good."

"Have a nice evening," she said and clomped off to greet a new customer.

I snatched my hand back, more than a little embarrassed. He looked amused.

"And how is Colin related to Jasper?" I blurted. What was I thinking? Playing one-up with a waitress who flirted with my lawyer. A man who just happened to be incredibly good looking?

Alex didn't seem to notice my inner discomfort. "He's the son of an old friend of Jasper's who died in Vietnam."

"I thought you said Jasper was a draft dodger."

"That doesn't mean he didn't have friends who served."

I started on the pie, thinking an apple a day is pretty good when it's cinnamon spiced, sweet and baked in a golden crust.

"Did they know each other?" I asked. "Jasper and Colin?"

Alex nodded. "He spent summers in Sedona when he was a teen."

"Then he knows something about the rock business?"

"A little, but if I remember right he was more interested in girls."

"Yeah what teenage boy isn't? Well, at least we won't be totally flying blind. Has he been running the store since Jasper died?"

"No. It's been closed." He pulled out an American Express card. "He's been living in Kansas working as a civilian employee at the Fort Riley Army Base. Said he had to give notice and train his replacement before he could make the permanent move to Sedona, but he's been down a couple times since the funeral. His final relocation should happen in a couple of weeks."

Okay, two years wasn't an eternity. I just hoped we'd get along for the duration. And if it got unbearable, I could always do something else. My father used to say, nothing ventured, nothing gained.

I saved the best bite of pie for last. The tip. Even though it was Denny's, the crust was light and flaky. The apples cooked just right. Not too soft, not too hard. I closed my eyes and swallowed the final morsel. "I accept."

"Good. Jasper would be pleased. Family loyalty meant everything."

"I like that," I said.

"You do? Well, we're on the same page there." For the first time he didn't seem the handsome lawyer, but a man whose friendship I could value.

"Maybe I can repay his generosity by solving his murder."

Alex leaned back, a furrow creasing his forehead. "It might be dangerous and I wouldn't want to see you hurt. Leave it to the experts."

"Some experts. After two months they don't even have a decent lead."

"Chief Stone won't put up with an amateur mucking up his investigation."

"I'm not an amateur. I have experience in criminal investigations."

His face turned dark. "Pretty women and murder don't mix."

Wrong comment, but I wasn't about to get into an argument, so I smiled and said, "Thank you for the feast."

"Sure you've had enough? Or do you want to order something else?"

"I'm good."

"One last thing." He handed me a check for two thousand dollars.

"What's this?"

"An advance."

"Wow, okay, thanks." Instantly I had it spent in my mind. First order of business after I settled in Arizona would be to legally revert my surname to Renault. It was time to get back into the game of life and stop feeling sorry for myself.

"When will you be ready to relocate?" he asked.

"I should be good to go tomorrow afternoon."

He raised his eyebrows, but didn't comment. Instead he slid out of the seat and headed to the cash register. I followed. After he paid the bill, he walked me to my car like the perfect gentleman on a blind date. The air had finally cooled and I was wishing I'd brought my sweater.

"You could fly back with me on Sunday."

"Thanks, but I'd rather drive." What I didn't say is that I was more terrified of flying than driving.

"You plan to drive all the way in this?" he said and double-slapped the hood of my battered Escort. A piece of the trim clattered to the ground.

I pretended not to notice. So my car wasn't a Rolls Royce. Twelve years old with 180,000 miles on the odometer. A few dents front, back and on both sides. But she was a reliable car considering she'd been in two accidents. And I owned her free and clear. "All she needs is an oil change."

"Jasper left a pickup and a car. They're both old, but in great condition. You don't need this heap."

"I like my car," I snapped, annoyed with myself for letting my guard down and starting to like him. Give a man an inch and they go all macho on you. Telling you what to do and how to do it.

He bent down and examined the tires under the streetlight. "You'd be safer flying than driving this wreck cross country. I wouldn't trust these to get me out of L.A."

The newly re-empowered-me said, "I prefer to drive. Case closed."

CHAPTER FIVE

ccording to Google maps, the drive from L.A. to Sedona is an easy seven hours and forty minutes. Well, Google maps didn't take into account a new radiator in Blythe, four tires in Quartzsite, and a timing belt in Sun City. I arrived in West Sedona after a brutal road trip at two thirty-five in the morning. Almost broke.

With a huge chunk of my two thousand dollars spent, there was no way I was going to use my last cash on an overpriced motel room. Not for half a night's rest when I was co-owner of a business property with attached living quarters that at the moment were unoccupied.

All I had to do was locate my new home. Which should be easy, considering Sedona is a relatively small town.

Alex had arranged for me to pick up the key from a Carl Morton, but I didn't think the man would appreciate a phone call in the middle of the night.

No key, not a problem. During my short stint as a public defender before moving to the D.A.'s office, one of my clients taught me how to use a credit card to jimmy a lock. I didn't have a credit card, but my laminated driver's license should work.

A perfectly legal act, because I co-owned the building.

"It's not a crime, because it's mine," I belted out like I was a television talent contestant.

For some reason, I kept singing the words like a jingle while driving slow to squint at the dimly lit street signs. Everything about my new hometown, Sedona, looked surreal. Golden streetlights glowed at intervals in the shadows.

The road wound up a low hill into West Sedona where THE ALABASTER was located. At the top, the black pavement expanded to four lanes. Just when I'd gotten used to navigating the roundabout intersections they gave way to traditional stoplights. Red and green lights glared at two-block intervals as far as I could see.

Alex had said the business was located in the modest shopping district for locals, so I knew I had to be close. Little strip malls squatted on both sides of the street, packed with familiar big city business franchises. In the dark, the majority of buildings were low-level and looked like they were built of brick or stucco or a combination of both.

This meant THE ALABASTER should be easy to spot. To quote Alex, it had a great location on the north side of the 89A highway, two blocks east of Safeway.

Safeway loomed on the right. Which meant I'd missed THE ALABASTER on my first pass. I flipped a U-turn across all four lanes of the deserted street. Rolling down my side window I let in the cold fresh air to clear the road buzz from my brain.

Something ran from the shadows into the street. I slammed on the brakes. A big dog? No, something wild. A coyote. It stopped dead center in the middle of the road, its eyes glowing red in the reflected glare of my headlights. We stared at each other. After a long moment it turned and loped into the shadows.

I shivered. My breath formed a wispy fog that swirled and disappeared beyond the reach of the pale light. I lifted my foot from the brake and the car inched forward. That's when I spotted THE ALABASTER. It stood alone, a huge single-story stucco building minus the usual security lights. I would have missed it all together except for the small hand-painted sign caught in the glare of my high-beams.

What had I been thinking? That moving to Arizona would be my salvation? Even in the dark, the place looked like a ramshackle dump.

Instead of becoming the co-owner of a thriving business, it seemed that I'd descended into a new level of low.

A cyclone gate stretched across the entrance to THE ALABASTER. I parked on the street in front, turned off the engine and rummaged in the glove box for a mini-penlight before getting out. Slammed by exhaustion, I wondered when this ordeal would end. My eyes felt dry and irritated, like someone had poured sand in them. Blinking hard failed to activate my stubborn tear ducts.

The place looked like a cockroach hostel, which meant my suitcase and other stuff stayed in the car. I'd sleep in my clothes. I got out. Locked the doors. It was freezing cold and I didn't have the energy to climb the six-foot gate. Still, what choice did I have?

Penlight in hand, I approached the cyclone gate that was attached to two massive steel posts. The obvious high-tech security meant to keep out unwanted night prowlers. Not that it had kept out Jasper's murderer. The shiver that skittered over my chest and into my belly wasn't from the cold.

My eyes traveled beyond the sentinel posts. I squinted so hard my cheeks cramped as I moved closer for a better look. What? Shaking my head in disbelief, I started to giggle and then hooted like a wild woman. The overkill gate wasn't attached to a fence on either end. It just blocked the entrance to the parking area.

Laughing energized me and I scooted around one side. As my eyes adjusted to the darkness I got a better look at my new home. Even in the dark, the cracked stucco walls and broken tiles on the roof were clearly visible on the Spanish hacienda. And then a sobering thought hit. My laughter died. It was pretty clear there was no security. Why would a vagrant break in when there were dozens of more prosperous businesses in the area?

That creepy premonition was back, tickling my neck.

Uncle Jasper had been murdered here less than two months ago. What if it hadn't been a random vagrant? And if it was a local thief, why hadn't they taken the five thousand in the safe? Maybe the night of the murder they'd run out of time, not greed. With the building sitting empty and the police tape gone, maybe they'd come back. My pulse throbbed where the strap of my purse cut into my shoulder. I started to pant like a woman in a Lamaze class as my imagination gave birth to the potential evils concealed by the night. Suspicious shadows began to lurk in the dark corners. Clandestine shades seemed to stare through the big dark showroom windows.

"Stop it," I told myself. It was perfectly safe. I ordered my exhausted imagination to quit running wild, but my brain refused. Scenario number two— the murderer didn't want the cash. He or she wanted something else. Something specific that Jasper had or knew about. And in the process had gained an enemy. I hated to admit it, but maybe my uncle Jasper wasn't the nice guy Alex had made him out to be.

Scenario number three— I was back to the vagrant, long gone a thousand miles from here. I was safe. Jasper's murderer was not lurking inside waiting to get me. It's just that my exhaustion kept spinning an endless stream of stupid what-ifs. I needed to get some sleep. That was it. Sedona was a small town whose inhabitants had good old-fashioned values like in the *Little House on the Prairie* books I'd read as a kid. Where right was right and wrong wasn't tolerated. A wholesome haven, impregnable to violence.

A safe town. . . where my uncle had been murdered.

"Quit it!" I chided myself. "Just get inside and get some rest. Things will look a lot better in the morning."

I crept toward the building. Random rock mounds loomed up along the walls. My senses went back on high alert. Someone or something could easily hunker down behind a pile and no one would be the wiser. I shined the penlight on the closest pile and moved to the next. Satisfied that I was alone, I relaxed.

"You are a sly one, Alex Farmer," I said, thinking that he must have exaggerated the value of the business. "The only cash flow here is for the lucky someone who trips, falls, and sues us for every penny of Jasper's estate. And the lawyer who represents them."

"Oooooooooooo," howled a lone beast in the night.

My god, the coyote. It had come for me.

I rushed for the front door. The muffled thuds of my feet pounded in mock imitation of my racing heartbeat.

Stumbling, my right hand flew forward in a vain attempt to minimize the damage of my fall. I landed hard. Pain stabbed into the soft flesh of my palm, shooting upward to my shoulder.

"Ooooooooooooo!" Another howl ripped the silence. Closer.

I scrambled to my feet, ignoring my stinging palms. I wasn't going down without a fight.

Let the starving coyote try to devour me, I thought and hefted a hand-sized boulder. Maybe the same rock that had tripped me. Clutching it, I raised my arm like the Statue of Liberty and shook the rock with false bravado.

"Come on, I'm ready for you!" I shouted.

I stood in the Liberty pose until my arm started to ache, and I realized I was standing there like an idiot. What a great way to introduce myself to my neighbors. My face grew warm in the cool night air. At least no one had witnessed my foolishness.

Enough nonsense; it was time to get inside and bed down before dawn. I moved to the front door and pulled out my driver's license.

The license slipped between the door and its frame and at the same time I jiggled the locking mechanism. Suddenly a shadow loomed over me. I gasped shifting sideways. The whoosh of something sliced the air just inches from the side of my head. It slammed into the wood with a deadly crack. That's when I saw that it was a metal baseball bat. One smash to my skull and. . .

"My god," I gasped. Jasper's killer had come back and was trying *to kill me.*

I spun, hollered a battle cry, and kicked out with my leg like I'd seen in an old Bruce Lee movie.

My foot connected with soft flesh. The intruder swore. I kicked again, this time I heard a loud crunch. He crumpled to the ground, rolling onto his back, writhing and clutching his arm. I kicked him one last time for good measure and grabbed the bat.

"Move, and the next hit's to the head." I said. "This bat of yours will crush it like an overripe watermelon." I pointed the penlight into his face. I wanted to get a good look at the man who had murdered my uncle.

The man blocked the light with his hand, obscuring his face. At the same moment the welcome flash of red lights from a cop car swung up to the gate. Its high beams spotlighted the scene and I breathed relief. The bad guy would be going to jail for a long time.

The officer jumped out of the car.

"Freeze," he ordered. "Drop your weapons."

I half-turned toward the deep voice, but kept an eye on my attacker.

"Now," the cop said. "Step away from the man on the ground."

What? The cop thought I was the intruder? I released my grip on the bat. It landed with a hollow clunk at my attacker's feet.

"Step back. Empty your other hand."

Complying, I moved and dropped my driver's license. It fluttered to the ground.

CHAPTER SIX

"**M**ove away from the man," the cop ordered. His gun pointed straight at my chest. "Put your hands on your head."

I stared in disbelief my mouth slack jawed.

"Hands up," he said.

"You're making a mistake," I shouted and jerked my arms over my head. "He attacked me."

The beam of the cop's flashlight seared my retinas. Wincing I glanced toward the dark building. The whole time he kept his gun trained on me.

I blinked hard as he finally shifted the beam away. My tear ducts kicked in and the welcoming relief of soothing saline tears flooded them.

The officer stopped just short of arm's reach. I squinted to get a look his name

tag, which was totally futile. My vision was still off from the blast of light, but I saw that he was about my height. This made him a little short for a cop. Dark blond hair, washed-out gray eyes and a scar over his left eyebrow. Not the slightest traces of smile lines.

"You're making a mistake," I said. "Officer. . .?"

"Stone." To the man on the ground he said, "Colin, you okay?"

Colin? My eyes snapped open and my stomach did a double flip. "Oh, shit."

Eyes finally re-adjusted, I got my first real look at my new business partner sprawled on the ground. That's when I noticed he was naked except for a pair of boxers emblazoned with the Playboy logo. Really? The Playboy Bunny. Who did he think he was, Hugh Hefner? Oh my god, what was I thinking? Who cares what kind of boxers he wore. At least he was defending the place from potential intruders. Our place.

Colin rolled to a sitting position, still clutching his arm.

"I'm so sorry," I said, almost too embarrassed for words.

He winced. "I think my arm's broken."

"I didn't mean to hurt you." I reached down to help him to his feet. "I thought—"

"Stop or I'll shoot." Stone's cop voice was low, steady and chilling calm.

I froze, my hand still outstretched. My eyes locked with Colin's. He was blond, blue-eyed, and good-looking in a movie star kind of way. Not bad for a man in his forties. To my chagrin, I giggled. A total nervous reaction. My hands flew to my mouth, but I couldn't stifle the unladylike guffaws that split the silent, cold night.

"Back. Away. Lady." Each word came out slow like Stone thought he was talking to a brain-impaired drunk, which I admit I probably sounded like. "Take it slow."

A full-throated laugh gurgled in my throat and morphed into uncontrollable brays between my gasps for breath. I don't know what was so funny, but my lack of sleep made the whole situation suddenly hilarious. Still, I complied like a nocturnal sloth on rewind.

Great first impression, Allie, I thought. *You maimed your new business partner and are being arrested for breaking into your own property.* A snort erupted from the back of my throat.

Neither man saw the humor of the situation. Colin struggled to his feet, looking at me like I'd sprouted seven heads and a tail. The scowl on Stone's face placed his humor score at a minus twenty.

While I ruminated, he pounced.

Before my addled brain registered what he was up to, he'd grabbed my hands, spun me, and I felt cold metal cuffs snap around my wrists.

"Officer, you're making a mistake," I babbled between cackles. "This is all one big misunderstanding."

"The only mistake here is your trying to break into my property," Colin said, resting his injured arm on a porch rail. He ran his good hand through his hair, smiled, and posed for some invisible photographer to snap his photo.

A déjà vu moment, I thought, as the laughter died in my throat. I recognized the series of gestures. Had laughed at them. Loved them. Had grown to hate them. And even though Colin looked nothing like my ex-husband, at that moment my new partner could have been him. My humor drained. Anger raged in its place.

"Your property?" I said and glared at him. "Have you forgotten that you are only a co-heir to Jasper Marlon's estate and that you have a part-ner? What are you doing here? You're not supposed to arrive for another two weeks."

Instead of answering Colin looked at his arm, winced and groaned.

I was still too angry to feel guilty. Yet.

"You have the right to remain silent," Officer Stone said.

"I'm fully aware of my rights."

"Anything you say can and will be used against you in a court of law."

"Un-cuff me," I said. "I'm Allie Renault. Or use to be. Renault is my maiden name. Jasper Marlon was my uncle." I tried to sound calm, cool and collected.

Officer Stone ignored my words and continued to recite my Miranda rights.

"I'm one of Jasper's heirs."

Colin smirked.

"If you cannot afford an attorney. . ." Officer Stone droned on.

"I co-own this property," I said.

Officer Stone stopped mid-sentence.

"Un-cuff me. I have every right to enter my place of business, day or night. By any means I deem suitable."

"And I have every right to do my job," he said. "Which is to arrest you for suspicious activities."

"I have not committed an arrestable offense. Cite me with disturbing the peace if you want, but when I'm done with you in court you'll either look like a fool or a total jerk."

Stone's expression hardened into a mask. "Are you threatening me?"

"Stone, can we get on with this? I think I need to see a doctor."

The officer ignored him. "Lady, do you have identification?"

I nodded to my driver's license on the concrete in front of the door. "It's there."

Stone picked up my California license and studied it a long moment.

"My copy of Jasper's will is in my car at the curb. I suggest you go get it before this farce escalates."

Stone held my license in the flashlight's beam for Colin to read.

Colin looked chagrined. "She's right. She's Jasper's niece."

"Do you want to press charges?"

"For what?" Colin and I said simultaneously.

"For assault?"

"That's ridiculous," I said.

Colin groaned. "I need to get some ice on this arm."

"You're right," I said. "I really am sorry. But you attacked me first with that baseball bat. You could have killed me."

His lips curled up, but somehow the smile didn't reach his eyes. Was it the pain or something else? "Looks like our partnership has started off as a big hit."

I nodded.

Stone stepped closer, his fingers reaching for my upper arm.

I jerked back. "Touch me and I'll file charges against you faster than you can spell sexual harassment. Believe me, it's a real career stopper."

He held up a little key. "Thought you wanted the cuffs off."

"Oh, sorry," I said. My face flamed.

"It's nice to meet you, too." He removed the official bracelets.

The skin on my neck suddenly flared unbearably hot. The planned triumphant arrival in Sedona had morphed into a total disaster. My new self-esteem was in tatters. Still I tried to smile. The guy was just doing his job. Under any other circumstances, I'd be glad to have him there.

"Sorry."

Stone broke into a genuine smile and then started to laugh. "They say a lot rides on a first impression, but ... under the circumstances I think we should start over." He held out his hand. "Welcome to Sedona."

"Thanks," I said. His strong hand enveloped mine, his clasp firm and somehow his words warmed me.

Okay. So maybe he wasn't the bad guy.

"Colin, let's get you to the hospital," Stone said.

"Want me to come?" Why did I say that? Hospitals were right up there on my list of favorite things. Like flying. Both terrified me. Not to mention I was totally exhausted and just wanted to go to bed. Still I felt responsible for Colin's arm.

"No, I'll take him." The tough cop act was gone. "You're obviously tired. I'll give Brian Scully a call. He owns the Eagle Inn. It's late, but I'm sure he'll rent you a room for the night."

"That's okay." I wasn't about to tell him I was low on cash. Colin had probably already commandeered the bedroom, but a couch would be fine. "Thanks, but I'll stay here."

"Suit yourself." He turned to Colin. "Let's get you dressed. Don't want to give the nurses heart palpitations."

Colin's face lit like a lascivious light bulb. He winked at some invisible camera before opening the front door to the store and led us in. He flipped on the lights. Overhead fluorescent bulbs pulsated to life. The air vibrated with their low-pitched hum.

"Here it is." He swung his good arm with a showman's flourish and winced. "May I present, THE ALABASTER."

My mouth flopped open. I grappled for a hold on a nearby shelf as I reached out to steady myself. I took another step and smeared a distorted handprint in the thick gritty grime. Narrow aisles ran between cluttered shelves. Dust coated everything, even the dead flies that littered almost every flat surface in sight.

"Oh. My. God." Each word came out like its own sentence of doom. "How long since the store was closed up?"

"Since Jasper's murder," Colin said in a dry voice. "A couple of months."

"Two months? It'll take six months to sort out this mess."

"It's not as bad as it looks. The dust is cosmetic. Part of Jasper's marketing strategy."

"The dust and dirt strategy?"

Stone chuckled as the two men rapidly moved toward the back of the store.

Colin talked over his shoulder. "Jasper said people liked to discover hidden treasures under what appeared to be years of neglect. Made them think they were taking advantage of a feeble old man who didn't know what he had and that they were getting a super bargain."

I trailed behind taking in my new future.

"Mind if I look around?" I asked, curious to see the place.

"Take all the time you want," Colin said. They exited through a door, leaving it open. "It's half yours. Just turn the lights off when you're done."

"Thanks," I said and stared the store in numb amazement.

The place looked like it'd been abandoned for at least a year. Make that a century, judging from the mammoth arachnid colony overhead. It was an incredible feat of magnificent engineering. If you like spiders.

I bumped into an ancient magazine rack. It teetered a full two seconds before toppling to the floor. Magazines fanned out in a distorted mosaic of glossy colors.

Something crashed to my right. My head swiveled toward the sound, saw movement, and froze. In the corner, a fat rat scampered up and over the face of a strange carving of an Aztec god. It leered at me through black obsidian eyes.

A rush of imagined little rodent feet raced down my neck, leaving rat-bumps in its wake. Shivering, I decided I'd seen enough for one night.

Clutching my arms around me I was ready to call it a night. Still, I found myself stopping dead in front of the cash register. I couldn't resist leaning over the glass countertop to stare at the murder scene. In spite of my years prosecuting homicides, bile erupted into my throat. Dried brownish red blood stains streaked the wall, the floor and the back of the counter.

CHAPTER SEVEN

I stared at the crime scene. First, I felt sick. And then I felt sad for Jasper even though I hadn't known him. Then I was annoyed. Why hadn't Colin bothered to clean after the police had completed their investigation? Or hired someone to do it? Didn't he have respect for the dead? Was he so heartless that he wanted to stand on Jasper's blood to ring up customer's purchases?

At the same time, I realized that his laziness gave me the opportunity to draw my own conclusions of the crime scene. Stone may have turned friendly when he realized who I was but he didn't seem like the type to share information from an official police investigation with a civilian. Not even one with high success in the investigating and prosecuting of criminals.

My eyes lingered on the dark dried puddle staining the wooden floor. It was weird that blood could look like an oil spill, all cracked and flaking from age. Jasper must have lost a lot before dying. Fast. Obviously the result of a stab wound to an artery. My eyes started to water. I wasn't sure if it was grief or exhaustion. Either way, it was clear the crime scene wasn't going anywhere until I scoured its existence into oblivion. After a good sleep would be soon enough. My mind would be fresher.

I spotted the door the guys had gone through at the rear of the store and headed for it, remembering that Colin had said the living quarters were at the back of the storage area.

I prepared myself for the worst and wasn't disappointed. The storage room was lit by an inadequate number of naked light bulbs hanging precariously from black wires. They gave off an eerie yellow light. The room was cavernous and perfumed with a stale, cloying musky odor mixed with old dust. An indoor junkyard maze of boxes, old bicycles, hubcaps, drawers, cluttered bookcases and lumpy sacks filled with who knew what.

My inheritance had morphed into a bad dream with nightmare potential.

As I stepped over the threshold, it felt symbolic. I'd slipped from the bright lights of the store into an ominous shadow world of hidden danger. Menacing dim shapes lurked behind plywood partitions randomly nailed to the floor.

Okay. So I was going overboard on the dramatic symbolism. It's just that I'd let myself get all amped up, thinking I'd inherited a thriving business. A bright new future. Yet since I'd arrived in Sedona, I'd been almost arrested. My new partner showed signs of being a serious jerk. And tomorrow I would have to scour my dead uncle's dried blood from the walls of my new home.

Not the triumphant arrival I'd let myself imagine.

Up ahead, a faceted glass doorknob twinkled in the gloom. The door opened. Stone and a dressed Colin emerged. I hurried across the storage space to them.

"Welcome to Chateau Jasper," Colin said, opening the door wider. "Extra blankets in the hall closet, unless you want to share the bed."

I'd been about to apologize again about his arm, but instead said, "The couch will be fine."

"Suit yourself," he said. "But you owe me, big time. You can work it off. Cleaning."

Wrong answer, I thought.

"We should get moving," Stone said.

"Speaking of cleaning," I said, "why hasn't the crime scene been cleaned?"

"What, and have my new partner think I'd high-graded the valuable stuff?" He flashed me a smile, all teeth and no substance. "Besides, I figured you being the female half of this partnership would want the honors."

I was about to lambaste him for being a heartless and sexist pig when he bumped his arm. He winced and his face turned white. Guilt slammed me. This wasn't the time to lay down the ground rules of our partnership. He needed to get to a doctor.

Tomorrow would be soon enough to establish our working relationship.

They left out a side door and I entered Jasper's apartment. It was small, but at least three times the size of my L.A. motel room and looked immaculate compared to the rest of the place. Not bad. Cozy, even.

I wondered if Uncle Jasper had been such a serious businessman, why had he been so lackadaisical about the store? Had Alex lied about its ability to turn a profit? Then again his murderer had thought he was making money.

After a quick search, I located the extra blankets and bedded down in Uncle Jasper's old leather recliner.

Why had Jasper saddled me with Colin?

IT WAS STILL pitch black when what sounded like a gunshot woke me from an uneasy slumber. I shook off my sleep-haze. No, my imagination must still be on overdrive. Not a gun shot, but a car door slamming. Colin?

Low voices drifted though the open window. It seemed like the conversation lasted forever. If it were Stone and Colin, what could be so important to talk about in the middle of the night? They'd had plenty of time to discuss my unexpected arrival.

Maybe it wasn't them. Maybe the talkers were a pair of thieves planning a break-in? Maybe it was the same guys who'd killed Jasper and assumed the store was empty and had come back for more loot.

I glanced at the clock's glowing red numbers in the corner— 3:30 a.m. Panic raced through my veins. I thrust down the footrest of the recliner. My afghan-blanket slid into puddle on the floor. Cold air replaced my warm cocoon and brought me fully awake. If I'd known how cold it'd get, I never would have opened the window. It was freezing. But I was glad I'd left it ajar because otherwise I would have slept through a possible break-in.

Wide-awake, the whole meet-and-greet Colin incident came back. My Ninja kick to his chest. His broken arm.

The car's motor idled next to the building. That would be a dumb move if it were crooks. Thieves would hardly be stupid enough to advertise their presence. It had to be Colin. So what could be taking him so long to say goodnight? Maybe it wasn't Stone who'd driven him home, but a girlfriend, and my being here put a cramp in their style.

Colin's voice drifted on the breeze through the open window. "Thanks for the lift."

"Anytime," Stone voice, loud enough to hear. "Good luck with the new partnership."

The car roared off. Which meant Colin would come in any second and I wasn't up to another awkward conversation. I grabbed the afghan, returned the chair to its pseudo bed position and pretended to be asleep.

I waited.

He didn't come inside.

Curious, I slid the footrest down again. Wrapping the afghan around me, I tiptoed to the open window. I couldn't see him anywhere. I listened. Nothing — then came the flip of a cigarette lighter belching a tiny flame.

The faint flare lit his face for a moment. Even smoking hadn't erased his attractive features. The planes of his cheekbones became sharp-edged shadows and looked a little creepy as if chiseled by Goya. Another trick of the night's light and my over-active imagination. Then only the glow of his cigarette gave away his position. The unpleasant pungent aroma of tobacco floated through the window. Was he actually being considerate and smoking outside? Maybe he wasn't a total jerk. I hoped not. We had to work together for at least the next two years.

Besides, Jasper had trusted him and I should, too.

A little ashamed to be spying on him like an immature peeping Tomasina, I moved away from the window and felt my way back to the easy chair. I settled and hoped to get back to sleep.

"Sorry to wake you," Colin said.

I jumped. I hadn't heard him come in. Guiltily, I sat up.

He wasn't there.

I crept back to the window and looked out. He was leaned up against the building, still smoking as he talked.

"Hold on," he said, and then his voice dropped to a whisper. It was as if he knew someone was listening. He glanced at the window and I ducked.

Who could he be calling at three in the morning?

"I know it's a God-forsaken hour," he whispered in a heated voice. "Yes I am angry. Jasper's niece showed up and it changes everything."

I peeked out the window again. Who was he talking to? He'd moved into the moonlight, pacing back and forth with his good arm clutching his cell phone to his ear. The other hitched up in a sling.

"Of course she can't hear me. Think I'm stupid? I'm outside freezing my butt off." He threw down his cigarette and crushed it under his heel, grinding it into the pavement. "You should have given me the heads up."

He turned away and all I caught was, "Our mutual business arrangement."

Pause.

"Don't threaten me. You want me to blow the whistle?"

Long pause.

"Okay."

Pause.

"She's an airhead. I can handle her."

Was he talking about me? I may sound a little dingy when I'm sleep-deprived, but I'm no airhead. He had another thing coming if he thought he was going to *handle me*.

"I'll call you tomorrow." Swearing, he kicked a rock and it clattered against the wall.

I scooted back to the chair. When he came in, I snored softly in rhythm to every third racing heartbeat. He stood by my chair and even though my eyes were closed, his stare felt palpable. It took every ounce of disciplined self-preservation to maintain my pretense of sleep.

He remained motionless for what seemed like an eternity before he retired to the bedroom.

Ten minutes passed before I dared move. By then the calves of my right leg had cramped and my left hand had gone numb. I flexed the fingers and tried minimal isometric stretches to relieve the strain of tight muscles while my mind raced with a zillion questions. Questions I could only guess the answers to. Whatever Colin was up to, one thing was clear. He was setting up a secret financial deal that didn't include the sharing of its profits.

Some new business partner I'd inherited. Thank you, Uncle Jasper. You weren't such a good judge of character after all. But then what had I expected? He'd named me a co-heir knowing my track record.

Oh just go to sleep, I told myself. Figure it out in the morning after a decent rest. I closed my eyes and started deep breathing, willing myself to relax. It didn't work. Still, I must have fallen asleep because the next time I opened my eyes, bright sunlight filtered through the window and I got my first good look at Jasper's home. Rather, my new home.

Along the wall sat a small faded loveseat flanked by two brass floor lamps. A scarred coffee table squatted on a faded blue and orange Turkish carpet. Tucked into the corner stood an ancient roll top desk with its brand new swivel chair. I knew it was new because the sales tag still dangled from the arm.

I struggled out of my makeshift bed and stretched. Assuming Colin was still sound asleep, I crept around the apartment in stealth mode.

After two days in the same clothes I was in desperate need of a shower. As gross as I felt and knew I looked, I didn't want to drag all my stuff from the car until Colin and I had a serious talk. The apartment was too small for both of us. Even if it were larger, I doubted the wisdom of sharing the same domicile.

After his late night phone conference with his other mystery partner, I had a feeling that working together would be enough of a challenge.

For now, I'd concentrate on my immediate needs—the bathroom and a serious infusion of caffeine. I doubted there'd be any milk, so I'd tough it out and drink my coffee black. That is, if there was any coffee.

The small efficiency kitchen was a pleasant surprise. Wow. The counter tops were spotless. The stainless-steel sink gleamed and the stove looked almost brand new even though it was a gas model from the sixties. A shopping list hung on the refrigerator under A Star Trek Enterprise magnet.

For a moment I wondered if Colin had cleaned the place, but discarded the idea. If he'd been that ambitious he'd have cleaned up the blood in the store.

A quick survey of the fridge confirmed my earlier suspicion. No milk, not even curdled. Jasper's shopping list was dated 9-29. He must have written it just days before his death. Maybe it held a clue to his murder.

Rice, bread, tuna, coffee, sugar, honey buns. Milk.

Honey buns. No way. Did they still make them? They'd been my Saturday morning favorite when I was a kid. Just remembering their sticky sweet taste, washed my mouth with saliva. At the moment I would have killed for one.

I opened cupboards, hoping against hope. To my amazement, every shelf was neat and organized. Even the canned goods were categorized by food type and positioned with their labels facing out. A quick search revealed peanut butter, coffee, and a mug, but no honey buns. Oh well. I'd live. Plus I'd learned one more thing about Jasper. He might have been a disorganized shopkeeper, but he'd been meticulous in his personal life.

It wasn't long before I was sipping coffee and eating chunky organic peanut butter with a spoon. The thick salty nut paste tasted heavenly and I groaned. It made even the un-doctored bitter coffee palatable.

I settled at his roll top desk while I ate, wondering what secrets its drawers would reveal. A man's desk is sort of like a woman's purse. It's a catch-all for a lot of personal stuff that reveals character.

That's when I spotted the photograph, displayed in a gold frame on the wall. How had I missed it? I jumped up, kicking a brass-headed cane leaned up against the desk. It clattered on the floor. Its dog head leered up at me in amusement. My face grew hot as I scooped up the cane and leaned it back against the wall.

"Colin, you son of a gun," I said between gritted teeth as I stared at my high school graduation picture.

Colin had to have seen it a dozen times. More if he'd visited Jasper in the last fourteen years. He must have recognized me last night. So why hadn't he stopped Stone from cuffing me?

The more I learned about the man, the less I liked him.

I shifted the bottom corner of my high school graduation photo an inch to the left. Yep, the wall underneath was a brighter shade of yellow. It had hung there forever. Proof positive, as soon as Colin had got a good look at me, he had to have known who I was last night, before Stone cuffed me. That I wasn't a random stranger-thief.

My blood boiled as I glared at his senior photo hanging next to mine. Mr. Big man on campus, good looking even back then and wearing the look of smug satisfaction of knowing he could have any girl he wanted.

"You may still be good looking, but you're a total jerk," I said to the photo. "You must have gotten a real kick out of seeing me cuffed and treated like a criminal."

He had more in common with my ex-husband than just a few gestures. I was half tempted to go wake him and give him a piece of my mind. But then I'd have to deal with him before my second cup of coffee and before I got a chance to get a good look around the place.

I poured another cup and slipped into the storeroom. The disorganized mess looked just as daunting as the night before. But on closer inspection, it looked like someone had rummaged through it. Bright dustless patches in the otherwise grimy gloom revealed where things had been shifted or moved. Maybe someone had been hired to take an inventory of the estate for tax purposes. Too bad they hadn't done a little cleaning as they went.

I made a mental note to ask Alex for a copy of the inventory when he returned to town. Not that anything looked valuable, but after last night I knew I couldn't trust Colin to tell the truth, the whole truth, and nothing but the truth when it came to our new business partnership.

Steeling myself, I went into the store proper and avoided the kill spot. I'd examine it later. Now I just wanted to get a feel for the store and its merchandise. Looking around I realized nothing was labeled or priced.

Most everything looked inexpensive except for maybe the carvings, a crystal ball and some silver jewelry in a locked case. That stopped me. If Jasper's murder was the result of a random break-in, why hadn't the killer taken the jewelry?

I rubbed gray dust from the face of a cold smooth stone and it rewarded me with a bright flash of blue. I picked it up and took it to the front window. Amazing. The play of color shifted like light bouncing off the back of a CD. Tilting the rock to the right transformed the bright blue to a coppery yellow. Cool. A natural hologram.

I had to find out what it was called. And all the other stones in the place. It would be like going back to school again. I had a lot to learn.

For the first time, I could see why Jasper had spent his life in the stone business.

Pounding sounded on the front door. I flinched and almost dropped the rock.

"Yoo-hoo," the voice called. "I can see you."

I moved over to the glass door. Facing me stood an elderly woman dressed in a black fitted polyester pantsuit. Her wavy iron gray hair was cut short in a no nonsense style. She stood ramrod straight and smiled like she expected to win first place in an octogenarian beauty pageant.

"I'm sorry," I shouted and returned her smile. "We're closed."

The lady grabbed for the doorknob. Before I could react, she'd pushed open the door, knocking into a little bell that hung from the ceiling.

Strange. I thought Colin had locked it last night.

"You must be the niece," she said and reached out a black, gloved hand to shake mine.

"Nice to meet you . . ." I matched her firm grip, unsure if I should call her Mrs., Miss or Ms. I settled on Ma'am. "We're not open for business just yet. Have to clean first and then figure out what's what."

She waved at an ancient black Dodge parked next to my Escort. Two more elderly ladies emerged from the car. They dressed in similar, sensible, out-of-fashion attire. One wore green and the other maroon.

"This nice young woman is going to open up for us. What is your name?"

"Allie, but we're not open for business."

"Let me present my two sisters. This is Miss Edna and Miss Rose. And I'm Dorcus. Dorcus Sedona Kincaid. I think it's wonderful that you and the young man are going to continue Jasper's dream," she said, pushing past me. "You don't mind if we shop for a little bit, do you?"

"I'm sorry to disappoint you, but--"

"I've had a vision. What I need is a special piece of alabaster so I can

49

channel Jasper." Dorcus moved like a Sherman tank through the store, picking up one stone, slamming it down, and grabbing up another.

I stumbled after her.

"I just know it has to be here."

"I have no idea what alabaster looks like," I said, not wanting to make a snap judgment, but thinking the lady was seriously out of her mind.

"That's okay, I'll know it when I see it." She swiveled, aimed her finger at Rose. "Open '*The Book*'."

Rose pulled a well-worn book from her crocheted shopping bag. An artist's rendition of a huge purple crystal dominated its cover.

"It's time Allie learned all about alabaster."

"That's okay," I said. "Maybe you could come back later, when my partner is here. He knows more about the rocks than I do."

"Page thirteen."

Miss Rose set the book onto the counter, put on the glasses that dangled around her neck and flipped pages until she found the spot. Miss Edna wandered over to a shelf that housed a pride of small dinosaurs carved out of a pink rock.

"Alabaster," Miss Rose read in a high whiny voice that would drive me nuts if I had to listen to it for very long. "The Egyptians cut and used it for mystical purposes. It is said to help the seeker unlock the ancient secrets of mankind and to help one to communicate with departed spirits. It also stimulates meditation when carved. And can energize other minerals. Medically it aids in treating disorders of the heart by diminishing one's anger."

"What kind of book is that?" I asked, trying to keep the skepticism out of my voice.

Dorcus sniffed. "It's the most complete book of rock mysticism and properties ever written. Isn't it wonderful that you will be embracing the power of the rocks every day?"

"Yeah, sure," I said.

"Here it is," Dorcus cried and held up what looked like a small hand-sized paperweight. "This is the one. Just look, it has a sweet flower carved on top of a pyramid. I can already feel Jasper's presence descending."

The phone jangled.

I jumped.

"Jasper here," a man's baritone announced.

I about died until I realized it was the answering machine.

"I'm out, about and the store is closed. Leave a message if you're so inclined. Just remember, if you bite the bullet, you'll pass lead."

Beep.

"Aaaaaaaaa," Dorcus cried out as if she somehow had summoned the answering machine to speak and clutched the stone to her chest. "Jasper, I'm listening. I'm an open channel."

CHAPTER EIGHT

M y jaw dropped open like a cartoon version of a shocked are-you-kidding look. Did this old lady seriously believe a rock would allow her to communicate with the dead? Or was it a desperate act to knock me off balance?

Dorcus didn't look like a killer, but my time as a lawyer had taught me that anyone is capable of committing murder. Even nice old ladies. Until I knew what really happened to Jasper, I couldn't trust anyone.

Dorcus clutched THE ALABASTER paperweight to her chest and stared, glazed-eyed at the ceiling. Her eyes moved slowly, canvassing the counter and floor of the crime scene. Maybe her masquerade as a crazy old lady had a purpose. Maybe she was looking for some miniscule incriminating evidence she'd left behind after stabbing Jasper. If she were the killer, had she dropped something in her haste to flee the scene? Something that could link her to the crime? Evidence that the police had obviously missed. Not that Chief Stone seemed too motivated to solve the crime.

"Jasper," her voice keened. "Speak to me. Tell me the person who's stolen your life force and wrenched your soul from this plane of existence."

"What's going on here?"

Dorcus snapped out of her trance.

I turned. Colin stood bare-chested in the doorway between the store and the storage room. My new business partner and a probable con man. Although Jasper named him a co-heir, and he had an alibi for the night Jasper died, there was something about him that didn't seem quite right. His movie star aura looked at odds with the dreary neglected merchandise on the shelves. Like he'd appeared for a sophisticated film shoot and found himself trapped in an old lady séance.

"Oh!" exclaimed Edna and dropped the little dinosaur carving she'd been examining. Its tail popped off as it hit the floor. Her wrinkled face turned a bright shade of pink that clashed with the color of her polyester top.

Dorcus blinked hard several times, shook her head, and raised her arms as if to ward off the visage of his nudity. "Young man! You're upsetting the aura of the stones and have broken my contact with the other side. I'm sure Jasper would not approve of you coming in here half-dressed." She shook her finger. "Edna, stop staring. Young man, put some clothes on. This is not a hoochie house."

I stifled a giggle. Compared to last night, he was overdressed. In addition to his boxers, his cast covered his right arm from wrist to elbow.

"Beg your pardon, ladies," he said. "I heard noise and thought someone had broken into the store again."

Dorcus sniffed, averting her eyes from his well-sculpted torso. "Well, I guess your state of undress is understandable under the circumstances, but now you see we're customers and not thieves. I suggest you remedy the situation."

"I tried to explain to the ladies," I said, "that we're not open for business yet."

"Nonsense," Dorcus said. "Colin, you know I've been one of Jasper's favorite customers for years. And a good friend. He'd be pleased if I were your first customer. Especially if it means that I'll be able to contact him on the other side." She produced a handkerchief from her sleeve and blew her nose. "I just have to have this carved bit of alabaster. How much do you want for it?"

"I have no idea what it's worth," I said.

Colin took the carved paperweight from her and examined it. His brow wrinkled and he pursed his lips. Finally he said, "I can let you have it for seventy-five dollars. You can pay Allie while I go get dressed. The tax is on us."

Wow. It didn't look like a seventy-five dollar paperweight to me, but Dorcus beamed. She dug into her purse for the money.

Colin pulled me aside and whispered, "Watch Miss Edna. The skinny one. She's a kleptomaniac." As he spoke, I saw her slip a small tyrannosaurus rex carving into her clutch bag.

I cleared my throat, starting toward her. He grabbed my arm and shook his head. "It's okay. It's cheap. We can afford the loss. I doubled the price on the paperweight. We're good."

"But you can't let her just take things."

"She's harmless and usually only snags one item per visit. As long as it's not something too expensive. . ." He shrugged.

"That's crazy."

"It is what it is. Jasper always said it was just part of doing business with the old girls." He frowned.

Was this a possible motive? I could imagine Jasper growing tired of Edna's stealing. Maybe he'd talked to her about it and threatened to press charges if she didn't stop. Dorcus, being the take-charge sister of the trio, wouldn't let that happen. She might not be able to stop her sister's petty thieving and saw only one possible solution. Stop Jasper before her delicate sister was thrown in jail and all three of the sisters' reputations could be ruined.

"Why did you let the ladies in?" Colin asked.

"What?" I said, startled out of my musing. He repeated the question and I replied. "I didn't."

"You're telling me they just materialized?" He laughed. "Maybe there's something to all their rock mumbo jumbo after all."

"I doubt it. It's more likely someone left the door unlocked last night. I wonder who that could be?"

"Not me. I locked up."

"Then why was the door open this morning?"

"I don't know. Maybe you sleepwalk."

"Or maybe, you just thought you locked the door." I stared at him a long minute. His bravado vanished. Tension lines appeared. Was that fear I saw in his eyes? Or had his pain medication worn off? Either way, the over-confident Colin seemed to have vanished.

"Maybe we should call a locksmith," I said.

"Maybe I will." He spun round and left me to deal with the ladies.

I looked at my watch. Five minutes had passed and the sisters showed no sign of leaving the store. I wanted to scream as they leisurely explored. I remembered the blood stains near the cash register. I grabbed some newspapers and spread them across the counter and on the floor. There was nothing I could do about the dried streaks on the wall other than to hope they didn't notice.

"I'm sorry," I said. "I have a few errands to run and an appointment with Carl Morton this morning." Okay. It was a little white lie. I didn't have an actual appointment, but Alex had arranged for me to pick up the keys for THE ALABASTER from the man when I got to town. "The morning is slipping away."

"The colonel?" Dorcus sniffed. "Why didn't you say so? It's most impolite to be late for one's appointments. Especially with the colonel. We can come back later to browse."

I didn't know if her colonel and Alex's Carl Morton were one and the same, but I wasn't about to ask. I didn't want to delay her exit.

She moved to the cash register. "I feel Jasper's life force straining to communicate with me on this very spot. His presence is strong."

I eyed the newsprint that covered his blood and had to choke back a hysterical bark of nervous laughter.

She set down the paperweight and pulled out a wad of bills. "To save time, we can add up together. One. Two. Three." She timed the placement of each bill, Washington side up, to coincide with her precise, enunciated count.

As the stack grew, I was amazed that it didn't topple.

"Seventy-five." She looked up. "Very satisfactory, indeed."

Edna joined us. She stared at the pile of cash, and bit her lower lip. She noticed me watching her and her gaze darted away. "What is that?" her voice squeaked.

Oh no. She'd seen the streaked blood on the wall. I stepped in front of it to block her view.

"It's a rat!" Edna shrieked and her face turned white.

A rat? Before I could even react, a large brown rodent ran down the counter, dropped to the floor, and raced over Edna's open-toed Birkenstocks before it disappeared into a pile of boxes.

Edna stood rooted to the spot, staring down at her exposed toes.

I shivered for her and hoped it was the same lone rat that startled me last night. Hoped that there wasn't a horde of them living in the store. Or living in the apartment. I shivered a second time imagining a pack of them running across my face in the middle of the night. Mentally I added rattraps to my shopping list.

Rose's voice trembled. "Oh!" Her face transformed into a mask of fear and she raced for the door, clutching the book.

"Don't be so squeamish," Dorcus said. She stared down her nose at me. "You need a cat. Edna," Dorcus grabbed her sister's arm, giving it a hard shake. "Snap out of it. You've had enough excitement for one morning. It's time we went home."

"It touched me."

"I'm sorry," I said. "That's one more reason we're not ready for business." Silently I cheered the rat. I'd make sure the rattrap would be a humane one.

I walked them to the door. Rose was already in the car.

"We're not opening until we get rid of the spiders, rodents, and whatever else is lurking in the corners," I said and hoped they wouldn't return until the window sported an open sign.

Once they were gone, Colin reappeared dressed in a sleeveless muscle shirt and pair of skin-tight Levis. He held out his hand. "I'll take my cut."

"What?"

"My half of the seventy-five. I'm feeling generous so you can keep the change." He ran his hand through his hair and checked himself out in the reflection of the glass case.

"Colin, we have to talk."

"About what?"

"For starters, why didn't you tell Stone who I was before he cuffed me?"

He gave me a wide-eyed, 'who me?' look. "I don't know—"

"Cut the bull. You had to have seen my photo on the wall right next to yours. It's kind of hard to miss."

He gave me his version of a charming smile that I'm sure worked on most of the ladies. "It was dark and I was in pain." His smile faded. "So when did Alex find you?"

"Two days ago. Maybe at first, you didn't recognize me, but once you saw my face you had to have known it was me."

He raised the elbow of his cast. "A little payback for the broken arm."

I stared at him hard and wished I'd kicked him harder. It would be a miracle if we survived six weeks working together, let alone two years.

The front door opened and the little bell tinkled. My fault. I should have locked it.

"Hey!" said a man's voice. It was deep and tinged with the underlying mellow seductive tone that really good disc jockeys spin on the airwaves. "Anyone home?"

The owner of the voice could talk fleas off a dog. He stood framed in the doorway. Instantly I saw why Dorcus had called him the colonel. He looked like a dead ringer for the famous Colonel Sanders of KFC fame; an older man in white, from his bushy snowy hair under a broad Panama hat down to his polished white patent shoes. He wore a white suit, white shirt and a white tie. On closer inspection, I noticed that he sported a white mother-of-pearl tie tack and matching cufflinks. Only a gold pyramid lapel pin and his intelligent chestnut brown eyes sported any color. Intense dark brown eyes that reminded me of someone I'd met recently.

"Hi," I said, making the connection. "Are you related to Alex Farmer?"

"Uncle and business partner. Now retired," he drawled and removed his hat. Stepping closer he clasped my hand in his. "And you must be the long lost Allie."

"Guilty as charged."

He chuckled. "Welcome to Sedona." He turned to Colin. "I just dropped by to tell you the Pyramidion council met last night and we approved your application. All we need is your bona fides and it's a done deal."

Colin beamed. "Why, thank you, sir. I'll get right on it. Allie, we can talk later. I have some personal business this morning."

"Excuse me," I said to Carl and turned to Colin. "Can't it wait a day? We have a lot of things to sort out."

"You can start on the clean-up," he said and pointed to his cast. "I'll be out of commission for at least six weeks." He gave me an exaggerated Groucho Marx wink. "By then everything should be ship-shape."

"And what will you do while I provide the slave labor?"

"Go over the books. Look through Jasper's records. Stuff like that. You wouldn't want to worry your pretty little head over numbers and such." He raised and flexed the bicep of his good arm. "It's man's work."

Not wanting to start a down-and-out brawl in front of Alex's uncle, I gave Colin a fake, "ha ha," bounced my eyebrows a couple of times, and returned his wink. "You know what they say… all brawn and no brains makes Colin a dull boy. I'm not so sure your pretty little brain-cell muscles can handle the challenge, either."

Carl let out a belly laugh. "She got you there. Come on, Allie. Why don't you join me for breakfast? My treat. Let Colin start on the paper sorting and filing."

"I'm not exactly presentable to venture out in public."

"Nonsense. You look just fine. And you have to eat."

My stomach rumbled.

"I'll take that as a yes." He chuckled again and looked at his watch. "We can walk. It's just down the street."

"Okay, let me grab my purse."

I rushed back to the apartment and made a beeline for the bathroom. I checked myself out in the mirror and confirmed my suspicions. Carl was a bald-faced liar. I didn't look *just fine*. I looked like crap. Dark circles under my red eyes gave me the anemic-raccoon-look of a binge drinker. The fact that I'd worn the same clothes for almost two days and had slept in them didn't help either.

I wished I could shower before I made my debut in town.

My hair was at that awkward limbo stage. Too long to be short. Too short to be long. I rummaged through my purse and came up with a pair of tortoise hair-combs and jammed one behind each ear. I so wanted to brush my teeth, but my toothbrush was in my suitcase in the car. I wet a tissue and rubbed it over them. It didn't really work, so I popped a piece of spearmint gum in my mouth, slapped on some lipstick and mascara. It'd have to do.

When I returned to the store Colin's smirk had disappeared and his perfect-formed body slouched like a deflated blow-up toy. He looked more like a little boy recently chastised than the macho guy he pretended to be. Carl's color seemed high and he looked more than just a little annoyed. I wondered what Colin had said or done to earn the disapproval. Whatever, it looked like the elder man had won the scuffle,

When Carl saw me he smiled.

"Hope I didn't take too long," I said.

"I never mind waiting for a pretty lady," Carl said.

"You are a charmer," I said, laughing. And meant it. The same words from Colin would have set my nerves on edge, but from this kind man it felt nice, like a warm blanket on a cold night. It seemed like a real stretch to view him as a suspect to Jasper's murder. From what I'd heard so far, it sounded like their friendship had gone way back. Still, who knew what secrets they may have shared? Maybe a secret Jasper was tired of keeping?

"But I sure am getting hungry." Carl motioned for me to go first. At the door he paused and turned back to Colin. "Don't let yourself get side-tracked. You have forty-eight hours."

Colin saluted with his good arm. "Yes sir, Colonel."

Outside the air pricked my skin, but the bright sun promised a nice day. We headed west walking just a hint faster than a stroll.

"I noticed that everyone calls you colonel," I said. "Should I?"

"No, Carl's just fine. That's what Jasper called me. He was a good friend. I'm sorry for your loss."

"I wish I could have met him. He sounds like a remarkable man."

"He was. As you've probably already surmised, he remained a man of principle no matter what. He objected to the war and stood his ground. Cost him his family."

"If I'd had known he'd existed, I would have stayed in contact. Hard to believe my mom could keep a secret for more than a day, let alone years."

Carl patted my arm. "That's because you're more like him than her."

We walked the next half block in silence. Him maybe remembering his friend and I thinking about the generosity of an uncle I'd never met.

He paused in front of a long, single-story brick building. It had a set of triple wide cement steps and a broad covered porch. The signage indicated it housed two businesses: the offices of Morton and Farmer Attorneys at Law and the *Sedona Charitable Trust, a nonprofit at large.*

"Mind if we stop here for a moment?" He nodded to the lone black BMW in the parking lot. "That's my daughter's car. She's early. I'd like you to meet her."

"Sounds great," I said, again wishing I'd had time for a shower and change of clothes. Still, the opportunity to meet more players in Jasper's life was an opportunity I couldn't let pass. Not with my growing suspicion that his murderer was an acquaintance, a Sedonite who had wanted Jasper dead. The few facts I'd learned so far supported this scenario more than Stone's theory of a transient thief.

Instead of entering the law offices, Carl led me into the nonprofit agency next door. The warm yellow tones of the room infused the atmosphere with comfort and hope. A slew of framed pictures filled one entire wall, all headshots of children from various ethnic groups. Name, age and country of origin were neatly printed under each smiling face.

One corner of the room had been fenced-off for a play area. It overflowed with bright colored toys guaranteed to appeal to the one-to-five crowd. Near it a cozy seating area situated for hopeful parents. A couch, two olive-green armchairs and a coffee table with parenting magazines spread out in a fan.

A white ash receptionist desk with two guest chairs was discretely tucked between two doors that led to what I assumed were private offices or interview rooms. No one manned the desk, but the door on the right stood open.

Carl didn't bother announcing our arrival. Instead he marched in without ceremony. A dark-haired woman sat in front of a computer monitor with her back to us.

"Ming, I have someone I want you to meet," he said.

She swiveled her chair to face us and I tried not to look surprised. Her name couldn't suit her better with her perfect porcelain skin, almond-shaped eyes, and petite features as refined as a priceless Ming vase. I guessed her to be in her forties.

"Allie, this is my daughter, Ming," Carl said. "Allie is Jasper Marlon's niece."

Ming reached across the desk to shake my hand. She looked fragile, but her grip firm. "Nice to meet you. I'm sorry for your loss."

"Thanks. Did you know my uncle well?"

Ming paused. "Only as my father's friend."

"Ming was just a wee bit of a girl when I brought her home from Vietnam," Carl said. "I found her in a burned-out hut, the sole survivor of a military rampage that destroyed her village. She was about two. By the time we got back to base she'd already wormed her way into my heart. I couldn't leave her behind."

"So you're a veteran," I said.

"A decorated veteran," Ming said. "A true officer and a gentleman. My humble father pulled rank and brought me home when his tour of duty ended."

"So you were a real colonel?" I said, realizing I'd jumped to the conclusion his nickname had come from his attire and not his status. "Somehow I assumed because you and Jasper were close friends you shared . . ." Suddenly I didn't want to reveal how shallow I'd become. Judging a man by his appearance before I had a chance to assess his character.

Mentally I kicked myself. I'd have to see beyond the obvious if I wanted to solve Jasper's murder. Carl seemed nice on the surface, an old trusted friend of Jasper's, but if he'd been a colonel in the Vietnam War he also had to be a man of steel nerves. Someone capable of killing to survive.

Carl laughed. "You wonder how a military man and a draft dodger could become fast friends? Well, age has a way of changing one's viewpoint. There's no such thing as winning a war. Everyone loses. Even the victors. So you see, Jasper and I had more in common than you'd think."

I didn't know what to say.

Ming's smile brightened. "Great meeting you, but I'll have to shoo you two out. I have a teleconference in five minutes. We're building a new orphanage in Romania and it seems there's a new problem every week that has to be ironed out. Dad set up the orphanage trust and now I get to do the trouble-shooting. Let's get together for a coffee once you're settled."

"Sounds good," I said.

"We'll leave you to it," Carl said. "Allie and I have a breakfast date." He gallantly raised his elbow in a gesture that I couldn't mistake.

CHAPTER NINE

D uring the short walk to the restaurant, I considered how best to quiz Carl about Jasper's murder. I hoped the fact that we'd both practiced law would smooth my way. The *Calico Café* sat next door to Carl's office building.

"This was Jasper's favorite breakfast place," he said. "We ate here four out of five mornings every week for the last twenty years."

Just walking into the building made my mouth water. The robust aroma of coffee mingled with tantalizing temptations. Cinnamon. Bacon. Fresh bread. Sausage. Melted butter. More amazing is that the place looked as delicious as it smelled. Every table had little calico cat salt and pepper shakers and its own pot of jam. Pink calico print curtains framed the large windows making the room bright, clean and inviting.

There was only one other customer. A man seated at a table under a window at the back. He waved when he saw us.

"You're running late this morning," the man called from his table. He looked to be about Carl's age, but that's where the resemblance ended. This man wore wire-rimmed glasses, had a smaller frame and looked like he still worked out. "Join me. I'm done eating, but still have coffee to finish."

"Doc," Carl said and saluted the man. "I was up with the birds, but had some important fish to fry this morning."

A short, middle-aged Latin-looking man bustled out from the kitchen to greet us. He smiled and finished tying on what appeared to be a triple extra large white apron. His feet were shod with what had to be sensible orthopedic man-shoes. Another possible suspect?

"Morning, Colonel," he said, eyeing me.

Carl took off his Panama hat and hung it on the hat stand by the front door. "Looks like you're the cook, hostess, and waitress this morning, Mel."

The man shook his head in exaggerated disgust. He spoke with a slight accent, like someone who'd learned English as a second language. "You know Beth. She'll be late for her own wedding. I expect she'll get here in time to serve you breakfast. Now introduce me to your lady friend."

"Mel, this is Allie, Jasper's niece. She's going to run the rock shop with Colin." To me. "Mel's the best cook in the Verde Valley."

"Nice to meet you," I said. The morning had turned out to be one massive meet-and-greet, all before nine.

"Likewise," he said. "You the one Jasper looked for the last couple of years?"

I nodded.

"Too bad you didn't get here before he died. He was a good man. A bit of an original, but a good man." He paused. "Want your usual, Colonel?" He handed me a menu.

"Is the Pope Catholic?"

Mel laughed and Carl led me to the table. The wiry man jumped up and pulled out the chair next to him. "You've been holding out on me, Carl." He winked at me. "How long have you been keeping this young beauty a secret?"

"Doc, meet Jasper's niece," Carl said, sitting down.

Doc waited until I was seated before he sat next to me. I immediately noticed his Old Spice aftershave. It might have been a bit strong, but I didn't mind. It reminded me of my dad and although he'd been gone for years, I still missed him.

"What's good," I asked, reading the menu.

"Everything. Take your time," Carl told me. "There's no hurry. What got you up so early this morning, Doc?"

"The sun," Doc said. "Seemed like the perfect day for flying, so I buzzed on down from Flagstaff. Plus I need to talk to that daughter of yours about the fundraiser next month."

I studied the menu while the men chatted. What really sounded good was the double cheeseburger with chili fries, a green salad and a piece of chocolate cream pie. Unfortunately, lunch wasn't served until eleven.

"What are you having?" I asked, interrupting.

"A chili omelet with hash browns, biscuits and gravy and peach cobbler." Carl winked and patted his stomach. "Ming insists that I have fruit once a day, so I like to oblige."

"More like the heart attack express," Doc said. "My old friend you need to start eating better."

Hang the calories and Doc's warning words. I was starving. "I think I'll have the same."

"It's your funeral," Doc said. He looked at his watch and stood up. "Hey, I've got to go. Nice meeting you, Allie."

Mel had eagle eyes. Before my menu hit the table he bustled out of the kitchen with a pot of coffee and two steaming mugs. He plunked them on the table. I doctored mine with a healthy dose of sugar and cream.

"I'll have what he's having," I said.

"It's big," Mel said.

"I'm hungry."

The waitress chose that moment to breeze through the front door. The *Beth* who'd be late for her own wedding.

She wore a pink striped uniform a size too small and looked about my age. A pretty blond, baby-blue eyes, curvaceous and just bursting with energy.

"Morning," she called out in a sweet breathless voice and hurried over. "Forgot to set my alarm. Let me get that, Mel."

Mel frowned, but I noticed amusement in his eyes. "Table four needs salt and pepper shakers."

"I'm on it," she said and left us.

"If she wasn't such a good worker, I'd let her go." Mel went to cook our breakfast.

I took another slug of coffee. "So tell me. How did an old draft dodger and a decorated Vietnam vet meet?"

A far off look came into Carl's eyes and he chuckled. "I first met Jasper in a card game almost forty years ago. He took me for forty bucks."

"You mean he cheated you?"

"No. Out-played me. Every Friday night a group of us got together for penny-ante poker night. Still do. Doc brought Jasper into the game."

"The Doc I just met?"

"Yep. Doc Shore. Our county coroner."

"I'd like to ask him some questions about Jasper's death. Do you think he'll talk to me?"

Carl shrugged. "Can't see why not. You've made a good impression on him already."

"I think you have the gift of exaggeration." I smiled, thinking of the coroner's disapproval of my food choice. "So. How did they know each other, Jasper and Doc?"

"Doc knew your Uncle Flint. I did, too. We were all in the same unit in Nam."

I felt a pang of regret. I'd lost two uncles I'd never met.

"I'll never forget the day your uncle Flint died. We'd humped fifty clicks into the jungle and walked into a sniper ambush. "That's when he bought it. We were under heavy attack. While we did our best to fend off the enemy, Doc tried to save him. But the boy was shot up bad. Doc couldn't staunch the bleeding and *Evac* arrived too late."

"Wish I could have known him. And Jasper."

"Both were good men. Anyway, Jasper tracked Doc down here. He had questions."

"About what?"

"How his brother died." Carl's face transformed into a mask of rutted worry lines. "It was a war that we should never have fought. Both armies corrupt. Unspeakable killings. Orphaned children. Widows. Devastation of lives on both sides. Vietnamese and U.S. soldiers." The muscles of his face relaxed and once again he looked like the jovial Colonel Sanders. "I was one of the lucky ones. Same battle a sniper's bullet got me a purple heart, stateside and an honorable discharge."

"When I came home, I dedicated my life to finding homes for orphans of war. It's been wonderful to see Ming pick up the ball now that I'm all but retired. What about you? What's been your life dream?" Obviously, he didn't want to talk about the war anymore. But my interest had been piqued. Plus I didn't want to admit that my dreams had been sizzle-fitzed, so I asked. "How long after the war did you meet Jasper?"

"During."

"When the draft was still in effect?"

He nodded.

"I thought he went to Canada during the war."

"He did, but then he came here looking for Doc. Flint had written letters to his kid brother. In them, Flint said Doc was a guy he could trust."

"Wasn't Jasper taking a huge risk he'd be arrested?"

Carl shrugged. "When you're young and have a bee up your boxers, you're invincible. Anyway, he found Doc. Liked the area. Became one of the boys of Jerome."

"Jerome? Was he a cult leader?" Even as I asked the question, I knew it didn't sit with the impression I'd formed of my uncle. Or maybe he had joined a cult like the Hare Krishna's and that's why my mom was ashamed of him.

Carl smiled. "Not a person. A place. Today it's a tourist town up on the hill west of here. Back in the sixties, it was an old ghost town. The perfect place for draft dodgers who didn't want to relocate to Canada." He chuckled. "Your uncle lived in the jail before it slid down the hill. Said that way if they came for him, he'd have already served his time."

My turn to laugh. "And the authorities looked the other way?"

"At the time, the Verde Valley wasn't a tourist destination. Too isolated, kind of a country into itself. The sheriff's only son had been sent home from the war in a box. It gave him a soft spot for the young men hunkered down in the old mine shafts on the hill."

"History books sure paint a different picture."

At that moment six men straggled into the cafe and sat together at a table by the front window. Beth greeted each by name, took their orders and returned to top off our coffee.

"You're going to love living in Sedona," she said.

A bell dinged in the kitchen. Beth reacted like a well-trained Pavlovian dog and scooted to retrieve our breakfast.

"When did Jasper move to Sedona?" I asked.

"In seventy-seven Carter granted amnesty to the conscientious objectors. That's when Jasper opened his rock shop."

Beth brought our breakfast all in one trip, balancing the plates and more coffee like a pro.

"Just let me know if you need anything else," she said. "I'll bring the cobbler out when you're done with this."

I took my first bite of a biscuit drenched in savory sausage gravy. Its spicy flavors exploded in my mouth. This was the best breakfast ever. Better than the steak at Denny's.

"It's good to see a young woman with a healthy appetite," Carl said. He split his biscuit and curlicues of steam rose from his plate. "Ming eats like a sparrow. She thinks a dry piece of whole-wheat toast and a sliver of paper-thin cantaloupe is a wholesome breakfast."

"Everything is delicious."

Carl slathered grape jelly on his toast.

"So what can you tell me about my uncle's death? Information that the police haven't released to the general public?"

"Let's not ruin Mel's fine cuisine with murder talk."

He had a point. But then again, maybe he had a reason to put me off. Maybe he needed time to decide what information to disclose. I wouldn't put it past him to edit what he knew about the murder, if for no other reason than to protect my feminine psyche.

"You know, I used to be a prosecutor?" I said. "I'm not a stranger to crime scenes or all that squeamish."

"I am," he said and attacked his omelet. He took a bite, closed his eyes and sighed. "If Mel ever relocated, now that would be a real crime."

He smiled and reached into his breast pocket. Out came what looked like a shiny tri-fold advertisement for tourists. "Almost forgot to give this to you."

"What is it?" I asked, his message clear. He would not talk about

Jasper's murder over breakfast. So I backed off for the moment, but it didn't mean I'd given up.

He handed the slick pamphlet to me. "Just a run down of what Sedona's Chamber of Commerce has to offer its members. You should consider joining."

"Was Jasper a member?"

He shook his head. "No. My old friend didn't hold with what he called the Chamber's plan to turn Sedona into a New Age Mecca. Said the beauty of Red Rock Country should be enough to attract the tourists. It didn't need a bunch of vortex mumbo jumbo."

"Vortex, what?"

"People believe this area is one of the few places on the planet where the earth's energy is so strong that it can amplify an individual's core being. People come from all over the world to recharge their physical, mental, emotional, and spiritual needs."

"And that's what the Chamber is all about? I don't see how THE ALABASTER fits in. It's a rock shop. I have to agree with Jasper. You don't honestly believe in that stuff, do you?"

"Like the Chamber, I believe in the economical health of our community. Personally, I'm an old ager, not a new ager, but if the New Age enterprises bring tourist dollars to town, it can't be all bad business."

I took my last bite of toast and pushed my empty plate to the side, waiting for Carl to finish. I studied the Chamber's brochure and a thought popped into my head.

Greed is high on the murder-motive-scale along with love and revenge. The excessive love of money could easily outweigh one's normal moral compass if threatened. Had Jasper actively tried to stop the New Age movement in town? And in doing so, threatened someone's livelihood?

CHAPTER TEN

Beth brought the peach cobbler to the table, steaming and topped with a generous scoop of vanilla ice cream that had already started to melt. Even though I'd eaten my truck driver breakfast, the cobbler tasted heavenly. Sweet. Fruity. The top crust paper thin and flaky like Phylo dough.

"About how many businesses in town are New Age?" I asked between bites, expecting a short list of possible suspects to interview.

Carl squinted as if mentally counting. "Can't say. At least a hundred. Maybe one fifty. You'll have to check with the Chamber for a current count."

"You're kidding." Mental groan. "Sedona isn't that large."

"It isn't. But it's big business and brings solid cash into our little community. Not to mention the ancillary jobs associated with tourism."

We finished the cobbler in silence, both of us deep in our own thoughts. I considered all sorts of New Age murder possibilities. The most plausible: Jasper discovered a charlatan preying on people's hopes and fears with what he called *mumbo jumbo*. Some snake-oil salesman who pulled in big bucks for fake cures. What if Jasper threatened them with exposure? Not that all New Agers are charlatans. In all walks of life, there are the good ones and the bad ones. Good teachers. Bad teachers.

Incompetent teachers. Good cooks. Bad cooks. Salmonella cooks. Good cops. Bad Cops. Crooked cops.

Yes. Fear of exposure could be a powerful motive for murder. Maybe I should plan a trip to the Chamber for the list. The sooner the better. It was long shot, but if my other ideas didn't pan out it was a good backup plan. I'd start as soon as I finished cleaning Jasper's blood from the murder scene.

"Now that we've finished eating," Carl said. "I'm ready for your questions. Don't know much, but go ahead and ask away."

"Okay." I had so many. Where to start? "Stone is a play-it-by-the-book kind of cop. Am I right?"

He raised an eyebrow. "You've already met him? I thought you just got to town."

"About three this morning. He thought I was breaking into the store." I rubbed my left wrist, remembering how the cuffs had bit into my skin. "He read me my rights."

Carl chuckled. "Sounds like Stone. But he is an honest cop and usually his instincts are good."

"So his theory that Jasper was killed by a passing vagrant is plausible?"

"The facts support it."

"What facts?"

"Fact one: the only disturbance in the store was by the cash register. There was no sign of a physical altercation anywhere else. Fact two: the front door was jimmied. Fact three: the cash drawer was empty, but there was still $5,000 cash in his safe in the next room."

"Why is that significant?"

"Because the local panhandlers knew about the money in his safe. He always bought this-and-that from those guys. They'd only take cash. If it were one of them, they would have forced him to open the safe for that money. They didn't. Which means it had to be a stranger."

I considered what he said. It did make sense, but I couldn't shake the feeling he was wrong. "When was the last time Jasper was seen alive?"

He shrugged and broke off his gaze. "Not sure, but I talked to him on the phone about ten o'clock that night. He wanted to meet for breakfast the next morning." Carl took a deep breath and I could feel his sorrow. Is that why he turned away? Or was he afraid of what I might read in his eyes? "I had no idea it was the last time I'd ever talk to him."

"What if someone staged the crime scene to look like a random break and entry?" I said, testing his reaction. "Maybe Jasper knew his murderer. Maybe it was someone he trusted. That's why there wasn't any sign of a struggle. It must have been quick."

"Not really. He received two stab wounds."

"Two?"

"The coroner said one superficial wound to his thigh and the fatal wound in his lower abdomen."

"Then it wasn't quick." I dry swallowed. He must have known it was coming. How horrible it must have been to die slowly, frightened and alone. Now I felt even more determined to find the person responsible.

Carl looked thoughtful. "It doesn't make any sense. Who would want to kill Jasper? He didn't have an enemy in the world. Everybody loved him."

I'd heard the words before, almost verbatim. Before I could stop myself, the same reply escaped my lips. "Not everyone."

AS I APPROACHED *THE ALABASTER*, I groaned. In the fresh daylight, it looked like a mammoth wild thistle in an otherwise well-manicured business district. Its cracked stucco walls were in serious need of repainting and re-plastering. Worse, the front yard resembled a rubbish dump more than a business. The city fathers must love this eyesore. How had Jasper managed to ignore Sedona's obvious strict building codes and regulations? Even the McDonald's down the street had been forced to conform. Instead of golden arches, it sported low-level turquoise ones.

The current store must have been grandfathered in before the expansion and development of West Sedona's mini-strip malls. In the birth light of day, I realized the hacienda-style building was huge. Which shouldn't have surprised me. It housed the rock shop, a cavernous storage room, the apartment, a room filled with rock equipment and two additional partitioned spaces. I smiled. There would be plenty of room for a second apartment once the superfluous junk was removed. It might cost a fortune to refurbish, but in the end would be worth the cost and effort. At least for me. Private space sans Colin would seem like heaven.

As is, the place was a lukewarm mess.

Maybe someone had wanted to get rid of the eyesore, one way or another. Possible murder-motive-theory number three. Now with Colin and me as new owners, I wondered what building improvements the city would enforce. At least that should speed up the permit process. Hopefully, a good cleanup and paint job would be enough to satisfy them.

One of us would have to contact the city offices. But first, there were a thousand other things that needed my full attention. Top of the list was a shower and a fresh change of clothes. Plus, I'd have to decide how best to deal with Colin. After overhearing his shady phone conversation and his chameleon behavior earlier, it was obvious I couldn't trust him. Dishonesty fit him like a second skin. Which made me wonder about the veracity of his alibi the night Jasper died.

Someone had opened the gate across the driveway and a white Nissan van was parked out front. A good time to move my car off the street and onto the property. I hopped in, fired up the Escort and let her warm up before edging into the parking lot and past the van. I slowed to a stop, letting the car idle. Wow. From the side, the building seemed ten times larger. At least there'd be more than enough room for a second living-quarters on the premises.

Another surprise. Someone had painted a section of the building a bright red-orange in contrast to the rest of the faded chartreuse walls. In the center hung a long sign over a pair of double plate glass doors— black calligraphy on white.

I blinked several times, not believing my eyes.

FROM HERE TO ETERNITY
God's word will get you there

In the window to the right of the spotless double-wide glass doors, hung a neon open sign. Fake sunflowers and purple wisteria spilled out of the matching ceramic flowerpots flanking the entrance. The left door was propped open.

I parked at the back, sat for a moment and rubbed my temples with both hands. How in the world had I missed seeing this little business smack dab in the middle of THE ALABASTER? I had to have walked right past it when I left with Carl. Wait. We'd gone out the front door. Relieved that I hadn't totally lost it, I grabbed my suitcase, got out and locked the car.

Old time gospel music blared FROM HERE TO ETERNITY. On closer inspection, one had to admit the cheerful little storefront had curb appeal, especially in the middle of the ragged THE ALABASTER. Then I spotted the gold and blue letters adorning the show window that neatly spelled out "Bible Book Store."

"Oh my god," I blurted out. Please don't let this be another one of Jasper's enterprises. I felt as qualified to sell Bibles as a Hassidic rabbi selling razors.

"Is that with a little "g" or a big "G"?" a woman's voice with a southern drawl asked.

"What?" I turned.

A statuesque woman in her mid-fifties stood next to the white van with a box cradled in her arms. She had a kind face, creased with smile wrinkles. Her short hair was a combination of dark black curls subtly streaked with gray. She closed the van's door with her hip.

"Your god?" Her voice was soft, but firm. "Mine is the big G. God of the creation. Savior of the world." She shifted the box and grinned. "Hi. I'm Sarah. I'd shake, but my hands are full. Come on in."

I wanted to say no, but like a sheep being led to the slaughter, I followed. Suitcase in hand and wondering for the thousandth time what I'd gotten myself into. A buzzer sounded as we entered the store.

Inside, she set her box on a glass case and turned down the music. She waved her hand like a game show hostess indicating the merchandise carefully arrayed on her spotless shelves. "We have the largest selection of Bibles and Bible commentaries, spiritual self-help books, Christian novels, videos, music, Sunday school teaching materials and prizes in Verde Valley. Is there anything special you're looking for?"

She pointed to a rack of charm bracelets. "Aren't these darling? We just got them in."

She slipped one over her thin wrist and gave it a little shake. "Just look at the detail. It's amazing. This is Noah's ark. See the little animals and Noah and his family? Kids will love it. Of course, we also have Moses and the plagues of Egypt, complete with a pyramid and the parting of the Red Sea. This one has the Ten Commandments."

I smiled and held up my suitcase. "Thanks, but I'm not here to buy anything. I'm Allie Renault and I—"

"I'm sorry, dear," she interrupted, still beaming. "But my shelves are full. I don't need any new merchandise at the moment."

"I'm not selling. I'm Jasper's niece."

"Dear me." She grabbed my free hand in both of hers and squeezed it gently. "I'm sorry. I should have guessed. I knew you were coming. Just not when."

I smiled.

"It's wonderful to meet you. I know we're going to be friends."

"I hope so," I said, feeling a little overwhelmed by her enthusiasm.

"Your uncle Jasper was a charming man. Generous to a fault. I know this is a little awkward as we've just met, but I hope you and Colin won't be raising the rent anytime soon."

"Don't worry. It'll take Colin and me at least a month or longer to get things sorted out before we make any big changes. I'm sure whatever arrangements you made with Jasper will stay the same for now."

"Bless you."

Two teens, a boy and a girl, burst through the front door. They bore a remarkable resemblance to Sarah.

"Mom, you're not going to believe what Jacob did." The girl laughed so hard her long dark hair quivered.

"Shut up, Becca." The boy's voice cracked and his smoky gray eyes seethed. He jabbed his sister's arm to make his point.

"Hey. That hurt."

"Jacob. Becca. Not in the store!" Sarah said, her voice still calm, but now steely. "This is Jasper's niece and she's going to run THE ALABASTER. Ms. Renault."

"Allie," I said and smiled.

"Cool," Becca said, tossing her hair over her shoulder. "You get to hang with Colin. For an old guy, he's hot."

My smile cringed. "We're just business partners."

"Becca," Sarah said. "Take this box into the storeroom, and remember what I said about making inappropriate personal comments."

"Mom, old people can fall in love, too."

Rock music blasted from the girl's pocket and she pulled out her phone. "Hi, Tamara." She laughed, glanced at her mother. With one hand to her ear, she grabbed the box in the other and headed through a door at the back.

"Let me get you a check for this month's rent," Sarah said. "Actually, I owe two months' rent, but Jasper gave me an extension. I needed to buy new stock. I don't know if his records show that, but I know I owe it. Jasper said not to worry."

"That's fine," I said. Her over-anxious honesty sent her straight to the bottom of my mental suspect list.

"Bless you. Let me get my checkbook." She left me with Jacob.

"Nice to meet you," he mumbled. His fingers tapped his legs. Then he surprised me by asking, "Do you need any help in the store?"

I smiled. With Colin's arm in a cast, extra help would be nice. "I'll talk to Colin and get back to you. I'm sure he'll agree." And if Colin didn't agree, I'd insist he get down on his hands and knees and scrub the blood stains himself. Not that I would let Jacob even see the blood, let alone clean it. That was down to Colin and me.

Jacob hesitated. "If I can use the rock equipment, you don't have to pay me. I want to make something for a friend."

"You mean, your want-to-be-girlfriend." Becca snickered and pock-eted her phone. To me, she said, "I was just talking to my best friend Tamara. She's always watching that Pawn Stars show. She said she left a carved tiger paperweight at the store to get appraised. She thought it might be worth gobs of money. She wants it back. Have you seen it?"

"No, but I'll keep an eye out."

"Great. She'll be totally relieved. It belongs to her gramps and she will be in big trouble if it disappears."

"Don't bother Allie. She's just got into town," Sarah said, walking up and holding a check. "I left the payee blank. I wasn't sure who I should make it out to."

"Write it to *The Alabaster*."

She filled in the blank and handed it to me.

"Thanks." I glanced at the check. Three hundred dollars. Wow, that was a pretty sweet deal she had. No wonder she was worried about us raising her rent. It's not likely she'd want Jasper dead. Unless there was some reason for the low rent that she wanted kept secret. Which brought up the question, why had Jasper given her such a good deal? This kept her on my mental suspect list, written in pen rather than pencil, but still at the bottom.

"Nice meeting you," I said and headed for the door. She followed me outside.

A shiny red sports car roared into the parking lot, Colin at the wheel. Sarah and I had to scoot out of the way to avoid being clipped by a fender. The red muscle car looked fresh from the car lot. No license plates, front or back, just a white registration form taped to the window. He screeched to a halt next to my battered Escort and jumped out.

"How do you like my new wheels?" he asked, sounding like a school-boy. "It's the latest model Corvette."

"You must have inherited some money," I said, thinking he was spending our profits before we even had a chance to go through Jasper's books. "Are you sure you can afford the payments?"

He laughed. "What payments? I paid cash."

"Must be nice to be rich."

"You could say that." He puffed-up like he was competing in a muscle man contest.

Jacob and Becca came out of the store. "What a cool car," she said.

I handed him Sarah's check. He took it. Read it. Crumpled it into a ball and shot it at a black oil drum of green rocks.

CHAPTER ELEVEN

"**W**hat's wrong with you?" I asked Colin, watching the paper-check-ball smack the side of the drum and bounce into a precarious pile of black shiny rocks. "That's Sarah's rent money."

"No, it's not," he said.

Sarah watched as if she couldn't believe what had happened.

I climbed into the pile of razor-sharp rocks and looked for the check. It had fallen between two huge boulders. I reached down to move the smaller one and it bit me. Not literally, but blood oozed from a cut in my thumb. I stuck it in my mouth and tasted the unique metallic zest of fresh plasma. Which reminded me of Jasper's dried blood behind the cash register.

"You've got to be careful with obsidian," Colin said. "It cuts like glass."

"Gee, thanks for the advice." I retrieved the check and climbed out of the pile without any additional mishap. "What's your problem? It's her rent check."

"Too little, too late." He reached into his pocket and pulled out another check. "I've found a new tenant. A lucrative one that will improve our business at the same time."

He waved the second check in my face. I couldn't really read it, but saw a lot of zeros. Sarah's face went pale. She'd heard the whole exchange and seemed to catch his drift before me.

"Kids, go inside. Close the door." She waited for them to comply before she spoke again. "Are you trying to tell me, I have to close up shop? This is my life's work. Second to being a mother."

"Don't take it personally." Colin smiled like a doctor telling a patient that they'd get used to walking with just one foot. "I like you, Sarah. You have a nice little business, but you have to move it somewhere else."

"Jasper and I had an agreement."

"I'm sure you did, but Jasper's dead. *THE ALABASTER* is mine."

"You mean, ours," I said. Both looked at me like they'd forgotten I was standing there. "In case you've forgotten, we are co-heirs to Jasper's estate. This is a joint business venture, not a solo enterprise. You're not its C.E.O. Which means until we negotiate how we will operate as partners there will be no major changes."

"I thought we decided all that earlier," Colin said, his fake smile morphing into a sneer. "You clean. Wait on customers. I'll handle the business end of things."

"Not on your life," I said, stepping back and clenching my hands. I noticed my thumb had bled all over her check. "Sarah's paid her rent. Legally you can't kick her out."

"It's obvious you have no business sense," he said.

"And you do? If I remember right, Alex said you worked as a mainte-nance man on an Army base. Translation. Janitor."

His face blazed a dark angry red.

Sarah stepped in between us. "What if I pay what the other person has offered you to rent the space?" She'd laced her fingers together as if she was praying.

"Think you can sell this many Bibles?" he asked, showing her the check. "This is for six months. Paid in advance."

Her face turned whiter.

"Let me see that." I grabbed the check. It was made out to Colin for the sum of twenty-four thousand dollars. Okay, so four thousand a month was a lot more than her three hundred. Tempting even, but Sarah had an agreement with Jasper and I was determined to honor his wishes.

Not Colin's. He was not going to push me around. Not on this or anything else.

"I'm sorry, Sarah. It's all about the money," he said. "We can't afford to run a charity." He gave her a hollow smile. "I don't want to, but if I have to, I will take this to court."

"Ignore him," I said. "If he did sue, he'd lose. He has no case. I'm not sure about Arizona law, but in California there are rent-hike limits. If you like, I can look it up for you. Do you have a copy of your lease?"

Close to tears, she shook her head. "No. Jasper said it wasn't necessary. Said he didn't like putting his name on unnecessary legal documents. Said that the mutual arrangement between the two of us was good enough."

Colin laughed like an old lecher. "I get it. I bet it worked swell for Jasper, but you're a little old for my style." He thrust his hips forward and grunted.

Okay, that was seriously weird. I wondered if he had a multiple personality disorder or if this was the real Colin. What kind of a business partner had Jasper saddled me with? The crude, the rude and the greedy?

Sarah's face flushed. "I'm a moral God-fearing woman. And despite your lack of judgment, I will pray for you and your immortal soul."

She turned and stalked into her bookstore.

"Colin, you're a total jerk," I said, wondering what game he was playing. Then it hit me. Maybe his game was to disgust me enough so I'd leave. Give up my half of the business so he could inherit it all. Ahh… well, that wasn't happening anytime soon. If he wanted a fight, I'd fight. And win.

"Like it or not, we're partners for the next two years," I goaded him.

"We'll see," he said, his voice loud and angry. "Fight me on this and I'll make your life hell."

Refusing to react, I gave him my best courtroom smile. The one that says I have all the answers and nothing the other side says can faze me. "That sounds like a threat. And duly noted for the record. I'll call Alex. It's obvious we're going to need a mediator."

"That's an unnecessary expense."

I nodded to his new car. "It seems like you have plenty of money to burn." Inside I seethed. On the outside I remained calm, picked up my suitcase and headed for the front door.

"Don't walk away from me." He rushed at me, grabbed my arm and squeezed it so hard I knew I'd have a bruise by nightfall. "I'm not done with this conversation."

I yanked my arm free. "Well I am."

He grabbed me again.

I lost my cool and shouted for all of Sedona to hear. "As far as I'm concerned, you could disappear off the face of the planet and it would be a better place."

"You will not disrespect me!" he said.

"You disrespect yourself," I said through gritted teeth.

"Bitch!" His good looks morphed into a mask of ugly fury and he slapped me. If I didn't know better, I would have thought he was insane.

My jaw dropped in shock. Not even my jerk ex, in his worst out-of-control moment, had dared to raise his hand. "Touch me again and you're dead."

He narrowed his eyes and reminded me of a rattlesnake I'd seen in a zoo when I was ten. The handler had dropped a tiny white mouse into its cage. The snake didn't attack. Instead it watched. Waited. And then struck. The mouse hadn't had a chance, and I'd had nightmares for weeks.

Colin's features smoothed into a controlled smile, the momentary rage fading as quickly as it had surfaced. "Hey," he said, his voice suddenly calm, almost friendly. "Sorry. I was out of line."

"Out of line?" You have no idea, I thought. "That slap is grounds for a lawsuit."

He held up a palm as if in surrender. "I said I'm sorry. Come on, be reasonable."

"Be reasonable? I could file a battery charge."

"What are you, a lawyer?"

"Was," I said.

"Bully for you." His self-satisfied smirk surfaced. "I'm not returning the check. Sarah's out. So get used to it." He reached out as if to stroke my hair.

I flinched and batted his hand away. "I'm warning you. Leave. Me. Alone."

Someone cleared their throat to my right with a loud," Hhhhuu-ummmmmm."

Pause. Colin and I both looked at our audience of one.

"Sounds like there's trouble in inheritance paradise," Stone said as he came around the side of the building. "I could hear you two out front. So can everyone else on the block."

Stone's gaze darted from Colin, to me, and back to Colin. "So which one of you wants to tell me what's going on?"

Colin smiled. "Just a little misunderstanding about the chain of command. Nothing that can't be worked out once Allie realizes I have a better head for business."

"In your dreams," I muttered under my breath. Out loud I said, "You men sort it out. I'm going to take a shower." I headed for the front door, swinging my suitcase back and forth like I was winding-up to use it as a battering ram.

"Make it a cold one," Colin said.

"You're asking for trouble," Stone said. "Women have long memories and a way of exacting revenge. Right, Allie?"

"What? I didn't say anything out of line," Colin said. "She's just touchy. It must be the wrong time of the month."

"With your charming repartee, don't expect too many mourners at your funeral," I said.

I left the two men outside and resisted the urge to slam the door. Once out of their sight I gave into my anger and stomped through the store like an elephant on steroids. My suitcase banged into a display shelf. It rattled like it'd been hit by a 7.5 earthquake.

AFTER A SHOWER and change of clothes, I chastised myself for taking Colin's bait. The cop must think I was the same hysterical female he'd met last night, but Stone couldn't ignore the man's inappropriate sexist remarks. That aside, Colin's display of almost insane anger made me wonder. He was the only person I'd met since arriving in Sedona who truly seemed capable of murder.

Had he thought he was Jasper's sole heir? That made for a pretty good motive. It must have been a real shock when I showed up in the will. As far as the means, Colin's vanity had kept him fit enough to overpower a much older man who must have trusted him. It was easy to imagine him stabbing Jasper. That left opportunity. Colin could have faked his alibi. If all hung on some woman's word, that alone would prove suspicious.

I'd find a way to check it out.

It struck me. If Colin killed Jasper, the murder had been premeditated. And now I was in his way. Numbing pinpricks of imagined ice shimmied down my neck to spread across my torso. I'd have to be careful. Never let my guard down around him. A man who would kill once for gain wouldn't hesitate to kill again.

From now on I'd treat Colin like the opposing counsel. I'd be cool, calm, and businesslike. No more letting him bait me into an emotional response as he clouded the real issues at hand.

A quick rummage in my purse produced Alex's business card. If he hadn't wanted me to call him while he was out of town, he shouldn't have written his cell number on the back.

I dialed and waited.

No answer. A mechanical voice instructed me that the party I was calling was unavailable. I could leave a voice message. Send a fax. Leave a call back number. Or . . . I waited for the beep.

"Alex. This is Allie Renault. Can you give me a call me when it's convenient?"

I pulled out my copy of Jasper's will and settled at the desk. I'd only given it a cursory read in L.A. It was time to go over the details. Maybe I'd find a loophole in the set-up of the partnership. Midway through my read, my cell rang.

"Hello?"

"You called me?" Alex said. "Is there a problem?"

"You could say that."

"Well?"

Suddenly I felt like a kid about to tattle on a schoolyard bully. Maybe I shouldn't have called him. I remembered the one time I'd complained to the teacher about a girl pulling my hair in the third grade. It had made things worse. Whenever Miss Pond wasn't looking, the girl continued to pinch, kick and hit me—only harder. It went on for weeks. Until I'd had enough and punched her in the stomach and she threw up her lunch. After that that she left me alone.

Putting Alex in the middle of things wouldn't solve my problem with Colin.

"You still there?" he asked.

I hesitated. "Yeah."

"Not having second thoughts about running a rock shop?"

"No." I had to think fast. Didn't want him to believe I'd called him because I was desperate to hear his voice. Although now that he was on the other end of the line, he sounded pretty good. Picturing him as my shining knight was tempting and I could tell that he'd be more than willing, but it wasn't my style.

"You okay?" he said. "You know you can talk to me."

I looked at the chair I'd slept in and my excuse came to me in a flash. "Colin and I need separate living accommodations. Jasper's apartment is too small for the two of us." Then I added, sounding lame even to myself, "Even if it was bigger, it wouldn't look right. Two unmarried people living together."

"Don't worry. I'll be back before Colin arrives next week."

"That's the problem. He's here now. Last night I slept in the recliner. He'd already commandeered the bedroom."

"What? That's not right." The outrage in his voice came through loud and clear. "I'll call him and set him straight."

"Wait. What was the arrangement supposed to be when he arrived?"

"There's a camper out back. He's supposed to stay in that until a second apartment is built."

"Can't I just rent a place until then?"

He cleared his throat. "Rents in Sedona are really high and—"

"What about an advance from the estate?'

"I'm sorry. The will stipulates you both must reside on the property for the first two years."

Crap. "I'll take the camper."

"It's small. You'll be cramped."

"That's okay. Most of my waking hours will be spent in the store.

Cleaning to start with and then learning the business."

He laughed. "You're sure?

"When can I move in?"

"I'll give Carl a call. The keys are in my office."

"Thanks."

"How was your drive?"

I felt heat rise on my face. "Great. Got in last night."

"Heard about that," he said. I could imagine amusement dancing in his soft brown eyes. "I thought you would have arrived earlier in the day."

My turn to laugh, albeit fake. There was no way I was going to tell him about my car problems. "I guess I spent a little too much time sightseeing."

"Well, like I said. I'll give Carl a call." His tone shifted. "Allie?" When he said my name like that, I felt like a foolish schoolgirl all twitter-pated. "When I get back, would you like to grab dinner?"

"It's a date," I said and instantly regretted the word *date*. He'd said, grab dinner, which sounded more like a casual business invite. So I added, "Sounds great, I have some questions about the will. Living arrangements for one."

Pause. His reply turned professional. "Sounds good."

Did I just blow it? I charged on. "One more thing? Can you ask Stone to let me read the investigative reports on Jasper's murder?"

"Why?" He sounded taken aback.

"I just wanted more information about my uncle and his death. Like you said in LA, family loyalty comes first. Jasper is my family and I'm not going to drop this until his justice is served."

Pause. "You have enough on your plate without playing detective."

"Please?"

"Okay, I'll ask. But don't expect him to come through."

"Thanks." I hung up and let out a huge sigh.

What was it about Alex that turned me upside down? Was it his loyalty to family or was it the way we seemed to click? Or was it the humor I saw in his eyes when he took me to dinner in my fairy outfit? I hated to admit it, but I was really looking forward to him returning to town.

CHAPTER TWELVE

Alex must have performed his shining knight-in-armor duty and contacted his uncle because Carl called five minutes later. He said he'd bring over the keys to the camper within the next hour or so. Hoorah! Soon I'd have my own space, however small. Until he arrived, I decided to explore my new assets. Jasper had been a pack rat. Not only were there literally tons of rocks outside, it seemed he also had a penchant for collecting junk.

Inside, the store's merchandise was a real mystery. I was in trouble and I knew it. I could see no prices. No labels. I had no way to identify the rocks and didn't have a clue as to the value of even a single piece. Worse, I'd have to depend on Colin and, knowing him, that promised to be a real nightmare.

It was overwhelming. So much to learn. So much to do. My eyes traveled to the brown streaks of dried blood near the cash register. No point in putting it off. I found gloves, cleaning supplies, and set to work. I pretended I was cleaning up dried maple syrup and not my uncle's blood. At the same time I kept my eyes open for any possible evidence missed in the police investigation; that is, anything not covered in dust. Found nothing, but twenty minutes later all signs of the murder had been scrubbed clean. I stepped back to survey my efforts.

I hoped Jasper could rest easier now that I'd erased the memory of what had been done to him here in his sanctuary. Those stains were no longer visible. It didn't equal solving the crime, but as least it was progress.

Wow. It looked so good that I picked up a dust-encrusted white crystal, started to wipe off the grime and stopped myself. What if it was delicate and I ruined it? I took in a huge breath, held the hand-sized specimen an inch from my lips and blasted it with a stream of focused air. Dust flew back into my face like a mini-sandblaster. I gasped, inhaled in a deep gulp of microscopic dirt, and coughed. After a couple of gritty blinks I examined my find.

It was beautiful. A thumb-sized clear crystal sprouted in the center of a delicate forest of smaller versions of the same. Each was a perfect replication of the larger one. I grabbed a rock book from a display rack and flipped through its pages until I found something similar.

"Quartz," I read. "Silicon dioxide. A six-sided crystal with a six-sided point." I did a quick count, smiled at my successful identification and looked around the store. "One down, five million left to learn."

For fun, I went around the store looking for more quartz. By the time Carl arrived about an hour later, I had a whole shelf of them cleaned and gleaming. Large. Small. Singles. Clusters. When he came in, I was hand-printing a description of quartz to put with the crystals on the shelf.

"Doing your homework, I see," Carl said.

I laughed. "It helps to put things down on paper. Writing sets it in my mind."

He chuckled. "Must be in the genes. Jasper always jotted notes on any old scrap of paper. You'll find them as you clean. If you're smart, you won't waste time reading them or you'll be at it until you're my age."

It was my turn to smile.

"Should have given you these at breakfast." He held up a set of keys dangling from a Star Trek Enterprise keychain. "You're sure you want to live in the camper?"

I nodded.

"It's not bad for the occasional rock hunting trip, but awful small for a permanent residence. Most women wouldn't stand to be cramped up like that."

"I'll survive."

"The garage is out back." He scooped up the keys. "Follow me. You drive a stick shift? If not I can move it into the parking lot for you."

We crossed a dirt alley to a long, barn-like wooden shed. The neglected building cried out for a serious coat of paint. Its four doors faced the back of THE ALABASTER; three overhead garage doors and a regular-sized house door at one end. Mentally I measured up another few thousand feet of junk.

Carl unlocked the smaller door, stepped out of the sun and turned to face me. "Which door would the lovely lady like to try first? Door number one? Door number two? Or door number three?"

"I'll take door two, Alex," I said, though I knew I'd named the wrong game show host. Maybe it was a slip of the tongue. Or maybe it was because Alex Farmer hovered at the edge of my subconscious like the memory of an out of reach cookie jar in my mother's kitchen.

Carl activated an automatic garage door opener. The middle door squeaked up to reveal a couple of dozen black oil barrels.

"These should be full of amethyst, quartz and agates from Brazil," he said.

"You know about rocks?" I asked, thinking I'd rather ask him for help identifying the rocks in the store than Colin. "I need a crash course."

"Very little. It'd take half a nanosecond to exhaust my knowledge. Now Jacob, Ms. Sarah's son, is your man. The boy's helped in the store since he could walk and talk."

"I met Jacob this morning. Seems like a nice kid."

"He is. After his dad died of a long bout with cancer, Jacob attached himself to Jasper." He sighed. "Which door next?"

"Door number three."

The far right door rumbled up to reveal a canary-yellow sports car. I moved to run my hand over the sleek line of its hood.

"What is this?" I asked.

"A nineteen seventy-one, American Motors, Javelin."

"You're kidding, right? This does not look like a seventy-one car. It's hot."

"Drives like it, too. You'll have to fight Colin for her."

"Maybe not," I said, thinking of the red Corvette. "He already has a new set of wheels."

Carl's eyebrows went up. "Hmmmm." Pause. "Okay then, are you ready for door number one?"

I nodded.

He lowered the other garage doors before opening the last one.

I couldn't help myself. I burst into barking laughter. The round head-lights of a vintage 1962 turquoise-colored Chevy truck hood perched over a vanity license plate that read: ROCK ON. I couldn't quite see the camper. It was hidden in the shadows.

Carl climbed into the driver's seat and drove it out. On the small truck's bed someone had built a gypsy shack covered in faded wood shingles. He hopped out. It was strange, quaint and completely adorable. Like it had slipped from a fairy tale parallel universe.

He hopped out. "Let me demonstrate some of your new home's finer features," Carl said as he led me to the rear of the truck. "It's quite comfy inside, considering."

He flipped up a hasp, reached into a slot under the door, and pulled out a set of steps. Four evenly spaced round hooks slipped snugly onto a bar welded above the rear bumper. Setting the steps into place, he unlocked the double doors and slid them into built-in side pockets.

"Come on in," he said. "Went on a few trips in this myself."

I followed, eager to see my new home.

He flipped a light switch. A pair of bright fluorescents illuminated the high-polished cedar interior.

Like the apartment, it was small, immaculate and cozy. No clutter. Everything slotted in a well-designed space. A stovetop, sink, refrigerator, and cupboards nestled in the far right corner. A closet built into the left corner. Along both sidewalls were wide benches with hinged tops. He lifted the top of the left bench, leaned it against the wall and pointed inside to a long cushion.

"The bed. Fits either bench," he said. "And there's the bathroom."

"Bathroom? This has a bathroom?"

He pointed to what looked I'd thought was a closet. "Of sorts. A toilet and sink."

I lifted the lid to the other bench. "There's a lot of storage space."

"Jasper designed them to carry rocks. If you use them, make sure to put equal weight on both sides." He gave me a quick lesson on operating the stove and hooking up the water, propane and electricity. "You don't want to run down your battery when there's an outlet available." He looked at his watch. "Want me to move this to the parking lot so you can plug in?"

"That's okay," I said. "I'll drive her over."

He gave an exaggerated sigh. "It seems like you modern young women can do everything these days. Pretty soon you won't even need a man to father your children."

I laughed. "Thanks for bringing over the keys."

"No problem." He wiped his forehead with a white handkerchief. "Don't give her too much gas, or she'll stall."

"I'll remember that." I hopped into the cab and rolled down the window.

His cell rang. "What's up, Doc?" He waved and headed for his Crown Victoria while giving a rundown about my new home situation to I assumed was Doc Shore— who probably couldn't care less that I was taking up residence in the old gypsy camper.

I moved up the seat, adjusted the side mirrors and out of curiosity, popped open the glove box. It was stuffed with scraps of paper, maps and assorted candy wrappers. I grabbed the note on the top and recognized Jasper's angular printing. It read: 9-17 *Tiger Force.*

It meant nothing to me, but I hadn't had time to figure out what was important and what wasn't. Until I did, I'd keep everything. I reached for the rest of the scraps of paper and something clunked onto the floorboard. A smallish handgun.

I shivered. Okay, I'm not anti-gun, although that didn't mean I wanted to own one. My dad said picking up a gun meant you were willing to kill. I wasn't. Not even rattlesnakes. Using my thumb and finger, I gingerly lifted the pistol and checked to see if it was loaded. It wasn't. I didn't want it, but there was no way I'd trust Colin with a deadly weapon. Not after the psychotic anger I'd seen in his eyes. He'd switched it off soon enough. Still, I wouldn't trust him. Which begged the question, why had Jasper?

When Alex got back to town I'd give him the gun. Until then its presence in the glove box would be my little secret. I buried the gun under a pile of maps. I found the box of bullets wedged under the seat. It was as safe a place as any, so I returned it to its hiding place.

The pickup started on the first try. Five minutes later I had it parked, plugged into an electrical outlet and the water hooked up. Taking Jasper's notes, I made sure to lock the cab of the truck before settling down for the evening. Unloaded my stuff from the car and found everything a place in my new cozy little home. Then I spread Jasper's notes over the surface of a lift-up tabletop near the back wall and studied them. Like the note I'd found earlier on the refrigerator in the apartment, each had a date printed on its upper right corner.

- *8-16 sulfer xls - sycamore canyon*
- *7-5 gold filled & silver wire, 22 gauge*
- *6-11 soapstone carvings*
- *9-17 tiger force*
- *9-11 flint*
- *8-6 milk butter eggs bread carrots*
- *7-19 oxalic acid*

Acid? What could Jasper want with acid? And why did he date everything?

I arranged the notes into three categories - food, rocks, and clearly what must be collecting sites. Nothing important jumped out at me. Next I laid the notes in chronological order. Still, no meaningful pattern emerged. After an hour of trying to make sense of his scratched hieroglyphics, a dull ache wormed its way into my right temple. I rubbed it with the palm of my hand.

My stomach rumbled. I needed food and rummaged through the cupboard over the sink. Big disappointment. No honey buns here. Or peanut butter. Just a dozen tins of Tiny Tot Sardines and one lone can of tomato soup. I opted for the soup. While it heated, I studied the notes one last time.

Carl had been right. Reading Jasper's discarded notes wouldn't tell me how to run the business, but there was the slight chance they'd reveal a clue to his murder. Not that I knew enough to draw lines between the dots just yet. I shoved them in a white plastic bag and tossed it in a bin. I wouldn't throw them away just yet. Not until proof positive they were worthless. If only I could get Stone to spill a little information.

I poured the steaming soup into a brown ceramic mug. It was too hot to taste, but I sipped at it anyway and burned my tongue. The pain triggered a new thought.

Of course I couldn't make sense of the notes. I only had a few. I'd need all of them to spot a trail of evidence. After slugging down the rest of the soup, I rinsed my dishes and set them in the sink. Jasper's sink and now mine. He must have been remarkable. So why had Mom pretended he didn't exist all those years? Was it because my uncle Flint had served and died for flag and country and she viewed Jasper as a coward? That didn't make total sense. Lots of young guys had dodged the draft, and history had proved that the Vietnam War was a big mistake. You'd think she would have gotten over it. Wasn't one war hero in the family enough for her? Or had he done something else to shame the family?

It didn't make sense. Everyone I'd met in Sedona seemed to like and respect him. A lot. Had his past caught up with him? Something Mom knew, but wasn't telling. I looked at the clock. Florida time it was almost noon. My step dad should be on the golf course.

"What do you want now?" my mother's sharp voice asked when she answered the phone.

Great. She's started yet another day in a foul mood. I'd have to massage her ego before asking about Jasper. Otherwise she'd hang up and I'd remain clueless.

"I thought you might like to know I've moved to Arizona."

"Whatever for? Who in their right mind would want to live in the desert?"

I smiled. Mom was warming up to the conversation. "I called for some advice."

"Make it quick. I have a hair appointment in twenty minutes."

"If you're too busy, I guess I could call Aunt Charlotte."

She paused and I could imagine the calculating emotions that stormed and threatened to damage her most recent facelift. The threat was the one thing that would keep her on the line. She hated Dad's sister.

"Why did you call?" she asked impatiently.

"It's about Uncle Jasper."

"Oh." Her disdain scorched the airwaves. "If that's why you called, you've wasted my time and your dime."

"He left me half of his estate," I blurted before she could hang up.

"And you're excited about a paltry little inheritance? Really, Allie? You need to reassess your priorities. Maybe you should focus on reconciling with George. I have it on good authority that he and his new wife have already split."

"I didn't call to talk about George." I needed to get her attention. Fast. So I lied. "One million, seven-hundred-fifty-thousand isn't paltry."

She gasped. "Well, that is surprising. We never expected him to amount to much." Pause. "When do you collect?"

"In two years."

"Two years! That's ridiculous. It shouldn't take more than six months to close an estate."

"The other heir and I have to operate the business for two years before we can dissolve the partnership, liquidate the assets and go our separate ways. Until then we each receive a substantial wage and a share of the profits we garner."

"Just like him to ruin your life from the grave."

"George took care of that. Why you think he is Mr. Wonderful, I don't know." Why did I bring up George again? Focus. "Tell me about Jasper. Please?"

Mom sniffed. I could imagine her vain attempt to produce frown lines that refused to materialize due to her love affair with Botox. "Allie, you have no idea the sacrifices I've made for you. After your father died, it was just horrible. We barely survived and every spare dime was spent on you. I put my life on hold and did without, so you could have nice things and fit in with your peers. Your education didn't come free, either." Another double sniff. "I don't know why you're pestering me about Jasper. I know you're angry I remarried, but you have no right to be upset. I loved your father, but he's gone. I was alone for a long time before I met Harold. He's made me laugh again."

I dredged up an almost forgotten memory from just before my dad died. I was seven and surprised my parents by serving them breakfast in bed. I'd burnt the syrup heating it on the stove and we were out of butter. Undaunted, I served them blackened pancakes, hard like bricks. Mom bravely tried a bite. I spit mine out and Dad started a game of pancake Frisbee. Soon we were all laughing hysterically. Mom. Dad. And me.

That mom had died with my dad.

"I'm glad you're happy, Mom," I said and meant it. "I'm glad Harold makes you happy."

"You just haven't given him a chance."

"You're right." And she was. "Everyone deserves a chance and that's what Jasper's given me. A chance to start over. It feels wrong that I don't know anything about him except what I've learned from strangers. Can't you tell me something about him?"

Silence.

"I know he was a draft dodger. What else?"

More silence.

"Mom, please?" I threw in an extra nudge. "If you hang up, I'm coming there. One way or another you'll have to talk about this."

"You're so much like him," she said bitterly. "Always on his high horse. Never caring how his actions would affect the rest of the family. Our reputation. Dodging the draft wasn't enough. He had to drag the family's name even deeper in the mud."

"What did he do?"

"Because of him, we had to move to a place where no one knew us. It was my senior year."

The phone in my hand began to beep. I looked the battery indicator. No. Not now. Not when I was about to finally learn the truth.

It dropped the connection, and its screen went black.

"Crap!"

I raced into the store and grabbed the landline phone and heard Colin's voice on the line.

Noooooooooooo. I wanted to scream, *get off the phone*, but I didn't.

"I'll be there," Colin said.

"Don't be late," the voice said. It sounded like a man, low and almost a whisper.

I carefully eased the phone back in its cradle and waited three minutes before picking it up again. Colin was giving orders.

"That's it," Colin said. "End of negotiations. Good bye."

Click.

I slammed down the receiver and picked it up almost immediately.

A dial tone. Yes!

I punched in Mom's number and heard Colin roar off in his new muscle car.

Eight rings later her answering machine picked up. Either she'd gone to her hair appointment or she was refusing to talk to me.

I left a short message after the beep. Explained that my battery had died and gave her the number to THE ALABASTER so she could call back at her convenience.

Stupid cell battery. My gut told me that I'd missed my one opportunity. By the time I got a hold of her again her defenses would be reinforced with self-righteous pride. I had learned something though. Jasper's fall from grace involved more than just dodging the draft. It had forced the family to relocate during my mom's senior year of high school.

Maybe I should contact Aunt Charlotte. I tried her number. Talked to her housemate and learned that she was in Europe. She'd be home next month, which put my questions on hold. So with Colin absent, I'd search Jasper's apartment for clues.

CHAPTER THIRTEEN

I nside the apartment, I went directly to Jasper's desk. I didn't really know what to look for and decided to grab anything that might be important. If nothing else, I'd get an overview of his life on the days leading up to his death. Starting at the top left, I pulled out the contents of each pigeonhole. Most contained the usual desk paraphernalia: postage stamps, paperclips, tape, etcetera, etcetera. I'd reached the last little cubby when a car roared into the parking lot.

Shoot. I'd just gotten started. Had Colin returned already? I shoved everything back into place and raced to the window.

False alarm. Just some teen roaring through the parking lot like he owned the place. A mini-Colin in the making if someone didn't set the kid straight.

I let out the breath I'd been holding, but instead of feeling relaxed it put me into hyper drive. Colin could be gone for hours or only minutes. Who knew how he'd react if he found me searching the place? I grabbed a rag and some Windex from under the kitchen sink as a cover. Even if it set a bad precedent if he walked in on me he'd assume he'd won and I'd started on the cleaning.

I rushed back to the desk.

The last cubby held a stack of dated notes going back years, each with just a name and a phone number. I recognized a few. Alex's and Carl's. And wondered if Elvis's was the real deal. Not that it would do me any good, considering the superstar had vacated the building in the late nineteen seventies. Still, I decided to keep it.

On the back of each slip I penciled the word *desk*. Paper-clipped them together and slipped them in my pocket.

I thought I heard another car drive into the parking lot.

A quick look revealed an empty lot. My imagination was getting the best of me. But I couldn't help it. Colin was one weird guy. I took a couple of power breaths and returned to the desk to start on the drawers.

A slew of erect file folders stood in the bottom drawer labeled in Jasper's now familiar printing. I pulled out January. Inside held a sheaf of bills. All marked paid. My eyes widened at the amount of outgoing cash. THE ALABASTER must do a lucrative business. That or Jasper spent everything he made.

I found a business ledger, flipped through the pages and whistled. Another surprise. Jasper's bookkeeping skills belied the appearance of the store. Each month he'd faithfully recorded bills paid, stock purchased, and the store's monthly sales. Wow. If the store did this well in its present disordered state, it had the potential to do a whole lot better once we got the place cleaned. Strong emphasis on the *we*. Cast or no cast, Colin would be helping.

Maybe an on-line store would double the profits and keep Colin out of my hair.

I closed the drawers, leaving the bookwork and files where I'd found them. I glanced at the clock. Forty-five minutes had passed. Colin could return any moment. I needed to step up my game.

Where else to look? The kitchen. Like a thief, I pulled open drawers with both hands. Rummaged. Scanned the contents. No notes. Slammed them shut. I grabbed the shopping list from under the refrigerator magnet of a shiny plastic space ship, the Enterprise.

I checked the clock again. Time was ticking. Think. Where else would Jasper stash notes?

The little hall closet? I rifled the pockets of a brown corduroy jacket and caught an earthy scent of the man who'd worn it. Not unpleasant, but somehow comforting. Cinnamon spice mixed with pine and something I couldn't identify.

I found two notes. *11/5 soapstone, $1.00 lb,* in the inside pocket. *11/2 Ask Morty- tigers,* in the breast pocket. Three more notes in a denim Levi jacket. One, in a long ranger coat. The sweatshirts yielded zero. I scribbled a location note on each and set them on the dining table.

Two rooms left. Bedroom and bathroom.

I hurried into the bedroom. It looked like Colin had a rough night. The blanket had twisted into a wad, half on and half off the bed. The fitted sheet had popped off three corners of the mattress. His suitcase sprawled open on a side chair.

Added to that, the stale pong of aftershave assaulted my sinus cavities. One inhale squelched my *Helen Reddy* bravado and I found myself listening for the roar of Colin's car. Jumping at every imagined sound. Deep in my gut, I knew he'd be furious if he caught me snooping. Even though it was my legal right to go though Jasper's things. Frantically I tried to formulate an excuse for my presence.

I opened the floor-to-ceiling storage cupboard on the end wall. Inside, piled in neat square stacks, were sheets, blankets, towels, washcloths and dishcloths. No notes.

"Started on the inventory, I see," Colin said.

I jumped and whacked my head on the sharp edge of a shelf.

He swaggered in with the charm of the snake in the Garden of Eden. "FYI. The stuff in my suitcase is mine." He crossed the room and flipped his luggage shut and locked it.

"Didn't hear you," I said. "I needed some sheets and towels for the camper. Carl brought over the keys." I grabbed a set of sheets and some towels and turned to face him. To my surprise, he had a sheepish, almost embarrassed grin.

"About earlier," he started and looked down as if he were a wounded puppy. "I don't know why I was being such a jerk. I'm not really like that. It must have been the pain meds. My head's clear now and I want to apologize." He looked up. "And before you ask, I already served up my humble pie to Ms. Sarah."

"No offense taken," I said, thinking the pain medication was a convenient excuse. But considering he'd caught me red-handed in his bedroom

I'd keep my skepticism to myself. If we were going to last two years as business partners we'd have to get along. At least on the surface.

"Let's start our partnership over." I extended my hand from under the stack of linens.

"Agreed." He gave my fingers a gentle squeeze, holding on longer than was comfortable. "You know I could sleep in the gypsy shack." He paused as if to judge my reaction before adding, "You can have the bedroom."

My eyes traveled over his mess. "That's okay. I've already cleaned the camper and moved in."

"Suit yourself." He ran his good hand through his hair. "You want to sit down and go over the books?"

"It's been a long day," I said. If I hadn't already seen the ledger, I might have taken him up on it even if I did feel like I'd been pulled through a two-inch drainpipe. Backwards. "Do you mind if we wait until tomorrow to talk business?"

He nodded. "Sure."

I sidestepped my way to the door and escaped, relieved he didn't seem the slightest bit suspicious I'd searched the room. Gut instinct told me not to share Jasper's notes. Hopefully Colin hadn't decided to clean and spotted the stack I'd left on the dining table. I rushed into the kitchen. Whew! They were still there. I laughed. Which was positive proof I needed sleep. How could I have imagined he would have taken the initiative to clean?

"Hey," he called from the bedroom. "You want to go out and have a steak?"

I snatched the notes and sandwiched them between the towels.

He came out. "My treat."

"Thanks, but what I really need is sleep. It's been a long two days. I'm turning in early."

"You still have to eat."

"I picked up a sandwich earlier," I lied, thinking that now I'd have to forgo food. Or chance the Tiny Tots. I was tired. I should have thought up a more plausible lie that wouldn't leave me starving or stuck with another can of tomato soup. "You don't mind if I take one of these honey buns for my dessert?"

"Take the whole box. I don't eat packaged or processed foods laden in poisonous preservatives."

"Thanks. I don't have such reservations." Inwardly I whooped. Maybe my luck had finally changed. I went out to my cozy new home, ate two honey buns and settled in for the night. Before my head hit the pillow I was out like a rock, no pun intended.

I dreamt I slept in a hammock, rocked by the gentle sway of a balmy breeze. The sound of dishes rattled and I halfway awoke from my sleep-induced coma. The trailer's carriage squeaked as it swayed and then rolled to a stop. I opened one eye a slit. The trailer was still shrouded in darkness. The clock read 2:30 a.m. Rolling onto my right side, I bunched a handful of covers under my chin and smiled. *Just a gentle three-point earthquake. Nothing to get excited about.* They happen all the time in California. I had another five blissful hours before it was time to get up.

The next time I woke, bright sunlight backlit the thin window curtains. Outside doors slammed, followed by muffled bangs. More than one car arrived in the parking lot. I looked at my watch. 9:30 am. Wow. I really overslept, but I felt great. I stretched, yawned and swung my feet down into a sitting position. Coffee first. Get dressed. Breakfast. Then I'd be ready to take on Colin and our partnership.

I could only hope that now I was rested, it'd be easier to get along with him. He had apologized, both to Sarah and me. It's possible the pain meds had altered his good judgment. But that didn't erase the mysterious late night phone call or his false lack of recognition when Stone handcuffed me. Plus, I doubted that his alibi for the night Jasper was killed was as rock solid as Stone thought.

Outside an unfamiliar female called out in a low-throated, come-hither voice. "Just lean it up against the wall. I'll call you back when it's time to hang, but I expect that won't be for a week or two. The owner's promised to repaint."

I sat up in bed and peeked out the window. Two deliverymen staggered under the weight of a giant slab of plywood. What on earth had Colin ordered, now? The men disappeared from view.

"That's good," the sultry woman's voice said. "Just leave it there for now."

A loud plop followed. Minutes later the two men came back empty-handed, jumped into a white pickup and drove off.

What was going on?

I hopped out of bed, slipped into jeans, a T-shirt and tennis shoes, not bothering to check the mirror. Running fingers through my snarled hair, I hoped for the best and scrambled down the steps slick from morning dew.

I slid, my arms cart wheeling in the air to keep my balance, and smacked my left hand on the doorframe. "Oooh, ouch." Blood oozed from a long gash on the back of my hand. Using my other hand I clamped down on the wound to stop the gush of blood.

I could bandage it later after I saw what Colin had ordered without consulting me. His nice guy act last night must have been just another ploy. It was time for a serious talk. I refused to play his games.

A green Fiat was parked in front of *From Here to Eternity*, but there was no sign of its driver. Propped next to the store was a huge, bright purple-and-lime green billboard. I frowned.

Step into a new reality . . .

MADAME PATSY
CHAKRA PEDICURES
FOOT MASSAGE THERAPY
TOE READINGS

Discover your **LIFE TREAD THREADS**
Past, Present & Future
Where you've been . . . Where you're going. . .

WALK-INS WELCOME

"Toe readings?" I snorted hard and tears trickled down my cheeks. Instinctively I wiped them away with the back of my hand. Oh gross. Now I'd smeared blood all over my hand and probably my face, too. How could one little wound produce that much blood? It was crazy, but I had bigger worries. Clearly Colin's apology and promise that we were equal partners meant nothing. The fact that he'd supposedly relented on his demand to rent out Sarah's space was just more B.S. to placate me. It'd been stupid to imagine his peace offering had been genuine.

It was obvious his "toe reading" want-to-be-tenant deal was still on.

My hand started to throb. At least the bleeding had stopped, but it looked like I'd just butchered a flock of chickens. Thinking of birds, I'd kill three with one stone. I'd go wash, make coffee in the apartment and wake up Colin for a little impromptu partnership meeting. I'd insist that all future business arrangements had to be agreed upon in writing. No mutual agreement. No action.

If he didn't like it. . . too bad. I headed for the side door into the building.

A familiar van pulled into the parking lot with Sarah behind the wheel. Double crap. This was going to be awkward to say the least.

She got out, staring shocked-faced at the purple and green sign. She held out a paper coffee cup and a takeaway bag to me as she read the new billboard. "I hope you like chocolate chip cookies." Her voice was flat. "Becca baked them this morning."

"Thanks," I said, taking her offering as guilt surged through my veins, even though I had nothing to do with the toe-reader. My mouth watered at the tantalizing mingled aromas of spicy chocolate and fresh coffee. Using my blood-free hand, I retrieved a warm cookie from the bag, savored a bite and sipped coffee. "These are wonderful," I mumbled. "Did she use almonds instead of walnuts?"

Sarah's gaze hadn't left the sign. "I thought you said I wouldn't have to vacate."

"I don't know what this is," I said. "Colin seems to be under the misimpression he's lord of the manor and we're mere peasants, but a little litigation should bring him out of the dark ages.

She turned to look at me. "My goodness, what happened? You're covered in blood. Are you okay?"

"It's nothing," I said, showing her my cut. "Just had a little mishap."

"I have disinfectant in the store. Let me get it."

"That's okay. I spotted a bottle under Jasper's sink yesterday." I gave her a reassuring smile. "Seriously, don't worry about this toe-reading person. Colin can't move her in and you out, unless I agree. And I don't. Agree, that is."

"But he said he had a signed contract with that—" She pointed to the sign. "That person."

"It's not legal or binding without my signature. Besides, unless she's independently wealthy, I doubt she'll be able to come up with two grand a month giving toe readings."

Sarah frowned. "Obviously this is your first time in Sedona."

"What do you mean? Sedona looks like a thousand other small towns, but with incredible scenery."

She smiled, but it didn't light her eyes. "This is West Sedona. Wait till you go downtown and then you'll see that the good folk around here have been seduced by Satan. They're reaping tourist dollars spreading a host of New Age mysticism."

"Uh," is all I said, uncomfortable at the turn of the conversation.

Before she could infuse anymore God-wisdom, a milk-curdling scream erupted from inside THE ALABASTER.

Our eyes met.

"What on earth?" Sarah said.

Seconds later a woman burst around the front corner of the building, arms flailing the air and screeching like a police siren on steroids. Clad in an outfit that was half leopard and half streetwalker, the woman's bushy hair looked as wild as the shocked expression on her painted eyebrows. She spotted Sarah and me and made straight for us.

Up close she appeared even more outrageous. Too much makeup. Tight revealing clothes with way too much exposure for a woman in her late forties. And the dye job on her untamed platinum hair was an inch overdue.

"He's dead," she wailed. "There's blood everywhere."

What was she talking about?

"Who's dead?" I asked.

Her wild eyes fixed on my bloodied hands. She clutched her ample chest and backed away from me. Her lips quivered and a bit of spittle ran down her chin. "You," was all she managed to whisper before she tripped and fell backward into a pile of rocks.

Sarah and I both rushed to help her.

"Don't touch me," the woman shrieked and stabbed her finger at me. "You've permanently diffused his aura at this level of existence. His life essence has been absorbed into the vortex. Forever." She sobbed. "You killed him. "

"I haven't killed anybody," I said. "What are you babbling about? Who's been killed?"

She started to scream again. This time I slapped her face. Her shoulders shook and she whispered in a frightened little girl's voice, "His blood is on your face and hands."

CHAPTER FOURTEEN

Sarah clutched the cross around her neck and knelt in front of the hysterical woman. "You're safe now. Tell me what happened." Her soft southern drawl seemed to sooth the woman. "Whose blood are you talking about?"

The woman eyed me suspiciously and rubbed her face where I'd slapped her. Streaks of tear-stained mascara ran down her rouged cheeks.

"Go ahead." Sarah urged. "You can tell us. You're safe."

The woman's face crumpled in distress. She gulped out her words. "Colin. Someone shot him in the face." Her hands went to her cheeks.

"Are you sure?" I asked, my stomach tangled into a knot. We might not have hit it off and I'd wished he'd just disappear, but that didn't mean I wanted him dead.

She nodded, eyes wide, voice warbling. "Of course I'm sure. I recognized his snake tattoo. I designed it, you know."

I frowned. I'd seen him half naked twice and hadn't noticed any permanent ink art. "Where was this tattoo?"

Her white skin flared a pale rose. "By the tree of life."

I bit back a retort. This wasn't the time for clarification and I didn't want to embarrass or upset my real tenant any further.

"Call the police," I said to Sarah and raced around the front of THE ALABASTER. He could still be alive. The woman could have mistaken the blood on his head as a face shot.

Someone had propped open the front door at an ungainly angle.

I gingerly picked my way inside. Colin's body lay in front of the cash register, his blood melding into the floorboards with Jasper's. Even in death, Colin had style. He was shirtless as if posing for a Fruit of the Loom ad in G.Q. magazine. The forked tongue of a snake flicked from the low-slung waistband. His handsome face marred only by the bullet hole in the center of his forehead. There was no point in checking his pulse. He was gone.

This wasn't the first dead body I had seen, but it never got any easier. Especially when it was somebody I knew. We may have butted heads and our partnership would have been fraught with strife, but no one deserved to die this way. He couldn't have been all-bad. Otherwise, why would Jasper have named him a co-heir?

It took a moment to regain my composure and then I scanned the room for evidence. The absence of a gun ruled out suicide. Not that he'd seemed the type. Nor did the crime scene match that scenario.

From the looks of things, Colin had not gone peacefully to his demise. Merchandise had been swept off shelves. The floor was littered with broken items and papers. I squatted in front of the body. A glint of gold peeked between the fingers of his right hand. I bent forward to get a better look. I knew I shouldn't touch anything. Still, I wanted to know what he clutched.

I grabbed a pen from the counter and steeled myself. Using it as a mini pry bar, I slipped it under his index finger. Applying steady gentle pressure, his finger raised an eighth of an inch. Squinting, I saw what he'd clung to in the final minutes of his life. A medium-sized brass key.

Outside, a police siren screeched into the parking lot. Doors slammed. Footsteps thudded down the length of the building. Men's voices grew louder as they approached the front door.

Call it an impulse. Call it stupidity. Call it self-survival. I flicked the key from his grasp. It bounced with a dead clatter. I snatched it and scrambled to my feet seconds before Chief Stone entered the building. Following him was a second officer that I didn't recognize.

Stone's eyes went straight to my hands. "Don't touch anything."

Even if I hadn't pilfered the key, his suspicious stare would have inspired guilt. To shake the illusion, I went into lawyer mode. "It appears that he was shot by a small caliber gun at close range," I said. "There are powder burns visible."

"You haven't touched anything?" Stone said. "Or tampered with the evidence?"

His questions weren't worth a response, so I went on as a nonplused professional use to unpleasant crime scenes. Inside I felt sick panic, but I managed to keep it out of my voice. "It was obvious he was dead when I entered the room. From his skin tone and odor, I'd guess seven to eight hours ago."

Stone squatted next to the body and motioned for me to back away. The other officer moved in for a closer look and seemed mesmerized by Colin's dead face. His bronze tan morphed to a mottled ash gray. It must have been his first murder. I took advantage of their focus on Colin's body and unobtrusively slipped the key into my pocket.

Stone stood and took a step toward me, effectively blocking the body from my view. "Did you take his pulse?"

"No. Like I said. It was obvious he'd been dead for some time."

"Then what's with the blood all over you?"

I held up my injured hand. "I cut myself. This blood has nothing to do with Colin's death. I came in to see if he was still alive. He wasn't. Then you arrived."

"So you just happened to be in the wrong place at the wrong time. Again." Stone looked to the other officer. "Get her out of here, call for backup and secure the premises."

"Yes, sir." The young officer motioned me to follow him.

"Are you sure you want me to leave? I probably have more experience processing murder scenes than you."

Stone glared. "I said, get her out of here. Now."

"Suit yourself." I moved toward the front door.

"And don't go anywhere. As soon as the crime unit arrives I'll be taking your statement." To the officer he said, "Keep the ladies separated, Sam. Don't let them talk."

Officer Sam nodded. "Will do. This way, ma'am."

"And don't let her wash off that blood."

"Yes, sir," the officer and I said in unison.

"You don't have to be an a-hole," I added. "A simple DNA test will prove the blood's mine." Stone was a jerk if he tried to pin this on me. I didn't own a gun much less know how to fire one.

Wait.

A cold shiver ran down my arms. The gun in the glove box of Jasper's pickup truck technically could be mine. And then I remembered being rocked awake in the middle of the night. Was the weapon still there? Or had it disappeared with my fingerprints all over it?

"Do you have earthquakes in Sedona?" I asked Officer Sam.

"Just small ones. This area sits on two giant tectonic plates and they shift back and forth on a regular basis. It's what gives this place its energy."

A sick feeling crawled into my stomach. Why hadn't I locked the cab of the pickup last night?

"How about I go wait in the truck?" I said. I had to know if it was still there. "I'll sit on the passenger side so you won't have to worry about flight."

"I guess that's all right as long as you don't try to clean up."

"Seriously? You think I'm going to take a bath in the cab of a truck."

He shook his head and tried to stifle a grin. In the process his face returned to its bronze glow. He strode toward Sarah and the other woman. The one I assumed was the toe reader.

"Ladies," he said. "I have to ask you to stop talking to one another until we get your statements. One of you can go inside. The other stays out here with me."

Sarah went into her store. Officer Sam helped the sniffling woman to his police cruiser. Of course he would offer the scantily clad suspect a seat in his car, even if she was a good fifteen years his senior. Men were so transparent. At least he'd be occupied while I searched for the gun.

Acting nonchalant I went to sit in the passenger side of the truck. Luckily, the cab faced the building and was out of the direct line of sight of the cop car.

This was the moment of truth. I took a huge breath, held it, and reached for the glove box. Half afraid the handgun had disappeared. Even more afraid that someone had taken it with my prints all over it. Steeling myself, I used the bottom edge of my T-shirt and reached for the button.

Please, let it not be the murder weapon.

"Damn."

The gun lay on top, no longer buried under the maps. I leaned in and sniffed. A distinct acrid odor lingered on the muzzle. It had been fired recently.

"Double damn." I closed the glove box and leaned back in the seat. Breathe in. Breathe out.

In this day and age of TV detective drama reruns up the kazoo I doubted the killer would be stupid enough to leave prints. But if they had, I didn't want to smudge them. The gun had been fired recently and the odds were high that it was the murder weapon. Borrowed by someone who knew Jasper kept it in the truck.

Goosebumps pricked my skin. There hadn't been an earthquake. That gentle rocking in the middle of the night was caused by the person who shot Colin. The question was, had I been woken up when the murderer took the gun or when they returned it? Had they meant for me to wake? Or had they simply been careless in their attempt to frame me, knowing that my prints were on the weapon? No. That was ridiculous. No way anyone could know I'd handled the gun.

An hour went by and I had nothing to do but think about Colin's murder. Jasper's murder. And the gun. Wait. What about the bullets? I'd forgotten about them. I checked to see if I was being watched. Didn't see anyone so I leaned down and felt around. No shells. Check for observers again and then laid down on the seat, the top of my head on the floorboard and looked. The box was gone. It was a relief, but now I had to decide what to do with the weapon?

Turn it in? Or leave it where it was and hope its existence remained a secret? Or get rid of it before Stone had a chance to take it into evidence? The third choice tempted me because I knew that after failing to solve one murder, he'd be hungry for a quick arrest.

As a former prosecutor, I'd seen people convicted on less substantial evidence than fingerprints on a murder weapon. All the authorities had to do was provide plausible motive, means and opportunity. If a prosecutor was good enough, not-guilty-by-reasonable-doubt was tossed out the window.

In spite of the cool morning, beads of sweat formed on my brow.

My motive? There'd been at least four witnesses to our less than private argument yesterday. One being a cop. Plus, I now was Jasper's sole heir.

My means? Jasper's gun with my fingerprints was hidden in the glove box.

My opportunity? That was a given.

In the prosecution's eyes I'd make the perfect suspect.

That left me with no choice. The gun had to disappear. Or I risked going to trial for a crime I didn't commit, face the possibility of a guilty verdict, and live out the rest of my life in prison if I wasn't executed.

Flipping burgers in L.A. didn't seem so bad.

I glanced at my watch; another forty-five minutes sitting in the truck. My legs were getting stiff. I wasn't used to sitting around and I tried to stretch rolling my shoulders and flexing the muscles in my back.

Now that I'd made up my mind about the gun, my thoughts went to Jasper's murder. Who'd want to murder him? Everyone I'd met so far had said he was a stand-up guy. He had lots of respect. Held in high esteem. Generous to a fault, etc. Even dogs liked him. Colin was another thing. It seemed like almost everyone I'd met had a motive to off him.

As crazy as it seemed, the two murders had to be connected. It was too much of a coincidence that they were killed in the same spot even if the methods were different. Then again maybe Colin's killer had chosen the location to throw the police off the scent. Either way, I had to figure it out.

If they were connected, maybe Colin had stumbled on the same information Jasper had unwittingly discovered that got him killed. Something devastating about someone? It wouldn't surprise me if Colin found a way to use it to his advantage. And I thought about both of the phone calls I'd overheard him make. I fingered the key in my pocket. Would it lead me to the answer?

Someone rapped on the window. I started and felt my heart drop to my toes. Stone stood just inches from me through the glass, wriggling his right index finger in my face indicating that I was to get out.

Heart pounding, I rolled down the window. Either the man was part Indian scout or I was really losing it. How had he managed to sneak up without me noticing?

"You ready for my statement?" I asked, trying to sound like I was eager to help. I put my arm on the window jam and pretended to relax, figuring the best way to get him away from the vehicle was to act like I wanted to do the interview there.

"Please follow me."

"Can't we do the interview here?" I said. "As soon as we're done, I need to go get groceries. My pantry's a little light on supplies. I need coffee, sugar, a few cans of chili and--"

"A man's been killed and you're worried about groceries?" He shook his head as if disgusted. "Just get out of the truck."

"Okay." I sighed like it was a huge inconvenience.

He stepped back, giving me room to open the door.

I pulled my arm inside and rolled up the window. I glanced in the rear view mirror. He'd already turned and was headed toward the back of the truck. I leaned over to lock the driver-side door, opened my door, locked it, and hopped out in time to see him trip over the electrical cord and hose that ran from the building to my home.

He cursed and I stifled a giggle.

He nodded at the camper. "Don't tell me you are sleeping in this."

"The apartment's too small for two people. But Jasper's will stipulates we both have to live on the premises. So until a second apartment is constructed, Carl suggested one of us live in the camper. I volunteered."

Stone's frown grew tighter. "Good old Carl, skating on thin legal ice as usual." He reached down and yanked the gypsy wagon's electrical cord free from the socket and shut off the water.

"Hey. What are you doing? You have no right to do that."

"I don't suppose Carl bothered to inform you that taking up residence in a motor home in the business district is a zoning violation."

"You've got to be kidding," I said.

"I don't make the laws. Just enforce them. Plug in again and I'll write you a citation that carries a hefty fine."

"So where am I supposed to live?"

He smiled. "I guess once we process the crime scene, you can have the existing apartment all to yourself. But then, maybe that was your plan all along."

Obviously Stone didn't want to waste energy looking for another suspect. Not when he had me standing in front of him covered in blood with, in his mind, the perfect motive and opportunity. I had to see that he didn't find the means in the glove box of the pick-up truck.

He led me to the front of *THE ALABASTER*. The crime unit had arrived and stretched out flimsy black and yellow tape warning the unauthorized to keep out.

I tried to watch the investigation in progress through the open door and front windows. A photographer clicked a series of photographs while two detectives gathered forensic evidence.

Stone pulled out a notebook. "Tell me, when was the last time you saw Colin?"

"Before we begin, I'd like to consult Alex Farmer," I said.

"I thought you were a lawyer?" He raised an eyebrow. "I haven't Mirandized you. You don't need counsel."

"I'm sorry." I plastered a professional smile on my face. "You know as well as I do that small town police departments are notorious for taking liberties with the law. Trampling citizen's rights."

A tight frown creased his face. "A man has been murdered. I'm just trying to gather evidence."

"And I'm just trying to protect my rights."

He glared and I stared in return, hoping that he couldn't see through my posturing to the fear quivering in my gut like raspberry Jell-O. My plan was to keep him off balance so he wouldn't think to look in the glove box or search my pockets.

"Go ahead," he said, sounding disgusted. "Call Alex."

"Thank you."

I pulled out my cell. Alex answered on the second ring.

"Hi. It's me, Allie."

"What's up? I just got back to town."

"Colin's been murdered."

"What! What's happened? Where are you?"

I turned and lowered my voice so Stone would think I was trying to keep the call private, but I talked loud enough for him to hear every word. "I'm at THE ALABASTER with the police. Someone shot Colin last night."

"Stay put. I'll be right there."

"The police, in the form of Chief Stone, want to interview me. Can I trust him?"

"What do you mean?"

"Is he an honest cop?"

"He's a pain at times, but he's a straight arrow."

"Thanks. I didn't want to take the chance that Sedona has a corrupt police force."

I slid my cell in the pocket with Colin's key and smiled at Stone. "Okay. I'm ready to answer any and all questions."

Before he could start, another police car pulled into the lot and two men got out.

"Just a minute." Stone went to greet the new arrivals and shook the hand of the short thin man who'd been in the passenger seat. "Doc Shore. Hope your flight was a smooth one. Thanks for making it down from Flagstaff on such short notice."

The man laughed. "Nothing like a short flight to keep the Cessna and my heart humming. So what've you got?"

"Gunshot victim."

The rest of their conversation was lost as they went inside.

Shortly after, Doc came out and over to me. His aftershave seemed stronger than I'd remembered. Maybe it was how he masked out the smell of death.

"Allie, how are you holding up?"

"I'm okay," I said. "But it's been a shock."

"Always is." Pause. "I put his death between midnight and four this morning. Did you hear anything in the early hours? A gunshot? Or see anyone?"

"No. I was out here in the camper. I didn't see or hear anything." Stone stepped out the front door and glared in our direction. "Stone ordered me sit here and keep my mouth shut. He doesn't look too happy that I'm talking to you."

"I'm not anyone. I'm the coroner on official county business." He turned and waved. "He's just a little uptight. This is the second murder on his patch and he still hasn't solved the first one. If you think of anything, let me know. And don't worry about Stone. He's just trying to do his job. Hang tough."

He left and I thought, easy for him to say. Not to worry. He didn't have a gun, possibly the murder weapon, hidden in the glove box of his car.

I sat down on a petrified log to wait and considered my investigative strategy. First, although Stone thought he was interrogating me, I'd pump him for information. Second, somehow I'd hide the gun where no one could find it. But it had to be someplace where it could be retrieved. Third, what was Colin's key to?

Surely Stone couldn't overlook the connection of two murders committed at the same location in less than three months. While he'd probably waste valuable time looking for holes in my ironclad alibi for Jasper's murder, the perpetrator would have plenty of time to further muddy the waters. And if that someone had killed twice for something in THE ALABASTER, and hadn't found it, what was one more murder?

Then it hit me. Maybe it wasn't something in the store, but the store itself. The eyesore sat on a valuable real estate parcel. Perhaps a property developer had his or her eye on the place and was waiting for the Sedona Foundation to take ownership. It'd be worth more to them as cash.

If I was convicted for the murders, I couldn't inherit.

Four, I'd have to find out who was on the foundation's board. And if they were related to Stone. It would explain why he'd failed to solve Jasper's murder and why he was looking at me as a suspect in Colin's demise. I'd do a little digging of my own to see if he was an honest cop. Even though Alex had vouched for Stone's honesty, how well did I know Alex? He was attractive, made my heart flutter, but could I trust my life to emotion? NO. I'd check Stone out myself. This definitely justified my decision not to turn in the gun until I knew where he stood on the honesty scale.

Getting the business up and running would have to wait. That is if I could afford to put the store on the back burner and focus on my investigation. The only way to remove myself from Stone's radar would be to solve the crime myself.

My thumb brushed the key's outline.

At least I had a starting place. An edge on the police investigation.

CHAPTER FIFTEEN

I'd just worked out my plan for the gun's disappearance when Alex arrived. It was the first time I'd seen him without a suit and tie. He looked pretty good in a pair of well-worn jeans and a bright white T-shirt. Younger. More handsome.

"You okay?" he said and unexpectedly pulled me into a hug. The bigger shock is that it felt good. Really good. As in shivering-good that gave hope to a new and safe future.

"I'm fine," I mumbled, holding onto the moment like it was a lifeline. The stress of the last two days had played havoc with my emotions. I wanted—no needed—his protecting arms around me. Making me feel safe.

"You sure?" He released me and studied my face. "You have blood on your cheek." The concern in his eyes made me feel like a puddle of warm wax ready to be shaped and formed into a bright candle of light.

Get a grip, I told myself, followed by a spatter of rational thoughts. Snap out of it. You're misreading his intentions. You hardly know this man. Remember your first impression of him. It wasn't that great.

"It must have been a terrible shock to find Colin's body," he said.

"I didn't," I said.

"You didn't? Who did?"

"The toe reader."

"Toe reader?"

"Alex, you're starting to sound like a parrot."

He pulled me back into his arms and to my shame, I didn't resist. "Just tell me everything that's happened. You talk. I'll listen."

"Okay. I was talking to Sarah when this—"

"What part of *don't talk* did you not understand?" Stone asked, stepping back outside.

Alex released me.

Even though he stood next to me, suddenly I felt alone. "You said not to talk to Sarah or the toe reader. I haven't. Alex is my lawyer."

"Stop splitting hairs." Stone rubbed his forehead like he'd developed a whopping headache.

"I'm not leaving." Alex said. "Now, tell me what's happened?"

"Colin's dead, shot in the face," Stone said. "Now, I need Ms. Renault's statement. When did you last see him alive?"

"Last night. Around five-ish. He'd come to apologize and invited me to have dinner."

"Did you?"

"No. I was tired and went to bed early. That was the last time I saw him alive."

"Did he have any visitors last night?"

"Sorry." I shook my head. "I was sound asleep."

"You didn't hear anything suspicious? A gunshot? Or?"

I hesitated, thinking of the little earthquake I'd felt. If I told Stone I suspected it might have been caused by an intruder, I'd have to tell him about the gun, which was not on the menu. "No," I said. "I'm positive. I didn't hear a thing."

Alex interrupted, earning him a sharp look from Stone. "Think hard, Allie. You're sure you didn't hear or see anything?"

"Look," I said. "The whole building could have blown up and I would have slept through it. I was that exhausted."

"Do you own a gun?" Stone asked.

"No. I hate guns."

"What about Jasper?" Stone asked.

Coffee-flavored bile rose in my throat. It was over. As soon as Alex mentioned the gun in the truck I was toast. It was too late to mention the early-morning visitor who'd taken the gun from the cab, used it to kill Colin, and then returned it. Why had I insisted on calling Alex?

Alex shrugged. "Jasper hated guns. He didn't keep one, not even to scare off predators when he went rock hunting."

I tried not to look too relieved.

Stone shouted to the young officer. "Sam! Double-check for the firearm. Inside and out."

Stone returned his attention to me. I repeated the same answers to the same questions at least a dozen times. Obviously he didn't believe my story.

That was his problem.

Stone finally flipped his notebook shut. The interview was done. "The techs will get a swab of that blood and then you're free to go. You can't stay here, but don't leave town."

"What about the camper? It's not part of the crime scene," I said.

"No, but I want you off the property until our investigation is complete."

"Fine, I'll drive it to a town-approved parking location and stay there until you're done."

"The camper's not safe," Alex said. "You can stay at my place. I have plenty of room and an extra bedroom."

Stone clapped Alex on the shoulder and gave him a lecherous grin. "Still living dangerously, huh." He went back into the store, saying, "Just give my office a call and let them know where to find you."

Alex laughed and looked slightly embarrassed. "Ignore that comment. It was directed at me, not you. You see, I've been divorced twice and Stone can't ever get a second date. It's like our friendship is still stuck in high school mode. He thinks I'm a lady's man, but I assure you I'm not."

"You don't have to explain," I said, suddenly feeling awkward and not at all surprised at Stone's lack of popularity with the ladies. Not with his bull-headed lack of humor. "It really isn't my business."

"I know we just met, but I'd like to think we're friends. I know you didn't kill Colin. Jasper's niece would never commit murder."

"Excuse me," an ambulance tech said to me. She was in her early twenties, and seemed to take her job seriously. "I need to swab your hands and face for a blood comparison to the dead man's."

Alex's face hardened. "Do you have a warrant?"

"It's fine," I said. "It'll prove that this blood is mine and not Colin's."

"If you're sure," he said.

"I'm AB negative. Not too common."

She swabbed my right hand first, placed the giant Q-Tip in an evidence bag and labeled it. "That's true. You're in the one percent."

"Knew you were special," Alex said and gave me a sexy wink that felt wrong considering the situation. Colin had just been murdered. I was a suspect.

Still, my heart betrayed me with a flutter. "How long for the results?" I asked, trying to sound like I was making polite conversation. "Hopefully soon, so Stone can focus on the real suspect."

The tech smiled and took another swab from my cheek. "First we'll do a simple blood-type comparison later this morning. If the blood-type is a match, then we'll send it off to the lab in Flagstaff for DNA. That could take weeks."

"Then let's hope Colin and I don't have the same blood type."

"It's not likely, unless . . ." Her voice trailed off, her face red. She finished up and left us.

Alex touched my arm. "The offer for my spare room still stands."

"Thanks," I said, wishing things were different. That I didn't have a murder weapon to hide. "I think I'd rather be on my own. Can you recommend a reasonably priced place to stay?"

He looked disappointed, but he covered nicely. "The Eagle Inn is just down the street. How about I'll take you?"

"Thanks," I said. "If you don't mind, I'll follow you in the truck." I needed to get the gun off the premises before Stone thought to search the vehicle.

"If I didn't know better, I'd think you're trying to ditch me."

"No, that's not it," I said.

"That camper's a monstrosity. Just leave it here."

"All my stuff is in it."

"I could carry your bags," he said and winked.

"That's not the point. It'd be easier if I left them in the camper. They're already organized. Stone said it'd only be for a couple days."

"If you insist."

"I do."

"You know, that truck's a bear to maneuver. Want me to drive it and you to follow in my car?"

Wrong answer.

"Thank you very much. I'm not helpless." I hurried to my pickup, unlocked it and hopped in, totally annoyed at myself and at him. At me, for my weak moment of thinking he was attractive and interested. At him, because his obnoxious I-know-better-than-the-little-lady attitude had resurfaced.

I started the engine, inched forward and heard metal scrape the pavement. "Crap." I'd forgotten about the stairs to the camper. Leaving the motor running I got out, wrestled the metal contraption into its traveling position and got back into the cab. Hopefully no one had been watching. Especially not Alex. And if he had seen my brief stair-drag, he'd better not say anything. I was in no mood for a macho-man lecture. Still, I geared up for it and forced a tight, painful smile onto my face. To the world I looked happy. Inside my guts churned.

His silver-gray BMW trolled through the lot from out front. Good. Coming from there he couldn't have seen my little mistake. He waved for me to follow.

Tension drained from my tight muscles and I relaxed my grip on the steering wheel. Great. Now blood seeped through the bandage on my hand and a fresh red streak slithered down my wrist. I pressed the wound to the wheel and hoped the bleeding would stop before we got to the motel.

Alex turned right onto 89ALT West. I kept two car lengths between us and rubbernecked like a tourist. Parking lots lined the road on both sides, all teeming with activity. It seemed obvious West Sedona was the main shopping hub for locals. Customers bustled everywhere. Hopefully the high traffic would be profitable once THE ALABASTER was up and running again. On closer look, I realized half the cars had out-of-state license plates.

The Eagle Inn looked like a newer two-story stucco built in recent years even though its parking lot had several mature shade trees that hadn't grown over night. Alex stopped near the entrance. I parked toward the rear of the building where the camper should draw less attention. After locking up, I joined Alex. We went inside together.

The ultra sleek lobby greeted the weary traveler. A veritable desert oasis with large over-stuffed chairs upholstered in rich earth tones clustered around leather-topped coffee tables. In one corner a red rock fireplace blazed with gas flames. At the opposite end of the large open-beamed room, a discrete coffee machine rested on an oak counter with a stack of Styrofoam cups, sugar and cream packets and little red plastic stir sticks.

The small red-faced man behind the check-in counter somehow had employed a double comb-over combined with some sort of colored hairspray. If he thought it disguised his hairless pate, he was sadly mistaken. Someone should tell him that bald was in and that men both young and old shaved their heads.

"Nice to see you, Mr. Farmer. What can I do for you this fine morning?" the man asked, his voice sounding all neutral and business. Neither welcoming, nor friendly.

"Morning, Mr. Scully. Allie needs a place to stay for a day or two. Can you give her the local rate? She's the new owner of THE ALABASTER."

The smile on Mr. Scully's face grew strained and his eyes widened when his gaze turned to me. His upper lip curled downward as he stared at my blood-smears.

"I cut my hand," I said as a way of explanation. "You wouldn't happen to have any hand sanitizer?"

His lips punched together. He reached under the counter and plunked down a giant pump bottle of clear jell in front of me.

"Thanks." I pushed down on the pump. A blob of thick viscous gel squirted, missed my hand and splattered on the counter. "Sorry." I started to wipe it up with my fingers.

"No, no, no." Mr. Scully reached for a tissue.

Alex took the bottle. "Let me." He cupped my injured hand in his free one.

My heart did a little flutter in anticipation.

"It'll only hurt for a moment and then you'll be thanking me." He slowly pushed the plunger. Two large blobs of cool liquid plopped into my hand. He was right. It felt good until it made contact with my cut. Sharp tendrils of fire seared my open wound. I winced.

"It's okay, babe." His thumb massaged my palm. "It'll feel all good soon."

Babe? Did he mean like the blue ox or the pig? How could he be so sexy and annoying at the same time?

He leaned closer and whispered, "I love that fire in your eyes."

His warm breath caressed my ear and as much as I thought I should be exasperated with him, I wasn't. Not only did my hand feel better, the rest of me tingled with every thumb-stroke.

"Humph," Scully sniffed.

I pulled my hand free before I ended up in a puddle on the floor. "Thanks."

Alex chuckled and transferred his attention to the little man. "Allie's just moved to town. She's Jasper's niece."

"So you said." Scully dropped the soiled tissue into a wastebasket behind the counter and muttered just loud enough for me to hear, "Jasper had a lot of people fooled around town."

My sleuthing antennae tingled. The first person I'd met who'd made a disparaging remark about Jasper.

"So you knew my uncle, well?"

He sniffed, slid a Band-Aide and a registration slip across the counter. "Fill this out. Mind you now, I'm only charging for one person staying in the room." He gave Alex a pointed look. "The rate doubles for two."

"The room's just for me," I said. "Mr. Farmer is representing my uncle's estate."

Scully pointed to a security camera mounted on the wall. "The camera catches whatever my eyes miss. I'm serious about the room rate."

"Duly noted."

The transaction completed, Mr. Scully slipped on a pair of bright yellow plastic gloves. The kind you wear to do dishes. Then out came a giant Lysol canister. He spritzed the counter and wiped it down with a wad of paper towels. When he caught me watching him, his face reddened.

"Anything else?" he asked.

Thinking about what I needed to do, I said, "Thanks. I think I'll get settled and then run a few errands."

"Should I pick you up at six or seven?" Alex asked.

"What?"

"For dinner," Alex said.

"I don't know. I have a lot of things to do." Dinner with Alex sounded like heaven, but I had to get rid of the gun in the glove box before Stone thought to search the pickup.

"You have to eat." Pause. "You must be in shock."

Shock is one word for it. Panic was more accurate. I had to get rid of the gun. "No really," I said. "I'd rather be alone."

"You really shouldn't be by yourself this evening after what's happened."

"Yes I should." The first time a decent man was interested in me and I had a date with a murder weapon.

"You want to pay for a double?" Scully said.

"No," Alex and I said in unison.

The two men stared at me like they expected something and I capitulated.

"Okay," I said. "Dinner's on." I'd just have to work fast.

"Pick you up at seven."

"See you then." I waved him out. I was in a hurry to put my get-rid-of-incriminating-gun-plan into action.

"Let me help you get your stuff from the truck."

"I'll be fine," I said. Getting the evidence past the eagle-eyed Mr. Scully would be challenge enough. "I'll just be bringing in a few things. See you at seven."

"If you're sure?"

"Oh yes, quite sure," I said. I waited until he was headed out and waved him out of the lot.

Key in hand, I hurried down the long hallway that ran the length of the building to my room. I barely noticed the décor other than it was clean and color coordinated.

In the bathroom I scrubbed the blood from my face and hands and then got down to business. I pulled out the key I'd taken from Colin to examine it. It wasn't for an automobile, but it looked like a thousand other keys. I turned it over. Two round circles had been stamped into the brass. Someone had added two black dots so that it looked like two little eyes stared at me.

I returned it to my pocket. Maybe it was paranoia or just good sense, but I peaked through the curtains and saw Alex at the passenger side of the truck. Hmmm. . . What was he doing? Checking to see that I'd locked up properly? As I watched, he kicked a tire and I rolled my eyes. This Sedona macho man act was in over drive. Like there could really be that many helpless females in the county. I just wished he'd leave so I could get on with my plan to get rid of the gun. The sooner the better. Which triggered another thought. What if there was a security camera aimed at the parking lot? I'd have to check.

BEFORE I COULD PUT my plan into action I needed a few things from the store. I drove to a supermarket about two blocks down the street. Across from it was a pharmacy. Between the two businesses I should be able to get everything I'd need.

At Safeway I picked up some fruit, peanut butter, crackers, green olives, and gallon-sized Ziploc bags. I paid in cash and asked for a paper bag. The grocery clerk grumbled because her station only had plastic. Judging from her size, the few extra steps were probably the most exercise she'd gotten all week.

At Walgreens I bought aspirin, Kleenex, an eyeglass repair kit and surgical gloves. If anyone asked about the gloves, I'd say it was for cleaning up after the rat residents of THE ALABASTER. Everyone knew rodents spread disease.

Back at the inn, I returned to my parking place at the rear of the lot. I still had a gun to dispose of. A date to get ready for. And two murders to solve.

I'd have to work fast. Mr. Scully seemed like the snooping type.

CHAPTER SIXTEEN

Seated in the truck's cab I felt safe for the moment from Scully's prying eyes. But then again with my luck and his obvious nosey tendencies, I had a fifty-fifty chance of him coming out and catching me with the gun. Or worse. Stone showing up for a little more Q and A.

Better get a move on. I slipped on a pair of the surgical gloves and pulled a Ziploc from my store purchases. Hopefully this would be the only crime I'd have to commit in Arizona. Concealing evidence of a capital murder. I held my breath. Took one last check of the lot. No sign of Scully. Or Stone. Breathed out and opened the glove box. The gun lay nestled like a hibernating snake in the dark recess. Snatching it, I shoved it into the plastic Ziploc and buried it in the bottom of a large grocery sack. My Walgreens purchases went on top. Maybe the deception was overkill, but if Stone showed up to search my stuff, I doubted he'd check any new purchases.

I slipped off the gloves and tucked them into my purse for disposal later.

Then, and only then, I allowed myself to inhale a deep stress-releasing breath. I got out and grabbed the shopping bags. My clothes and personal items could wait for later. Two trips meant less risk of dropping the gun in the lobby.

I went inside. Scully hunched over the countertop phone and started dialing the moment he saw me. His hawk-eyed glare seemed to drill holes into my back as I traversed the lobby. Halfway across his party must have picked up because his voice rattled off a chain of frantic whispers. The only words I caught were, "She's here . . . Not sure if . . . Thought you should know."

In my room, I deposited the bags on the bed and grabbed the ubiquitous phone book every motel room in America seems to provide. I flipped through the yellow pages until I found the section I wanted. I used my cell and punched in the first number on the list. Didn't want Scully to eavesdrop. While I waited, I did a quick count of my cash. Fifty dollars. Probably not enough, but I had to give it my best shot.

"Red Rock Trailer Village," the voice said.

"Do you have space tonight?" I asked.

"Sorry. We're booked through the end of the month."

After six more calls I gave up. I was stuck at the Eagle Inn for the night. No one had a room for my paltry cash and they all required a credit card. I was trapped here. Hopefully Stone's men would finish up A.S.A.P. Until then I was stuck with Mr. Super Snoop.

Wow. Time had flown. It was already four o'clock. Suddenly I felt exhausted and still had the gun to conceal before my dinner with Alex.

I double-checked the deadbolt before deciding where best to hide the gun. Then I spotted the perfect place. Okay, maybe it wasn't a totally original hiding place, but the odds of Stone looking there were super low.

I slipped on the gloves from my purse and got to work. First I removed the light bulb from the oversized wall-mounted reading light. Next I detached the glass shade and went to work with the mini-screwdriver from the glass-repair kit.

"Damn." The screwdriver slipped and a tiny scratch appeared on the fixture. One that Scully was sure to spot. What had I been thinking? The cheap little toolkit was worthless. I should have bought a real screwdriver. Now it was too late to go and get one. Stone might get wind of it. The risk wasn't worth it.

Wait. Jasper must have tools in the truck.

"Yes!" I punched the air and tossed a pillow on the gun, bumping my purse in the process. It tipped and change spilled on the carpet. Scooping up a dime gave me pause. My dad always used them to tighten the odd loose screw. Said it was *making your money work for you, instead of you working for the money.*

I tried it. Yeah, it worked. The fixture slipped from the wall. Behind where it had been was a three-inch round hole just big enough to accommodate the small gun. A satisfactory repository until when and if it was ever needed for evidence against the real killer. It'd be a little hard to retrieve, but not impossible.

The gun clunked into place. I reattached the light and once the scratch was painted, no one would suspect it'd been fiddled with. The gun with my prints now officially disappeared. It would have been easier to wipe the gun clean, but even with my newly acquired larcenous bent, if on the odd chance the killer had left prints on it as well, I couldn't bring myself to destroy evidence in a murder case.

I was on the winning team again and laughed, but stopped myself. This wasn't a game I was playing. Someone had tried to set me up for murder. To get me out of the picture? They'd killed twice to remove obstacles in their path. With the failed set-up to get me out of the way, would I be the next murder victim? A chill swirled down my spine sending a tsunami of shudders in its wake.

What I needed was a hot bath. It was 5:30 and I still needed to get ready for my date with Alex. Too late to fix the scratch, but no one should enter my room until I checked out the next morning. That gave me time after dinner to repaint.

The bathroom was decadent. The huge Jacuzzi tub looked über tempting, but I was afraid I'd never want to get out and Alex would be there in a little over an hour. He seemed like a *type A* and probably would be early. I didn't want him to catch me unprepared. So I opted for the blue tiled shower stall. It had decent pressure and an endless supply of hot water. I lathered and washed myself three times. When I finally shut off the water, the room was hot and steamy like a sauna.

I left the fan on to suck up the mist and returned to the bedroom, shed the towel I'd wrapped around me like a strapless dress, and slipped on a large oversized T-top. I belted it with a leopard printed scarf and slid into my best jeans. I didn't want to overdress. At the same time I didn't want to look too drab so I applied mascara and lip-gloss.

At 6:15 I headed to the lobby, settled on a comfy couch and people-watched while I waited for my date. Scully spied on me. I tried to ignore his censorious glances. Or was I mistaken? Was there something more sinister in his glare? He hadn't liked Jasper and it was obvious he didn't like me.

Muted CNN news whispered from the flat-screen TV mounted on the wall. As predicted, Alex arrived early dressed in a gray suit, gold cuff-links and dark blue tie that made his brown eyes swim. He didn't notice me and stopped to speak with Mr. Scully.

I stood up and went over to join them.

"You're early," I said.

He looked at me in surprise. "No problem. I can wait while you get ready," he said, eyeing my outfit.

"This is it," I said, grinned and held up my hands like a game show hostess. "I gave all my party dresses to charity."

"Sorry," he said. "I'm over-dressed." He removed his tie, slipped out of his coat and slung it over his shoulder like the beginning of a male model strip tease.

"I have to say I like the casual look on you. To be honest, it's a relief. I'm a more casual guy myself."

He opened the door and led me out into the cool night air. Five minutes and two roundabouts later, Alex parked under a huge sycamore in front of what looked like an old Mexican village.

We got out of the car and headed for an arched entryway. Trailing vines covered the high stucco walls as if to prove the place's ancient authenticity.

"How quaint," I said. "I hadn't realized Mexico had settled this far north."

"Gotcha." He grinned. "It's only been here since the 1970s."

"You're kidding. It looks centuries old."

"Originally this was an artist community."

We passed under the arch and into another world.

"Welcome to Tlaquepaque," he said. "It means the best of everything. You fit right in."

Before I could blush, he took my hand and led me down a cobblestone walkway past several shops and art galleries. Wow. Everything about the place was upscale, which made me regret my T-shirt and jeans. Well-dressed tourists strolled in and out of little trendy storefronts.

We went through another archway into a courtyard. In the center stood a fountain full of bright vibrant-colored pumpkins and gourds. Water glittered like diamonds as it splashed down from the top.

"This place is amazing," I said.

He squeezed my hand and let go.

A warm quiver rippled up my spine. This attraction I felt for him was crazy. I hardly knew the man and yet it was like I was fifteen and on a dream date with the school quarterback.

"I thought you'd like to see your competition for the tourist dollars." He took me into a small shop that specialized in original art and jewelry. Purple and white crystals had been positioned about the salesroom as visual accents. The white ones I recognized as quartz. Although better displayed and totally dust free, they looked to be about the same quality of the ones I'd grouped together at *THE ALABASTER* earlier that morning.

Alex pointed to the price tag on one and I did a double take. One hundred and-eighty-nine dollars? Maybe I hadn't inherited a worthless pile of rocks after all.

He leaned in and whispered. "Here, part of the price is the ambiance. But even if you charged only a quarter of that, you're sitting on a good living."

His breath tickled my ear as another round of shivers rippled down my neck and spread yet another wave of heat to my face.

Leaving the store, we continued down a narrow passageway to a larger courtyard.

A delicious blend of aromas teased the breeze. Whatever cooked on the grill, it smelled heavenly. Sautéed onions. Sizzling meat. Roasted chili peppers.

"Hope you're hungry," he said. "The *Oak Creek Brewery and Grill* has the best BBQ Pork Ribs in Arizona. Or you can do half chicken and half ribs. Both are fantastic and their homemade BBQ sauce is the best I've ever tasted. Spicy and sweet." He winked. "Like the new owner of *THE ALABASTER*."

"You're a real comedian," I said, hoping it wasn't obvious that I was drooling. And not just for the food.

The restaurant was on the second floor. Near the entrance a lot of people waited for tables, but when the young hostess saw Alex she grinned and waved for us to follow. She seated us next to a window with a picturesque view.

I smiled as I noticed her painted fingernails. Even though Halloween was long past she'd painted them white with purple tips and each nail had a tiny black scorpion.

She must have sensed my interest because she waggled them and said, "It's Spirit Week at Red Rock High. And even though I've graduated, I like to show my support. I used to be a cheerleader."

She started to hand me a menu.

"We don't need menus," Alex said. "If that's okay with you?"

"Sure." I was happy to let him decide. I'd made enough decisions for one day.

She smiled. "Great. I'll let your server know you're ready."

The waiter was a young man, college-aged, with a bright smile. "Mr. Farmer, you want a pint of your regular lager?"

Alex nodded.

The server turned his attention to me. "And for you?"

"Can you recommend a light beer?" I asked.

"Doc's Pale Ale."

"Sounds good," I said, not sure what to think about our date. Was it real or something else? Was Alex as nice as he seemed or did he have a hidden agenda?

The light conversation and alcohol eased away the tension I'd been feeling. We laughed. Swapped war stories. Played accidental footsies under the table. To my surprise I realized that I had to stop thinking every man was a clone of my ex. Not all men had ulterior motives or were cheaters.

The ribs were scrumptious, as in finger-licking good. Which I did. My mom calls it a nasty habit, but there is nothing better than licking the sweet remains of a perfect meal.

"Any dessert?" the server asked as he removed our plates.

"Not for me, I'm stuffed," I said. "But I will have some decaf Earl Grey if you have it."

"I'll have coffee," Alex said.

He leaned forward. Reflected lights danced in his eyes. Was he going to hold my hand? Wow had my life changed. Less than a week ago I had been alone and flipping burgers for minimum wage. Now I was imagining a shared future with the handsome guy sitting across the table from me.

"We need to talk." His warm hand enveloped mine on the tabletop. "Things are moving fast."

Pin prickles erupted at the base of my neck. Was he going to ask me to spend the night? Not that I would. But it was nice to think I could attract a good-looking, successful and single man.

His eyes turned a dark shade of umber. "It's time to plan your defense."

"My defense?" Did he think I was resisting his come on?

"For Colin's murder."

I felt my loopy grin slip. Boy had I misread his signals. Suddenly I was self-aware and felt bloated and embarrassed. And totally stupid. What had I been thinking? That this was a romantic interlude?

In less than a nanosecond I was cold sober. Pulling my hand free from his grasp I said, "I don't need a defense . . . or your services."

"You've got to be prepared. Stone plans to charge you with Colin's murder. It's only a matter of time before he arrests you.

CHAPTER SEVENTEEN

I stared at Alex across the table. My warm fizzes dissipated like bubbles popping in a sink of dirty dishes, leaving behind a scum of regret. Regret I'd been foolish enough to think he was falling for me. Greater regret because I'd thought I'd finally met a man I might be able to trust with my heart. I should have known better.

Okay. Supposedly he was trying to help me, but I didn't like being managed. Emphasis on *man*. My track record for falling for the wrong kind of guy netted me a big F on the report card of love.

I wouldn't allow myself trapped under the thumb of any guy. Never again.

Time to return to reality. I'd only known the man for less than three days. This was not a date. We were not an almost-couple--regardless of what seemed like mutual attraction. He probably had as much hefty luggage on the cart as I did. Which meant neither of us was ready for a serious relationship.

To preserve my self-respect, all I had to do was convince myself that I'd accepted his invitation to dinner to pump him for information. To find out if he'd discovered what evidence Stone had unearthed at the murder scene.

I forced a half-smile on my lips.

Alex leaned closer and his voice lowered. "Maybe we should talk somewhere more private."

I looked around the Brewery. Most of the dinner patrons had left. Only a few drinkers sat at the bar. The waitpersons bustled about cleaning tables and readying for the next day. Our waiter refilled a tray of salt-and-pepper shakers at a nearby empty table.

"This is fine," I said. "For the record, I had nothing to do with Colin's death."

"Maybe not, but Stone has you in his crosshairs."

"What do you mean, maybe not?" When he didn't answer I felt my dander rise. "You seriously think I killed Colin in cold blood? I hardly knew the man."

"Relax. I'm your lawyer. Whatever you tell me is confidential."

"I did not murder Colin. I don't need a lawyer."

"I know you didn't kill him, but Stone is motivated. Two cold-case murders, is two too many. And given the evidence you're his perfect suspect."

He was right, but my courtroom instincts wouldn't let me admit defeat in even the smallest detail.

Alex tried to reclaim my hand, but I pulled away and leaned back in my chair.

"You need to step back," I said. "You're not my lawyer." Or my significant other, I silently added.

"I am your lawyer and I'd like to be your friend," he said. "I can't protect you if you don't trust me."

"I don't remember hiring you."

"I represent the interests of Jasper's estate. That means whether you like it or not, you're my client." When I didn't answer he added, "You didn't have a problem calling me when Stone was about to arrest you last night."

"That was different."

"How?" His intent gaze made me uncomfortable.

"I needed you to verify my identity," I said. "You were my only contact in Sedona. When it comes to Colin's death, I don't need a defense."

"You don't know Stone."

Our waiter came over. "No rush," the young guy said. "We close in twenty minutes."

After he disappeared, I asked, "Have you actually talked to Stone?"

He nodded.

"When?"

"This evening. Before I picked you up."

"Then why didn't you tell me earlier?"

"Because I didn't want to ruin our evening."

"Little late for that."

"Allie," his voice pleaded. "I truly want to help you. Think about the evidence from Stone's P.O.V. You threatened to kill Colin in front of more than one witness. Including him."

"People say things like that all the time. I didn't mean it literally. I was angry and Colin was being an ass. He man-handled me."

He frowned. "From an outsider's view, your motive looks strong. With Colin out of the picture you are now the sole heir to Jasper's estate." He pulled out a little two-by-three spiral notebook.

"It's all circumstantial speculation on Stone's part," I said, going into lawyer mode.

Alex studied his notes. "You were on the premises. Have no alibi. To Stone it looks premeditated."

"Don't you think if I planned Colin's demise, I would have included an alibi for myself?"

"It could have been an impulse kill," he said. Pause. "You don't own a gun, do you?"

"Never had the need for one."

"You're sure you didn't come across one while exploring THE ALABASTER?"

"You said Jasper didn't own any guns."

"He didn't. But you're sure you didn't find one? Pick it up? Touch it?"

I crossed my toes for luck. "I'm sure." It wasn't a lie. Technically I'd found the gun in the pickup.

"Colin worked on a military post. He could have brought one."

"And we can't ask him," I said dryly. "Stone may think I'm involved, but he has no real evidence. Not even good circumstantial evidence. He's grabbing at gnats."

"I wish that was true." Alex's face went grim. "Stone got the results on the blood-type comparison. The blood swabs from your hand match Colin's blood type."

A sobering flutter churned in my stomach. "You're sure? Colin has AB negative blood, too?"

He nodded.

"An unlucky coincidence," I said, "but not a real problem. Without the official lab results, he doesn't have a case. And when he gets them, our DNA won't be a match."

"But the test results will take weeks. In the meantime Stone will focus on you. He's already pulled your disbarment file. He sees it as further proof of your lack of respect for the law. Just a small step away from murder."

I resisted rolling my eyes. "If I were the murdering kind, my ex would be dead. That should be proof that I don't have violent tendencies."

Alex smiled. "I do love that fire that sneaks into your eyes. Do you have any idea of how beautiful you are?"

Don't react to the flattery, I told myself. Stick to business. Ignore his sexy eyes. Still, I allowed myself a little smile.

"Stone jumps to conclusions," I said. "His fixation on me as a suspect is a repeat of Jasper's murder investigation. He decided it was a vagrant and stopped looking for the killer." And then to check his reaction I added, "What if the two murders are connected?"

A shadow of what could have been doubt surfaced in his brown eyes and disappeared with a blink and a shake of his head. "Not likely."

I stared at him while my palms turned clammy. "What if the killer plans to return for me?"

"That's not going to happen," he said.

My fingers went cold. How could he possibly know that? Unless . . . No I wouldn't go there. Besides, how could he possibly defend me against a ruthless killer?

The waiter came back with the bill. Alex scribbled a generous tip and we left. The walk to the car didn't seem as magical as it had earlier when we arrived. Lingering shadows took on sinister vibes. The air felt cooler. The clinging vines now strangled tortured-looking walls. Shops were closed and the narrow alleys dark and deserted. An atmosphere of danger lurked as we tripped along the cobbled walk. We hurried, our footsteps leaving a hollow echo in our wake. In my imagination, even the welcoming fountain trickled a series of warnings. *Go. Leave this place. You're in danger.*

I was shivering and goose-bumped by the time we reached the car. Alex cranked up the heater and blasted blessed heat by the time we'd reached the first roundabout.

"Would you mind stopping at Walgreens?"

"I thought you went shopping."

"I did, but I forgot to get something. If it's an inconvenience, I can go after you drop me off."

"Don't be ridiculous." He pulled into the store's parking lot.

I raced in, made my purchases and was back in the car in less than five minutes. At the Eagle Inn, he parked near the entrance, but not right in front. He kept the heater running.

"There's one more thing you should know," he said.

"What?"

"Stone needs a quick solve of the case. It's personal," Alex said.

"Why?"

"The short of it is that he and Colin were in high school together. They started out as friends. Colin chased the girls. Making one conquest after another. Stone was his sidekick. Then Colin seduced the wrong girl."

"Stone's girlfriend?"

"No. His younger sister. Within a week Colin had moved on. Stone's sister was devastated. Everyone at school knew about it. It was a real scandal. Then she tried to commit suicide."

"How awful."

"She went for treatment. Colin went back to Kansas. Old timers around here have long memories. It's the reason Stone needs a quick arrest. Otherwise people will think he's slacking on the job because of an old grudge."

"Maybe he should hand the investigation to someone else."

"Can't. The department's too small." His dark eyes studied mine. "Never understood how Colin managed it. All those women fawning all over him like he was a Greek god. Did you feel it?"

"What?"

"His magnetism?"

"No." Awkward pause number five hundred thousand. It was time to end our little less-than-romantic tryst. "Hey, it's getting late," I said. "I've had a long day."

"I know. Sorry to lay it all on you now, but. . ." His eyes went soft and he leaned over as if to move in for a kiss. "I don't want to see you hurt."

I grabbed for the door handle. It was like I'd hit the driver seat eject button. He hopped out, raced to my side of the car, and like the perfect gentleman, walked me to the front door.

"You know," he said, "once we prove your innocence, Colin's murder could be a lucky break. I know it sounds harsh, but he would have made your life hell."

"That's not what you said in L.A. when I asked you what kind of a partner he'd make."

"Back in LA, I didn't see beyond the fairy dust to the real you."

I felt a shiver on my neck and bit my lower lip to replace the seductive tingles with a dose of no-nonsense pain.

He didn't seem to notice the effect his words had on me. "It wasn't my place to prejudice you against your new partner."

"I understand. You were just doing your job." I really couldn't fault Alex for his professionalism. In fact, I was having a hard time staying mad at him, but I had to be strong. It was too soon to get involved with a man I hardly knew. Especially when I hadn't written anyone off as a suspect. "Still a heads-up would have been nice. My first impressions wouldn't have come as such a shock."

"I know I can be a little forceful, but don't shut me out. I'll do whatever I can to see that Stone doesn't railroad you." He held out his hand. "Friends?"

"Of course," I said and took his. He gave mine a gentle squeeze before letting go.

"I mean it," he said. His intense gaze almost hypnotized me into telling him everything. About Colin's late night phone call. The key I'd pried from his dead hand. The gun safely nestled in the wall of room 125. But I knew I couldn't. I didn't know if I could trust him yet. I had to do this on my own. At least for now. Maybe after everything was cleared up, I'd be ready to explore a relationship with this man.

"If you need anything, just ask," he said.

No time like the present to see if he meant his words. "I do have a few questions," I said. "Do you think you could convince Doc Shore to give me copies of Jasper and Colin's autopsies?"

He winked. "I'll talk to him, but I still think you should just leave things alone."

"Thanks."

CHAPTER EIGHTEEN

B ack in the motel room my mind raced like it had been injected with a pack of insomniac hamsters. I banned all thoughts of Alex and concentrated on Stone and his investigation. And, his focus on me as a prime suspect.

What rotten luck Colin and I shared the same rare blood type. On the other hand, it was good luck. Stone couldn't move on me until the DNA results were back. This gave me time to run my own investigation.

I slipped into an oversized Raiders T-shirt that served as my nightgown. Colin's key went in my travel kit. Not the best place to hide it, but it would do until morning. It had to be important. Why else would Colin have had it? I had to figure out what it unlocked.

Easier said than done.

I stared at the scratch on the fixture. Crap. I was too tired to trust my artistic skills. I'd do it in the morning. Still, I could prep for it. Pulling out the bag from Walgreens, I lined up a row of white nail-polish bottles on the bed stand. One of them had to match.

Starting on the left, I painted my left pinky with polish number one. Number two went on my ring finger. Soon I had seven white fingernails. In the morning, I'd do the color match.

After turning off the lights, I stretched out on the king-sized bed and lay there wide-awake for what felt like hours. Shifting from one side to the other. Propped up by pillows on my back. Face down on my stomach. My brain too tired to think. What is it about exhaustion that banishes sleep? Giving up, I reached for the TV remote and started flipping channels. On Turner Classics, *Rear Window* with Jimmy Stewart played across the screen. If only mysteries were easy to solve in real life. I drifted off as he wheeled his chair to the door.

Gunshots blasted in the room. I popped up like a Jack-in-the-box, disoriented and confused. Lights flickered on the ceiling and walls as machine gun fire rattatatted from the television set. I flopped back into the pillows and felt for the remote. It was wedged between the bedspread and the sheets. Pointing it at the television, my fingers blindly pushed buttons until the only sound in the room was the distant hum of a bathroom fan. I drifted back to sleep until the shrill ring of the bedside phone woke me.

Rolling onto my side, I eased onto my elbow, plucked up the phone and knocked nail polish bottles, numbers six and seven, to the carpet.

"Hello," I croaked into the receiver.

"Ms. Renault?" It was Scully. "You have a visitor."

"What time is it?" I mumbled.

"Ten a.m." His voice betrayed disapproval. "Would you like me to send her to your room?"

Her? Suddenly I was wide-awake.

"Who?" I asked, while trying to guess who had tracked me to the Inn.

"It's a Ms. Patsy Gaines." The 'Mizzzzzzzz' came out like an angry buzz saw.

Who was Patsy Gaines?

"Tell her to meet me at the Calico Café in thirty minutes."

Pause.

"She says she'll be there."

Click.

I didn't need the full thirty minutes to get ready, but I had the scratched fixture to take care of before I left the room. I speed-dressed; putting on the same clothes I'd worn to dinner with Alex.

Turning on all the lights in the room, I held up each painted nail to the fixture. My left index was a match. "Yes!" Holding my breath like I was putting on eye makeup, I brushed a thin line of quick-dry polish the length of the scored metal. Stepping back to survey my work, I was pleased at the result.

Practically invisible. Or was it? I squinted. If Scully looked close, he might see the raised line of polish. Shoot. I had to do the other twin wall light to match. When finished they looked pretty much identical.

The unpainted nails on my right hand looked odd, so I splashed them with polish, grabbed my purse and headed for the Calico.

Beth greeted me from the kitchen when I arrived at the restaurant. "Sit where you like."

The place was empty. Where was the mysterious Patsy Gaines I was supposed to meet? I chose a table at the back and sat facing the door.

Beth bustled out with a steaming pot of coffee. Today her uniform was at least two sizes too big. It made her look younger, like she was playing waitress. She stumbled when she reached me. Hot coffee sloshed from the pot on the table, my shirt and my arm.

"I'm so sorry. I didn't burn you, did I? Let me get you some ice and some soda water so the stain doesn't set."

"I'm fine. Don't worry about it." I pulled the wet shirt away from my skin. It had already started to cool.

"I don't know why, but I'm a total klutz today."

"Some days are like that," I said, wishing I had worn an old T-shirt. "But I will take a cup of that coffee if there's any left."

"It's the least I can do. On me. Are you sure you're okay?"

I nodded. That's when I noticed that the whites of her eyes were red. From allergies or a crying bout? Either way, it was none of my business — unless she was somehow connected to Colin's murder. Wait? Had she been one of his conquests?

"I guess you heard," I said. "That Colin is dead."

Her eyes brimmed with tears. "It's horrible. He was so nice."

"You knew him well?"

"We dated some. Just off and on. Not seriously, but I'm going to miss him." Tears trickled down her cheeks.

Even though it would add to her distress, I had to ask, "Did he have any enemies? Someone who would want to kill him?"

"No." Her voice quivered and I knew she was holding something back.

"You can tell me."

"Well . . ." She bit her lower lip.

"If you have a suspicion, please tell me."

Her gaze focused on the coffee pot. She swallowed as if to choke back a sob. Two bright red spots appeared on her cheeks. "You're the only one who profits from his death," she finally blurted. "I'm sorry, but it's true."

"I didn't have anything to do with his death," I said. As Beth walked away, I called after her, "But I'm going to find out who did."

Beth's shoulders tensed, but she moved on like she hadn't heard me.

The front door opened. Great. In came the toe reader. I hoped she wasn't going to make a scene and accuse me again of murdering Colin. I cupped my hand over my forehead, tilted my head down and peeked through a slit between two fingers. Please don't let her notice me sitting here.

No such luck. The woman spotted me and headed straight for my table.

"I'm sorry I'm late," the woman said and sat across from me. Today she'd left the leopard print behind and dressed in all black. No visible cleavage, but she still boldly supported the makeup industry. "I had a few errands. They took longer than expected. I'm Patsy."

I forced a smile and sat up straight. *Patsy Gaines, my appointment.* Other than recriminations, I couldn't imagine what she wanted to talk to me about. Well I wasn't going to let her ruin my breakfast.

"Oh my," she said spotting my painted nails. "You could use a manicure." She called to Beth. "I'll have coffee."

Beth came back to the table. "Anything else?"

"Heavens no," Patsy said. "I've already eaten and want to keep my girlish figure."

"I'll have the 'Cat's Meow,'" I said. I hadn't been a girl for a long while. Plus I had a great metabolism.

"Sausage, bacon or ham?"

"Can I have all three?"

"Sure." Beth scribbled on her pad as she went to place my order.

Patsy raised her penciled eyebrows. "You may get away with eating like that at your age, but I hope you realize that men don't find fat women attractive."

I snorted. This toe-reader packed at least thirty pounds more than my 120. Granted, ten of them were on her chest, but she was in no position to cast stones.

"You're probably wondering why I want to talk to you after yesterday." She pleated a paper napkin with her long red nails. "Finding Colin like that stripped my chakras to the core."

Okay, what more could I expect from a holistic toe reader?

"I want to apologize," Patsy said.

"It's not necessary. Murder is a stressful event."

"Be that as it may, the specter of death has never invaded my aura before. I was beside myself. When I saw your blood-streaked hands, my spirit and intellect split at the cosmic level. Unable to think rationally, my emotions exploded. I lashed out at you. For this I am truly repentant."

Her eye-lined, fake-lashed, and blue-shadowed eyes pleaded for absolution like some distorted character in an animated horror film. "You have to forgive me. It's the only way to realign my astral essence."

Was this an act or for real? My suspicious mind wondered what she really wanted. After yesterday's accusations, she'd gone to a lot of work to track me down. "It's forgotten."

"And forgiven?"

"Forgiven," I said, thinking maybe she might be able to give me the lowdown on Colin from a romantic-conquest-point-of-view. "Tell me, how did you and Colin meet?"

She stared at her hands encircling her coffee mug. Gently she began to swirl the cup as if mesmerized by the little mocha whirlpool she'd created.

Beth came back with my breakfast.

"It was true cosmic passion between Colin and I," Patsy said and blushed. "After my husband died, I didn't think I would ever share the joy of physical desire with another man. Then I met Colin." She looked up. "We were going to be married."

Crash.

My pancakes, sausage, bacon, ham and eggs splattered like road-kill on the tile floor. To my shame, I briefly wondered about the two-second rule in a restaurant.

Beth's face blanched white. "I'm sorry, I'm not feeling well." She clutched her stomach and ran for the restroom.

Mel materialized with an oversized dustpan and a roll of paper towels. He had no comment, just a series of muttered grumbles under his breath.

I helped him clean the floor and said to Patsy, "I need to wash my hands." What I really wanted to do was check on Beth. She squatted over a toilet, sobbing and puking at the same time. When she finished, I put my hand on her trembling shoulders and helped her to stand.

"You okay?" I asked, thinking the jury was in. Colin had been a certifiable jerk. They had had more than a few casual dates. I wondered how many other women he'd managed to bamboozle with his GQ charm?

I handed her a couple of wads of toilet paper. She wiped away tears and blew her nose. Her face looked blotched and puffy.

"Should I tell Mel you're sick?"

She didn't answer. Just looked so pitiful that I wished I could reassure her that everything would be okay. Tell her that she'd get over Colin's death and his betrayal, but I didn't have the words. All I could dredge up was the anger that still smoldered from my ex's philandering. "Men can be such jerks."

"He said he loved me," she said. Her voice sounded like she was five and had just found out that the Easter Bunny wasn't real.

"I'm sorry. I know this sounds trite, but by this time next year he'll be just a hazy memory."

"No, he won't. I'm having his baby."

"Oh," is all I managed to squeak. After she shed another bucket of tears I asked, "Are you going to be okay?"

She sniffed and rubbed her nose. "I've been sick every morning for the last two weeks. At first I thought it was the flu. But when I didn't get better, I bought a home pregnancy test kit." She gulped. "I was so excited to tell Colin. I knew we were going to be so happy together. The three of us. Now..." She started to sob again. "He's dead and never knew about our baby."

I hugged her and patted her back some more, not that it seemed to help. Nor did my repeated mumbled, "You'll be okay."

Finally her blubbering subsided and she seemed to take hold of her emotions. She pulled away, her face now a mask of sorrow shadowed in doubt.

"Do you think it's true?" she asked. "That Colin planned to marry her?"

"I don't know." I felt totally out of my league and a little embarrassed to see such painful raw emotion and not be able to offer any real words of comfort. "How about I tell Mel you have the flu and need to go home."

"Don't tell him I'm . . ." Her voice trailed off as she unconsciously rubbed her belly.

"I don't gossip," I said. Still, I couldn't help wonder if she'd known about his other affairs? About Patsy? The fact that Colin had knocked-up Beth and then deserted her for an older woman could be a powerful motive for murder. At the same time, I would swear that her shock at his betrayal seemed real.

I went to find Mel.

"Is she okay?" Patsy asked, when I came out.

"A touch of flu," I said and headed for the kitchen. Once I told Mel the same thing, adding the words *possibly contagious*, he told me to tell her to leave by the back door. "She's already cost me enough this morning." He handed me a steaming plate of food. "Here's your breakfast."

I took it and the coffeepot back to the table.

Miraculously, Patsy had recovered from her maudlin aura chatter.

"What I really want to talk to you about," she said, suddenly sounding business-like, "is when I can open? When is the Bible lady vacating?"

I dry swallowed, dreading her reaction to the news that Sarah wouldn't be leaving.

"I'm sorry, but Colin misrepresented the availability of the rental space," I said.

Her face turned hard. "That's not possible. Colin cashed my checks."

"Checks? As in plural?" I'd only seen the one.

"Yes. One for one-hundred-and-fifty-thousand dollars, and the other for five thousand."

I felt my eyes widen, but tried to keep the shock off my face. "What did you think you were buying into?"

"My half of the property. We were getting married. He said that if we treated the ownership of THE ALABASTER as a business arrangement, it would work better on our taxes. I didn't really understand it all, but then I've never had a head for financial finagling. The second check covered the first three months' rent including a security deposit."

I took a deep breath. "If you thought you were buying half the property, why would you have to pay rent?"

She shrugged. "I don't know. When Colin explained it, it made sense. Besides, he said it was just a formality for the tax man."

"So Colin didn't tell you that he only owned half of THE ALABASTER? That I was co-heir to Jasper's estate and co-owner?"

Her eyes popped open so wide that her green irises floated in white. Either she had amazing theatrical skills or Colin had snowed her good. Maybe it was a combination of the two. Because I'd just realized that once we'd started talking business, she hadn't inserted any new age mumbo jumbo into the conversation.

This had been a productive morning. In the short space of an hour, I'd discovered two women with good reason to murder Colin. And who knew how many others were out there? Women he'd romanced with false promises. And how many others had he financially exploited?

"You mean he lied to me?" Her voice grew shrill and I think I caught a glimpse of the real woman.

"I'm afraid so." I swallowed again.

Her face grew taut. Deep creases marred her forehead and the corners of her mouth. "So you're telling me my money has disappeared? And you won't rent the business space to me?"

"The business space is already rented. I can't throw out the current tenant."

"Colin said she was closing."

"Colin said a lot of things." I let that sink in before I added, "I think you should talk to the police. Maybe during their investigation they can locate your money." Then I thought of his shiny new red corvette. "Or at least some of it."

Her face crumpled. Streaks of mascara-tears ran down her cheeks.

"What am I going to do? I put everything I had into my business. My husband's life insurance. Our savings. I even took out a business loan for my startup costs. That alone was twenty thousand."

She grabbed my arm. "If I can't have the Bible store space, rent me a corner of the rock shop."

"I don't think that would work."

"Then rent me another part of the building. It's huge. Colin gave me a tour. It's mostly filled with junk, taking up precious space." She rattled on for five minutes. In the end I agreed to think about it because I felt sorry for her. She'd lost her fiancé, her fortune, and if she learned about Colin's tomcat habits, her self-respect would soon follow.

I went back to the Eagle Inn and reviewed what I'd learned that morning. I jotted notes using shorthand I'd developed. I studied the list of names and tried to decide on the next step in my investigation. Still had to visit the Chamber for a list of new age businesses. Still needed to talk to the coroner. Still needed to figure out what Colin's key unlocked. Plus I wanted to read all the press about both murders. Too bad Jasper did things the old fashioned way and hadn't owned a computer.

One thing was for sure. Colin had been more than just a middle-aged Lothario, and I doubted Patsy was his only victim. I remembered his late night call. He'd probably swindled more than just women. I'd bet my inheritance that he had a long line of people with grudges against him.

But that didn't explain Jasper's murder. Deep down I knew the two homicides had to be connected. I'd make up a list of potential suspects for both Jasper's and Colin's murder and see where they intersected. And how? Another possibility radiated chills down my spine. Maybe someone wanted to buy THE ALABASTER and Jasper refused to sell. Even though the buildings had run down, the land remained valuable. Especially when you considered the big open field behind the store right in the middle of the business district. I'd have to add checking real estate agents to my list.

Owning THE ALABASTER might be a dangerous profession.

CHAPTER NINETEEN

I decided to skip lunch after my late breakfast.

Back at the inn, I surveyed my temporary room. Had Scully had been in to snoop? It didn't look like it. Everything was as I'd left it and it was obvious the cleaning staff had respected the *Do Not Disturb* sign I'd hung on the door when I'd left. The bedding was rumpled, a towel lay on the floor and my row of nail polish still stood like sentinels on the bedside table. I plunked down on the side of the bed and reached for the house phone.

I didn't care if Scully monitored this call. I needed to save my cell's battery for emergencies. For some reason it kept losing its charge in Arizona. I smiled ruefully— maybe it was the power of the vortexes. Plus, I didn't like restricting my research to a little two-inch screen. Too hard on the eyes and visually limited.

A few minutes later I had the directions and hours of the Sedona Public Library. It had opened at ten. Until the police released THE ALABASTER crime scene, I decided to employ some legwork and expand my knowledge of the town with a little local reconnaissance.

At the library, I planned to spend as long as it took to read all the news reports and social chatter about Jasper's murder. Plus, I wanted to visit the Chamber and get a list of New Age enterprises.

Before I headed out, I jotted a list of the people I'd met in chronological order on a piece of the room's complimentary stationery—a pretentious golden eagle soaring over the embossed *Eagle Inn* lettering stretched out like a mountain chain. I made a mental note to grab a notebook at Walgreens on my way to the library.

Printing in small neat letters, I made the following list.

Alex Farmer: Lawyer of Jasper's estate. Professional. Friendly. Flirtatious. Why? Interested or involved?

Colin Phelps: Son of an old friend of Jasper's. His murder implies he's innocent of Jasper's murder but not an innocent man. A real Don Juan.

Chief Stone: Cop in charge of investigation. Knew both Colin & Jasper for years. Colin romanced his sister back in high school and dumped her. Still holds a grudge?

Dorcus, Rose and Edna Kincaid: I lumped the sisters together. Longtime customers at THE ALABASTER. Dorcus into the metaphysical power of rocks. Edna a kleptomaniac. Rose the "yes" sister. Spinsters?

Carl Morton: Long-time friend of Jasper who knew Flint. Retired lawyer. Former soldier. Started and supports orphanage charity. Friendly, forthcoming, but . . . secrets?

Ming: Carl's adopted daughter from Vietnam. Runs Sedona Charitable Trust. Oversees orphanages. Last name?

Mel: Cook and owner of the Calico Café. Last name?

Beth: Waitress at the Calico Café. Says she's pregnant with Colin's child. Last name?

Sarah: Bible bookstore owner and tenant. Super cheap rent? Why?

Becca: Sarah's daughter. Teenager

Jacob: Sarah's son. Worked for Jasper. Knows something about the rocks. May know other things about Jasper.

Scully: Runs the Eagle Inn. A real snoop. Seems self-righteous. Judgmental. Didn't like Jasper.

Patsy Gaines: Has best motive for Colin's murder. He bilked her out of her savings. Had he dumped her once he had her money? Did she know Jasper?

I reread my list. In Colin's case, it was easy to imagine him having a host of enemies. But Jasper? I couldn't see any one of them wanting to kill him, except maybe Scully. And thinking of Scully pulled my eyes to the light fixture. Hopefully no one would notice my repair job. At least not for another month or two, long after my stay.

I folded the paper and tucked it into my pocket. Before leaving the room I swept the nail polish bottles into a bag. No point in inviting curiosity. I picked up the towel and tossed it into the bathroom. Closed my suitcase, grabbed my purse and the polish. After double-checking to make sure the door was locked, I flipped the Do Not Disturb sign to Maid Service Please.

Miraculously after only one try, I fired up my new rock-hunting truck with its gypsy wagon and was on my way. Even stopping at every stop-light, in three-minutes I reached the first turn at Dry Creek Road. Top heavy, the truck careened around the next left at White Bear and rumbled into the Library's parking area. I navigated the creaking and groaning Behemoth into the center of two side-by-side parking places at the outer edge of the lot.

The hot sun felt good as I approached the building. The library had festive beige and red sandstone block walls. Near the entrance a bronze statue of a pioneer woman held out her hand in welcome. Inside, stained-glass windows let in warm natural light that played on the sand-stone pillars rising high to the open-beamed ceiling. Soft indirect light bathed the reference desk. It felt like a cathedral.

My footsteps echoed on the tile floor.

"Hi," I said to the lady behind the desk. "I'd like to use a computer."

"May I see your driver's license?"

I handed it over.

She studied my photo and then my face. "Just visiting Red Rock Country?"

"No, I'm a new resident."

"Then I suppose you'll be wanting a library card. It requires two pieces of identification and a cancelled envelope addressed to you local-ly." She waited expectantly for the required documents.

"Sorry. I haven't been here long enough to receive mail."

"A visitor pass will work for today. The computers are over there."

She pointed to a bank of computers. Only two were in use, but the click-clack of the keyboards sounded loud in the hushed surroundings.

The woman handed me a slip of paper. "This is good for one hour. If you need to print, it's ten cents a page. Black and white only."

"Thanks."

I turned and almost bumped into a book cart commandeered by two high school girls. I should have heard their soft giggles. Instead I was focused on getting started. That's why it surprised me when one of them spoke to me.

"Hi, Allie," Becca said. The girl with her was tall, dark-haired and pretty.

"You work here?" I asked.

"We volunteer here to get our community service credit. It's a graduation requirement."

"And better than picking up trash," her friend said.

"Oh," Becca said. "This is my friend Tamara. You sort of met when I was talking to her on my phone yesterday."

"Nice to meet you in person." I waved my research pass. "I have research and my time is ticking."

Becca leaned closer and said in a loud stage whisper, "I have connections. Take all the computer time you need."

"Yeah," said Tamara. "It's not like there's a line."

I smiled.

"Wait," Tamara said. "I hate to be a bother, but by any chance did you find a paperweight at the shop? It's white, round, and has a tiger head carved on the top. About the size of a donut. Oh, and an ice cream cone is etched on the bottom."

I shook my head. "Sorry. Becca asked me to look, but I haven't had time." I didn't add that it was a crime scene. If Becca knew, she'd probably already told her friend all the gory details. Plus a few speculative ones. "If I find it, I promise, I'll give you a call."

"Tam's obsessed," Becca said. "She watches *Pawn Stars* all the time."

"Pawn Stars?" I said.

"Yeah, that show where people take in old junk and find out it's worth gobs of money."

"I thought the paperweight might be worth something," Tamara said. "I took it to Jasper. He said he'd check it out. Then he died." A frown creased her pretty face. "I need to get it back. It's not mine. I borrowed it. My mom will kill me if she finds out."

"Moms can be harsh," I said, thinking of mine. "Don't expect them to change with time. Hate to be rude, but I need to work."

Both girls looked at me funny, like I'd been speaking Croatian with a Cuban accent and they only understood teen-speak.

"Wait. Why don't you sketch it for Allie," Becca said. "She's really good at art stuff."

"That might help," I said. "I'll be here for a while if you get it finished before I'm done."

The girls took off with their cart and I settled at a computer. First I started with everything I could find about Jasper's murder. There wasn't much information and what there was, I already knew. I hoped Alex would convince the coroner to talk openly with me. Once I'd read everything, I started on my potential suspect list.

I resisted the impulse to type *Alex Farmer* into the Google search engine. It'd feel too much like I'd be checking him out, a cross between voyeurism and outright cyber stalking. I couldn't chance finding out something that might subconsciously tempt me to move beyond friendship. It was hard enough to forget how his smile could turn my bones to putty. Or the quivers that rocked my core with the mere graze of his fingers when he'd helped into me the car for our non-date. I'd be strong and keep him at arm's length. No man would invade my good sense or threaten my new found confidence ever again. Regardless of charm or sheer animal magnetism. Come on, Helen; let's sing it again.

It was a waste, thinking about what wasn't going to happen.

Time to find out what skeletons dangled in Colin's baggage. There were over five hundred hits on Google for Colin Phelps if you counted the 'Colin's' spelled with a double 'l'—A doctor, lawyer, athlete, writer, town mayor, but none my ex-business partner. And none engaged in public nefarious activities.

Colin hadn't been in any serious trouble. Or hadn't been caught. A total dead end, but not a total waste. He didn't have any public enemies.

Next, I tried *Fort Riley, Kansas* where he'd worked in the maintenance division. I found the department that oversaw the hiring of civilian personnel, jotted down a couple of phone numbers. They were long shots. Military installations are usually tight-lipped.

A noisy group of boys entered the library.

"Quiet, boys," a man's voice said. "Remember, we are Scouts and good citizens, and this is a library."

I turned in my seat. A troupe of twenty or so tweens dressed in khaki-colored uniforms clustered around their adult male leader.

"You will need to work in pairs. You have ten minutes before we go on the computers. Find a book that you can use to earn your badge."

I looked at the clock. Crap. Even though Becca had assured me that I could take all the time I'd need, obviously I was about to be replaced by a pair of pre-pubescent Cub Scouts. And I hadn't even really started on the list of suspects.

THE ALABASTER needed its own computer, a laptop, and building-wide WIFI. But for the moment, I would make the most of the next nine minutes of my computer time.

This last hurried search netted me *The Prairie Post's* contact information in White City, Kansas—Colin's hometown. Crazy. A town with a population of just over six hundred people had its own newspaper. It should be easy to find at least one gossip in a community that size.

To find a likely candidate, I pulled up a recent issue of *The Prairie Post* when the computer screen started flashing, "TIME IS UP."

Great. So much for progress. The sweaty swarm of little boys headed my way.

I tucked my notebook into my bag and dodged eager little boys as I started for the exit. At least I had some possible phone contacts and it was still early in the day.

"Allie." Tamara held out a paper to me. "I didn't want to bother you while you worked, but here's the sketch of the paperweight."

I took the drawing. The savage face of a tiger glinted up at me from the page. Its face filled one circle. In the other circle she'd drawn what looked like an ice cream cone and some branches.

I'd seen nothing like it in the shop, but who knew what lurked under the dust?

"Becca was right. You can draw," I said. "Is this close to its actual size?"

"Yeah. The tiger is the top. The funny snow-cone thing is the bottom."

"You're a real artist."

She colored and looked pleased. "It kind of runs in the family. You should see my mom's paintings. And grandpa is a sculptor."

I slid the picture between two pages of my notebook. "I'll keep my eye out for this."

"Thanks. My number is on the back."

In spite of my plan to skip lunch, my stomach protested. It droned in unison with the truck's engine as I turned left onto the main road. On autopilot, I pulled into the McDonalds and smiled again at the turquoise arches. How many other places had they changed their signature logo to fit in? The drive thru looked narrow. I parked.

Okay, I told myself. I'd grab a burger, fries, a drink and then hit the phone until the battery died.

My purse had fallen on the floorboard and I reached down to get it. Someone rapped on my side window. I jerked up. Found myself face-to-face with Chief Stone and only a quarter inch of glass between us. He was dressed in civvies and wore faded blue jeans, Dan Post boots and a blue plaid western shirt to match his eyes. He must have wanted to be a cowboy when he was a kid and lived out the fantasy off duty.

I wasn't about to let him abort my lunch plans. At least not the eating part. I smiled like I was happy to see a familiar face, opened the door, said hello and sped toward the entrance.

He followed like a dog herding a wayward lamb. "I've been looking for you all morning. Where have you been?"

"Gee whiz, Dad, I was at the library." I pushed through the glass doors and stood in line. Couldn't help but think about the last time I was in a place that specialized in fast food. Last week I'd been behind the counter taking orders. Now I was a customer and placing one. The counter person was slow, and I wondered if they were new? Or if the cook crew was short handed? Regardless I'd remain patient. Even though Stone stood uncomfortably close, I wanted to get my food and bolt. I wouldn't complain.

I'd been there. Short staffed. Overworked. Underpaid. Berated by impatient customers.

The line inched forward.

The good police chief leaned closer. In a low voice just above a whisper he said, "In light of recently discovered evidence, I'd recommend you adopt a less combative attitude. I can arrest you for obstruction of justice."

I spun around. "What new evidence?"

CHAPTER TWENTY

Stone's new evidence turned out to be old evidence. Old, because I already knew my blood type matched Colin's. Of course Stone didn't know that Alex had already given me the head's up.

He corralled me to a table in the corner farthest from the door. So much for my escape. I watched him set his gray cowboy hat on the plastic bench across from me. He sat. Then he turned his blue eyes on me, I'm sure to study my reactions, but I didn't plan to give him any. Instead, I scarfed down a double quarter pounder with cheese and super-sized fries. He kept eyeing my two baked apple turnovers or whatever they were called. If he wanted one, he'd have to order it himself. I wasn't sharing with the enemy.

"We need a sample of your blood," Stone said.

"You already have my blood." I dipped a fry in ketchup and popped it in my mouth. "Your tech swabbed me yesterday."

He frowned. "Preliminary tests indicate that it's Colin's blood."

"No they don't. You're making assumptions before the facts."

"I can get a court order," he said. "Your refusal won't change the end results. Just delay the process. "He plunked his coffee down with such force it sloshed on the tabletop. "The blood on your hands was AB negative. Less than one percent of America's population is AB negative. Colin was AB negative."

I didn't react.

He watched me dip another fry. Then I took a long sip of my ice tea. I knew it was unwise to annoy him, but I couldn't help myself. I had another. Besides, this way I'd have a little more understanding of how he worked and a clear picture of his interrogation techniques. The stalling had the desired effect.

He switched gears. When he spoke his voice lost its hard edge. It was smooth, almost sweet like a mocha coffee blend. Made it sound like he cared. "Are you sure you don't want to amend your statement?"

This was great. He was playing a single-man-show as good-cop-bad-cop for an audience of one.

I shook my head and had another fry. Unfortunately I couldn't keep the game up much longer. The little white paper funnel was empty.

"Maybe he got a little too friendly," Stone said. "And wouldn't take no for an answer. You could plead self-defense."

He waited. Giving me time to reconsider and trust him.

This was fun. Stone thought he had me trapped. But what he didn't realize, is that I was the cat. And he was my mouse.

His *"Colin wouldn't take no"* comment wasn't a shot in the dark. I knew the assumption that Colin had pushed himself on me connected directly to what had happened to his sister. Which meant it wasn't ancient history. Or forgotten.

Of course Stone didn't know, that I knew what had happened to her. If he arrested me and I was indicted on bogus circumstantial evidence, it'd be my wild card in the courtroom. In any reasonable jury's eyes, it would cast doubt on his investigation.

From my online search of public records, Colin wasn't a registered sex offender in Kansas or Arizona. And there were no rape charges either. If there was some record of Colin's amorous misdeeds, it must be buried in his juvenile file. Something Stone could access. Why else the question?

Okay, I was ready to play. I took a sip of my ice tea and tried to look contrite and cooperative. "Did Colin have a history of mistreating women?"

"Why do you ask?"

"You brought it up. I assume for a reason."

He took the bait. "Did he try something with you?"

"No. I don't think I was his type."

Stone frowned. "Female."

"What?"

"His type was female. Legal-age."

"Then it could have been a jilted lover."

He shook his head. "I seriously doubt that."

"Why?"

"The ones I've interviewed are all devastated at his death. They still loved him. Haven't found an angry husband or jealous lover either. It seems Colin focused his attentions on the lonely and vulnerable."

"How many?"

"Twelve at present count. His funeral should be interesting."

Okay. I'd done it again. Judged someone's character on a faulty first impression. I'd assumed Stone hadn't bothered to investigate anyone other than me, but obviously he'd been busy. It didn't mean I thought Stone was a great guy, but I had to appreciate he was doing his job. Which meant he was even a more dangerous adversary than I'd assumed. There I went again with the assumptions.

"So I'm not your only suspect?"

A flash of humor sparked in his cold blue eyes. "No. Just my best one."

I tried another tack. The will hadn't gone through probate yet, and there was no other way for Stone to know its contents. Unless Alex had broken attorney-client confidentiality, Stone couldn't know that Colin's interest in THE ALABASTER had died with him. And, that any heirs would be out of luck. "It'd be awkward if a bunch of his illegitimate kids showed up."

He looked at me with fresh eyes. As if I'd just sparked a whole new line of inquiries. "That's not likely. The majority of his conquests were older."

"Any chance you'd give me a list so I can interview them?"

Now he looked at me like I was crazy. "Not on your life. You'll just have to see who shows up."

Okay obviously he had no leads there.

He lifted his hat and ran his finger back-and-forth over the felted edge. It seemed he figured he'd gotten all he could from me on that front and it was time to move on. To my amusement he looked like he'd won the dog bone and the milk dish.

I decided to egg him on, "Then are we done for now?" I asked meekly.

"No. There's still the blood test. Do you need a police escort to the clinic?"

"I think I can find it. And I hope you realize that I am cooperating. I'll give you a sample of my blood. But if I wanted to be obstructive, I could force you to get a court order."

He leaned back and a smug satisfied look appeared on his face. He must have thought he'd played me.

I peeled back the bandage on my hand and held it up as a visual. "The DNA test will prove that the blood your officer swabbed from my hand and face is my blood. From this cut. Even if Colin is my long-lost illegitimate brother given up for adoption before I was born, the DNA will not be a perfect match. Even though we have the same blood type."

His smug smile faded and reappeared on my lips. I picked up the brown plastic tray littered with the paper remains of my lunch.

"I'm not your best suspect."

"I'll wait for the official lab results."

"What a great idea," I said, unable to hold back the sarcasm. "Premature conclusions are always less than satisfying. Foolish even. Especially in murder investigations."

"More foolish is a suspect who muddies a police investigation."

In spite of his officious comeback, it was obvious that I'd rocked his working theory. "Hey, sorry if I seem rude," I said. "I don't mean to be." Okay, so it was a little white lie.

"Stress can do that," he said, return of the good-cop.

I sat back down and leaned toward him, my body language implied I was about to confide my deepest secret to a trusted friend. "In less than four days I find out that I have an uncle who made me a co-heir to his estate. I pull up stakes and move here. I barely meet my new partner and he's killed." Dramatic pause. "Now I'm a suspect for murder."

I picked up a napkin, blotted my eyes and blew my nose.

"Moving is hard enough under the best circumstances. And I didn't even get to know them. Jasper or Colin. And now I never will."

"There, there." He patted my hand awkwardly. "You would have liked Jasper. A real straight-shooter. Minded his own business. Believed bygones were *by-garsh-darn-gone*." Pause. "A good man who'd give a stranger the shirt off his back. Everybody loved him."

"That's what most everyone's implied. Wish I'd have known him." And each time I said the words I meant them even more than the previous.

How could have Jasper and my mom have been siblings? He'd left a selfless legacy and she'd always seemed selfish and self-absorbed.

"There is an exception," I said. "Scully at the *Eagle Inn* didn't love him."

"That's because Jasper refused to sell or exchange the property THE ALABASTER sits on. Scully thought he had a deal in the works for a resort and needed more land. Couldn't pull it together. The deal and profits went to another investor. He's been bitter ever since."

"Bitter enough to murder Jasper?"

"Maybe twenty years ago, but didn't have the gumption. Then or now."

I thought of the little weasel of a man. Stone was probably right. From what I'd seen, he wouldn't want to dirty his hands.

"Any evidence of hand-sanitizer at the murder scene?" I asked.

Stone looked at me like I'd lost my mind.

I plunged on. "Everyone says you think a passing vagrant murdered my uncle."

He stared me straight in the eyes and I saw signs of intelligent life in his gleam. "I'm not responsible for what people think. Although it can be revealing."

"So that's your game," I said. The words came out before I had a chance to think about their impact. To my surprise he laughed like we'd shared a private joke.

"My job is to investigate and link evidence." He shrugged. "If the public gets the wrong impression . . . I observe."

"Smart," I said.

"Just doing my job."

"Off the record, what was Colin like when you were teens? I'm sure I saw the worst of him, but he couldn't have been all bad if Jasper made him an heir."

"He spent July and August with Jasper during high school. Between his junior and senior year he dated my sister. That was the last summer he came to Sedona for extended visits."

"But he did come back?'

"For short visits. A week here and there."

"Were they serious?"

"The visits?"

"No, Colin and your sister?"

"Their romance cooled as quickly as it flared."

"Why was that?"

He rolled his shoulders as if to stretch his back and started tapping the fingers of his right hand on the table. "Don't really know."

Stone was a great liar.

No point in ruining our new found respect, even if it only floated on the surface. I let him off the hook, smiled and spun a little lie of my own to release the tension. "I remember my freshman year of high school. I fell in love with six different guys the first week. Young, dumb and susceptible to love. I'm glad I outgrew such foolishness. By the way, did Patsy Gaines contact you this morning?" I asked.

"No."

"I told her to call. You should talk to her again."

He looked annoyed. "Why? I hope you're not interviewing potential witnesses."

"She tracked me down. It seems that Colin made her a lot of promises that weren't his to make."

"Like what?"

"You should hear it from her. I have a feeling I got the edited version."

"Smart suspects don't interfere in ongoing police investigations." He cocked his chin up a fraction of an inch and leveled me with a look that would irritate a flea on a dog's hindquarter.

Bad cop back on the beat: obnoxious, rude and irritating.

"So, where do I make my blood donation?" I asked.

"The Sedona Medical Center. It's just down the street. I'll give them a heads-up you're coming in." He pulled out his cell, dialed and made the arrangements. "They said, come on down."

I stood. "Good. The sooner you eliminate me as a suspect, the sooner you can focus your sights on arresting the real killer." I paused. "When will I be able to move back into THE ALABASTER?"

"We finished with it this morning."

"Thank you for your prompt notification. Good day, officer." Talk about irritating. Were all men chameleons? Nice one moment, jerks the next?

I headed for the trashcan. Dumped my lunch debris. Slammed down the tray. Strode out to the truck. Without so much as a backward glance.

THE REST of my afternoon I buzzed around like a one-woman-show depicting a flock of chickens fleeing a crazed chain-saw-toting rooster.

I gave blood. Checked out of the Inn. Thanked Scully for his hospitality. Visited the Chamber for business fliers. Registered at the post office. Bought groceries. Bought more cleaning supplies. Returned to THE ALABASTER by quarter after three. The bookstore was closed. Sarah either didn't know the police were finished, or she was taking a holiday. I went into the apartment through the back door, avoiding the crime scene out front. Tomorrow would be soon enough to tackle the cleanup. Again.

Parked at Jasper's desk, I started making phone calls on the landline.

No one at the Fort Riley Army Base would give out any information about Colin. They'd only verify that he'd worked there for eighteen years and had quit two months earlier. This didn't jive with what Alex had told me. He'd said that Colin needed to train a replacement before he could make the move to Sedona. That my new partner wouldn't be here for another two weeks. Obviously Colin had lied.

So? What had Colin been up to in the last two months? If not on base, where had he been?

The clock read 4:30. I had time for one more call.

I dialed the *Pioneer Post's* number. It rang twice.

"Lincoln James, editor-and-chief of the White City's very own *Prairie*

Post. We always have a story for you." Pause. "Do you have a juicy one for me?"

Thank you, Mr. James, I thought. You just gave me the edge I needed.

"Hi. I'm Allison McArthur, a reporter . . ." I tried to think of the name of an Arizona newspaper and came up blank.

"Yes?" the man said.

"Actually sir, I freelance and am following a story down here in Arizona."

"Freelance work is how I got my start," he said. "And look at me now. I run my own newspaper. How can I help you?"

"I'm writing a background story on Colin Phelps. I understand that he grew up and until recently lived in White City."

"What has that boy done?"

"At forty, I'd hardly call him a boy."

"I'm seventy-five. Colin will always be a juvenile delinquent in my eyes. Now tell me. What trouble is he in?"

My pulse quickened, but I paused before answering. "He was murdered."

The man gasped. "I always knew he'd come to a bad end." Then he surprised me, belting out a delighted cackle followed by the sound of a slap. "I'm ready. Give me the goods. I just love it when I can scoop the *Junction City Daily Union.*"

CHAPTER TWENTY-ONE

When I got off the phone with Mr. James from the *Prairie Post*, my head reeled. The loquacious editor had enjoyed sharing his fount of rumor-laced innuendos. So much so that an hour later I had to lie and tell him that someone needed the phone to call 911.

The call confirmed Colin's *Don Juan* tendencies, but little more. My partner hadn't committed any real crime. His only serious trouble happened shortly after his mother's death. He'd been thirteen when she was diagnosed with cancer. She lost her fight shortly after his graduation from high school. At seventeen he became the sole heir of his mother's modest estate. Because of his age, the court had emancipated him. Unfortunately, he wasn't ready for the freedom of adulthood.

One balmy summer night Colin supplied the alcohol for a little party. He passed out in the back seat of the car. There were three other underaged drinkers. The driver, a sixteen-year-old girl, crashed the vehicle into a train. She and the other two boys died at the scene. Colin survived because he hadn't bothered to clip his seat belt and was thrown free of the wreckage.

The old tragedy didn't seem to shed new light on who'd want to kill him twenty-five years later. But some grudges don't have an expiration date. They just needed the means and opportunity.

A headache started to gather behind my eyes. I needed a mental break and fuel. Flipping though the yellow pages, I ordered a large pepperoni pizza from *Moondog's*. Didn't know if they were the best in town, but I liked their name. I half-expected a big dog to deliver my dinner. Instead it was a teenage punk in baggy jeans without the benefit of people-skills or manners. He sneered at my five dollar tip and I was tempted to refuse delivery, but the pizza smelled just as heavenly as *Angel's*.

The phone rang, just as I opened the box. Regretfully I closed it to keep the pizza hot and answered.

"Doc here."

"Hi."

"Can I ask you a favor?"

"Sure."

"I just got the lab results back from Colin's autopsy. Have you gone through his things yet? Did he have any prescriptions or drugs?"

"I haven't, but I'll be happy to check and call you back."

"If you could do it now, I'll wait on the line."

"Okay." I set the phone down and went to the bedroom. Had Doc implied Colin was on something? It would explain his erratic personality changes.

A quick search verified four things. One, Colin wasn't very neat. Two, he hadn't squirreled anything of a suspicious nature on the premises other than a box of Trojans. Three, he hadn't left any prescriptions behind. And four, he owned an impressive collection of boxers. Every color of the rainbow, pattern and style imaginable. He could have opened a men's underwear store. A quick stir through with a pencil— couldn't bring myself to touch them— and came up empty.

"Sorry Doc. Didn't find any medications, just clothes."

"Thanks for looking."

He hung up and I settled in front of the television with a slice of pizza. It's a good thing the Italian pie tastes good hot, cold and even lukewarm. Jasper didn't have cable or Netflix, so I was stuck with local programming. After the news I shut the TV off and curled up in Uncle Jasper's easy chair for the night. I'd considered sleeping in the camper, but didn't want to give Stone the opportunity to cite me.

Half plans drifted in my semi-consciousness before I slid into slumber. Tomorrow I'd clean the bedroom. Move my stuff inside. Mop up the murder scene. Track down the lock Colin's key fit.

At one fifteen, I awoke feeling anxious. Then I heard something. A muffled thunk. I sat up. It sounded like it came from the front of the building— from the store. Had someone broken in? Again?

I sprang out of the chair, tiptoed to the apartment door and grabbed Jasper's dog-headed cane. Not as lethal as a baseball bat, but it would have to do. Clutching it tight, I pressed my ear to the cold wood door and listened.

Total quiet. Except for my own shallow breathing sounding strangely feral.

Two men had been murdered on the premises. I didn't want to be the third victim. Wouldn't be one. Instead I'd take charge. Catch them in the act. I grabbed my cell, keyed in 9-1-1 for quick dial if I needed it, and eased open the door into the storage room. Just thirty feet of silent darkness hovered between me and whatever evil lurked out front.

Had my imagination morphed the midnight antics of a rat into an intruder? Or had someone managed to jimmy the front door? Why was it so silent? Had they heard me get up? And now they were standing perfectly still in the rock shop. Frozen. Hoping the careless bump hadn't betrayed their presence. Ready to flee.

I sucked in musky air through dry lips. Tasted the dust and mold. Crossed the fingers of my free hand and crept through the vast maze of Jasper's junk toward the solid wood door to the store. Reached it and paused. Indecision battled inside me. Open it? Or retreat to the apartment? I must have stood there for five minutes. Tense and ready for action. Still hearing nothing but eerie silence.

A cramp crawled up my right leg to my hip. I wiped my hands on my pants and gripped the cane tighter. My lips tasted of salt. This was ridiculous. Get a grip. Go in. Call 9-1-1. Or go back to bed. But I'd feel like such a fool if the police showed and it'd been my imagination. The noise was probably an induced hallucination from over-indulging in spiced pepperoni and melted cheese.

Like Dad always said *it was time to stop cutting bait and to catch fish.*

Indecision nets you nothing. It was go time. Catch a thief. Catch a murderer. Or prove it was my imagination.

I unlocked the door. Pushed it open just wide enough to reach the switch on the shop's wall and flipped on the light. Momentarily blinded, I blinked hard and stared down at the floor. My vision adjusted and to my dismay I realized my bare feet were planted in the middle of a generous sprinkling of rodent turds. Eeeewe.

I stepped into the store and wiped my feet on a yellowed newspaper. An early morning shower suddenly sounded like a great idea.

Fully and completely awake, my tense muscles relaxed. No prowler. Just dirty filthy rats. I attempted a half-hearted whistle. Its hollow tone mocked my imaginary fears.

There wasn't anyone in the store. No thief. No intruder. No deadly killer. I was done with paranoia. Let the rats have their fun until the traps arrived.

I flipped off the lights and retreated back through the storage room. My hand felt for the apartment doorknob when the second crash struck. It resonated like a dozen shelves had smashed to the floor. Even a thousand rats pumped-up on steroids couldn't pull that off.

With reckless abandon I shouted, "Who's there?" My fingers gripped the cane. "I've got a gun and I'm not afraid to use it."

More scrabbling noises. Things smashing to the floor. Thudding footsteps.

I scooted back to the apartment, slammed the door, locked it, and propped a kitchen chair under the knob. I raced to the window and peered out. Nobody in sight. An engine started out front and roared off.

They were gone. I breathed a sigh of relief.

My breathing slowed. It must have been a garden-variety thief who'd decided to do a little discount shopping. A thug who didn't know I was in residence. Hopefully the shelves he'd knocked over didn't include the new quartz display, which was a totally stupid thought to even consider at the moment.

It could have been the killer. I could have been just seconds from death.

Return of the creepy shivers.

Stop. This was not the time to panic. Breathe in. Breathe out. Stay calm. Don't overreact. I was safe, alive and obviously not the intruder's target. Of course if they had known I was in residence, their plans might have included removing me. Permanently.

I grabbed the phone. My trembling fingers hovered over the buttons, but I didn't dial. Terrified or not, Stone would probably think I'd staged the whole thing as a diversion. I'd had enough of his insinuations. No way I felt like being grilled by him a third time in less than twenty-four hours.

Besides, the intruder had left. Hadn't they?

Jasper's and Colin's murders had to be connected by some unseen chain of circumstances. But what possible link would cause a murderer to kill two men who were so different? It didn't make sense. My mind seemed stuck on the fact Jasper didn't have an enemy in the world and Colin had dozens. From that fact alone the obvious conclusion was that the murders were unconnected.

What was the connection? What was the catalyst? Don't let me be the pendant on that chain.

A cold sensation gripped and squeezed my gut.

I looked at the flimsy little chair propped under the knob. I heard the car drive away, but what if someone had stayed behind to clean up? Meaning me. The chair didn't look strong enough to stop a determined killer. But Uncle Jasper's roll-top desk would. I dragged it over to block the door, sending papers fluttering in its wake. My security measures might not pass a fire inspection, but I felt safer.

I gathered the papers and stacked them in a heap on the coffee table and then settled into Jasper's easy chair and listened, the cane clutched in my hands.

The last thing I remembered thinking is that I needed to call a lock-smith in the morning.

I woke late the next morning after a fitful night's sleep and was in desperate need of a caffeine infusion. After making a double-strong pot of coffee, I went outside with cup in hand and was greeted with an incredible view. The burnt red-orange hills glowed in the soft blue sky. The beauty almost dispelled the shadow of last night's intruder. Almost —but not quite.

How had they gotten inside?

I circled the building, checking every door and window. Cobwebs still intact. Nothing looked out of the ordinary except for the unlocked front door. This was the second time it'd had been locked at night and open in the morning. Had I forgotten to lock it like I'd accused Colin doing? No. Before going to bed I'd double-checked every door. And window. They'd all been locked tight.

That meant whoever broke in must have had a key. I shivered.

Back inside, I settled at Jasper's desk with a second cup of coffee. Even though it went against my personal resolve to distance myself and avoid Alex, I punched in his number. I sucked in a breath, vowing to keep my end of the conversation totally focused on business.

After a brisk "*hi*" and "*how are you,*" I eased into the real reason I'd called. "A lot of things need to be fixed around here. I was wondering. What's my operating budget?"

"What do you have in mind?" he asked. His voice seemed distracted and all lawyerly, but it still sent shivers down my spine. To my annoyance, I felt disappointed there wasn't a hint of flirtation in the exchange. I guess my message had been quartz-crystal clear. That I didn't want a romantic relationship and he'd translated that into no relationship. Couldn't his ego accept friendship?

"A dumpster or two," I said, matching my tone to his. "New locks. Computer. Wi-Fi. And I'm sure I'll need some other stuff once I get things sorted."

"Sounds reasonable, but what's wrong with Jasper's laptop? It's not that old."

"It may not be old, but it's not here."

"Are you sure?"

My retort came out before I could bite it back. "Moving to Sedona hasn't given me any special psychic powers, but I think I'd have seen a computer if there was one."

He sighed. "Maybe Colin used it. Have you looked in his things?"

My voice grew taut. He had a point. I should have thought of that. "No. Hold on, I'll take a quick look."

"Why don't you buzz me back? I've got someone on the office line."

"Sure, go ahead rack-up a few more billable phone calls on my account. How much am I getting charged for talking to you, anyway?"

Alex's response was dead silence.

I mentally kicked myself. For the next two years Alex held the purse strings. Insulting him was pretty stupid. Besides, it wasn't his fault that I didn't want a romantic relationship. Or that I was miffed that he'd given up on the potential relationship so easily. "Sorry, that didn't come out right. I didn't sleep well. What I meant is, I didn't realize Jasper had a computer. And I haven't seen one around. Now that it's out in the open, I need to know how much this is costing the business."

"We can sort that out later. Apology accepted." Pause. "I'm a little slammed this morning, but I'm never too busy to talk to you. I'll call Sedona Mutual Bank and have them issue you a debit card."

"Thanks, but it takes weeks to get a card. I hoped to get started today."

"No problem. The bank prints photo-ID debit cards in house."

"And my limit?"

He gave me the account balance.

"Great," I said and resisted a clichéd victory whistle. "It's more than enough funds to get started. And to paint inside and out. Order a new sign. Landscaping. Replace the missing roof tiles. And—"

He interrupted. "The estate will cover all maintenance costs for the next two years. You want me to make the arrangements?"

"No. If I'm going to be a successful business owner, I need to know how everything works first-hand."

"Okay. May I suggest you hire a cleaning crew?"

It sounded tempting, but I couldn't chance a clue to either murder getting tossed. "No thanks. Jacob, Sara's boy, has offered to help. And he's going to teach me what he knows of the rock business."

"Suit yourself. But before you buy paint, make sure you get the color approved by the city planning department."

"Thanks for the heads up." I should have realized that there was a reason all the buildings in town blended so well with the natural beauty of the place. Subtle reds. Cypress greens. Sandstone beiges.

My next two phone calls were to *Bell Rock Locks* and *Dumpsters R Us*. A forty- yard dumpster would be delivered tomorrow. The locksmith would come around noon.

I put three check marks on the to-do list I'd scribbled on a piece of scrap paper. I spun the yellow paper under my thumbnail while I processed the conversation. What had happened to Jasper's laptop?

It was definitely missing. Had Colin taken it? Or was there something in its web-search history that would point to either murderer?

My index finger gave the list a vigorous spin. The paper took flight and flipped. That's when I realized I'd written on the back of a receipt for a six-month mailbox rental at a UPS store in Cottonwood, Arizona. Strange. Why Cottonwood? The Sedona post office was just down the street. I smiled, realizing there was a 95% chance I'd just discovered what the mystery key unlocked.

I grabbed my dirty jeans from the day before and dug in the pocket for Colin's key. On close examination the little stamp that had looked like a pair of eyes morphed into the number eight.

A quick check of Jasper's files indicated that all his business corre-spondence had been delivered here, to *THE ALABASTER* itself, via the U.S. Postal Service. I studied the receipt. Box 8 was clearly marked as a mail-box, which matched the number on the key. Given the date, Jasper had rented it seven days prior to his murder.

How had Colin gotten possession of it? Had he found it in Jasper's things? Or had Jasper mailed it to him in Kansas? And why did Jasper have a secret mailbox in the next town?

Tingles exploded like fireworks in my skin.

"Mailbox eight, here I come!"

I called the UPS store for directions. It was only a twenty-five minute drive each way. I grabbed my purse and then looked at the clock. Shoot. It was almost eleven. A drive to Cottonwood and back before the lock-smith arrived was impossible.

I did have time to go to the Sedona Mutual to pick up my debit card. I made a dash to the bank and went through the motions, but the whole time my mind was focused on Jasper's secret mailbox.

If it turned out that the box held evidence germane to Jasper's murder, at least I'd have first shot at it. Hopefully it would put me one step closer to clearing my name, and solving his murder.

I smiled. Stone couldn't charge me with withholding evidence, because until I saw the contents, it wasn't evidence.

CHAPTER TWENTY-TWO

I looked everywhere I could think and netted zero for Jasper's laptop. I examined every spot in the storage room where the dust had been disturbed. Came up with nada. Next, I searched the garages across the alley. Double nada. Colin's new car was parked in the space Jasper's truck had occupied. No computer squirreled in it.

Where else could I look? There was no point in searching Jasper's vehicles. I already knew it wasn't in either. Which left one last possibility if it were anywhere on the premises.

I popped into the Bible bookstore. Sarah stood at the cash register counting change. She looked up and smiled when she saw me. "How are you holding up?"

"Okay," I said.

"I'm sorry about Colin's death." She sounded like she meant it in spite of the fact he'd tried to evict her. "Yesterday was just awful. Is there anything you need?"

"I'm fine," I said. "We'd just met, so it's not like I really knew him. I feel bad he was murdered. But it's not like it's a personal loss of someone I cared about." Okay, I was seriously babbling and needed to stop. But couldn't. It was like my personal-filter pipe had shattered. "But I'm sure we would have got along well, running the business once we'd gotten things sorted out." I pinched myself. "Jasper must have had a good reason to saddle us as partners."

I pinched myself a second time. Harder. It worked. The babble stopped its flow.

"Jasper was a wise man." She sighed and began fumbling with her wedding band. "Colin was so troubled. I've prayed for him for years."

Hmmmm. My suspicion antennae raised a notch. She and Colin must be about the same age. Was Sara one of his high school conquests? Had his threat to kick her out raised old memories and reopened dormant wounds?

"So you grew up around here?" I asked.

She shook her head and half-smiled. "No. My husband and I moved here fifteen years ago. Ten years ago I opened the store."

"Oh."

"Five years ago my husband died." Sorrow pinched at her lips and wet her eyes. "Death is cruel. It robs joy from the living as well as the breath from the dead. I hope Colin was saved." She shook herself. "Eternal death is worse. At least I'll see my husband again in heaven." She brightened.

I had the uncomfortable feeling she might be launching herself into a sermon. Her next words confirmed it. "Are you saved? It's never too late to get right with God."

This was awkward, but I didn't quite know how to get her off the subject without offending her. So instead of answering her actual question, I pretended to misunderstand.

"Yes. Jasper saved me from minimum wage drudgery. Did you know that he named the business after me? My given name is Alabaster."

"How lovely." Her smile looked genuine.

"My family has a thing for 'rock' names. My mom's name is Jade. And I had another uncle called Flint."

"Family traditions are nice. They tie generations together."

"I was wondering. . ." I tried to sound off-hand, like my curiosity wasn't important. "Any chance Jasper left his laptop with you?"

"Heavens no," Sara said, wiping her hands. "He never let it out of his sight. He was as attached to it as he was to his Star Trek."

I made a show of looking up at the clock on her wall. "Thanks. I've got go. The locksmith will be here soon. Do you want your door rekeyed for better security?"

"No. If anyone comes in and steals a Bible, I'll count it as a blessing."

We both laughed and I made my escape before she started preaching again.

In my absence, Dorcus had called and left a message on the store's ancient answering machine. She'd wanted me to know that she'd been in contact with Jasper's spirit and that he wanted me to get the shop opened ASAP. I was tempted to delete the message without listening, but decided that it would be foolish. What if she inadvertently said something that would point me in the direction of the killer?

I listened, growing increasingly edgy as her voice nattered on for over twenty minutes. It was all nonsense. I hadn't realized that the old answering machine could handle such long messages. The locksmith still hadn't arrived when I deleted her communiqué and started to clean.

The intruder's hurried exit had left a huge mess in the middle of the existing disorder. At least my quartz display looked good and hadn't been knocked over. The time I'd spent putting it together hadn't been for naught after all. The fate of several other shelves didn't prove to be so lucky.

I frowned. Another déjà-vu moment reared its ugly mug as I looked at the blood splotch on the floor. I retrieved the ammonia, gloves and two rolls of paper towels. To my chagrin, I thought that at least Colin hadn't bled all over the place. That in death he'd been more considerate than when he was alive. And then I felt ashamed of my callousness. No one, not even someone like Colin at his worst, deserved to be murdered.

Maybe it was mental. Or maybe it was real, but now the musty air seemed tinged with a metallic trace of blood. I considered opening the front door, but with my luck, it would invite unwanted customers like the old ladies from the day before or ghoulish lookie-loos who wanted a first-hand glimpse of the murder scene. Clenching my teeth, I breathed through my mouth and set to work. This time I pretended I was cleaning mold stains and not the blood of a second murder victim. When I finished the unpleasant task, I peeled off the gloves and had another irreverent thought. If the rock business went under, I could always hire out as a crime scene cleaner.

Or not.

There was at least another twenty minutes to wait. I donned another pair of surgical gloves and went in search of a broom and dustpan. Found them tucked in a small closet along with a case of black plastic trash bags.

Starting with the area around the cash register, I dusted the long glass-topped jewelry display case. A bright turquoise pendant caught my eye. Hmmm. Maybe I'd start wearing jewelry for advertising purposes. I pulled it out of the case and tried it on. There wasn't a mirror so I stepped outside and used the reflection of the front window. Looked nice.

Back inside, I wiped down the tall swivel highchair behind the counter. I plopped into the chair and stared at my handiwork. The tiny cleaned section shined like a precious jewel in the midst of a junk-pile from hell.

How had Jasper made a living out of this chaotic mess?

Closing my eyes, I rubbed my temples and contemplated having a snack or a caffeine boost. Anything to put off the inevitable, but this kind of procrastination wouldn't solve anything. The sooner this place was cleaned, the sooner I could open for business. Ergo, start making money.

I found a sheet of paper and started to jot down a plan of action. Don't ask me why, but writing lists is satisfying. Not to enumerate what has to be done, but because of the perverse satisfaction that comes from crossing off those things once they're completed. It also provides a little transition time between the thinking and doing. List making is not procrastination. For me, it's more like being my own self-help coach with a little pregame pep talk. Now that I was the sole proprietor and Colin wouldn't be a catalyst to egg me on, I'd have no one to blame if the business failed.

That wasn't going to happen. Jasper's legacy deserved to live.

If THE ALABASTER was going to be a success, I had to transform the place into an attractive business. A place where I'd want to spend the majority of my time. A place that I could take pride in owning.

The shop phone rang.

I picked up; afraid it might be Dorcus following up on the long message she'd left. I mentally added a new message machine to my shopping list and a hand mirror. One that limited messages to thirty-seconds.

"Ms. Renault. This is T.J. from *Bell Rock Locks*. I'm in the parking lot. You want me to let myself in?"

I laughed. "Go ahead. I'm in the store."

A few minutes later, a tall man of African heritage entered through the front door carrying a red toolbox. He wore pressed work overalls with an embroidered name tag that read, "T.J." It was hard to guess his age, but his infectious smile radiated timelessness. His grin grew larger when he saw me.

"Afternoon." He sat the box on the cleaned counter. "This is where Jasper and that young fella were killed, isn't it?"

I nodded.

He pushed his lips into a frown. "I'd want new locks, too. Why don't you give me a tour and we can see what needs to be done to keep you safe and secure. You might even want to consider a security system."

After I showed him what I wanted, he made a few suggestions. "You sure you don't want to just rekey the locks? It'd be a hell of a lot cheaper."

"Okay, but I want new dead bolts on all the exterior doors. And a deadbolt between the store and the storage area."

"Sounds like overkill, but you're the boss." He ran his hand over his tight curly hair. "You got it. Sixteen inner and outer doors to change out. I'd better get started if I'm going to finish before nightfall."

I hoped he was joking about the time it'd take to complete the job. The UPS Store closed at six and it was a good twenty-minute drive to Cottonwood. I didn't think I could stand waiting until the next day to check out the contents of the mailbox. I'd tried quizzing the UPS employee over the phone but didn't have any luck. The man had been adamant. "No key. No information."

No point in my stressing. It wouldn't make T.J. finish any faster and whatever reason, I didn't feel comfortable leaving him there in the store alone. I grabbed a quick peanut butter sandwich in the apartment and returned to the store.

The phone rang.

I swallowed, licking P.B.& J. from the roof of my mouth before picking up. "Hello?"

"Is this THE ALABASTER?" a breathless girl's voice asked.

"Yes. I'm sorry we're not open."

"Is that you, Allie? This is Tamara. Becca's friend."

"Ohhh. The soon-to-be-famous artist? That sketch you made me will be worth millions in a few years. You're not calling to get it back, are you?"

"Nooooo." Her laugh tinkled and I could tell she was pleased. "I hate to be a pest, but did you have any luck finding my paperweight?"

"Sorry. Not yet. But I'll look some more. It might be hiding under a layer of dust."

Her laugh this time sounded more polite than amused. "Thanks. It's just that I think Gramps has noticed that it's gone. I really don't want to be in trouble for taking it."

"If it's here, I'm certain it'll turn up."

"I could come over and help you look. I know I could spot it right away."

"I'm not sure that'd work for me today. Maybe next week."

"Please?"

"Sorry. But I have plans this afternoon." I felt bad, but I couldn't afford to be locked into her time frame. There was too much on the line. More important things than finding a missing paperweight.

"Don't stress. I'm sure it'll turn up."

"I sure hope so." She hung-up and I continued with *Operation Clean Up* with the added chore of keeping an eye out for the carved tiger paperweight. But first I had to do something about the oppressive musky air.

I opened a few windows, propped opened the front door with a chair, set the big CLOSED sign from the window on it and prayed the old ladies were out of town. It was worth the risk if it meant I wouldn't contract some dust-borne plague.

I decided to kill two rats with the same cat—tidy the shelves behind the counter and look for Tamara's missing treasure. There's no way Jasper would have set someone else's property out on a shelf and risk having customers think it was for sale. That would be stupid. Which meant this was a great place to look.

Whistling marked T.J.'s progress. By three he'd installed five dead-bolts—the store's front door plus all the doors connected to the store-room: i.e., the apartment door, the parking lot door, the rock cutting room door and the inside store door. Plus he'd convinced me to alarm them as well.

In the same length of time, I'd discovered enough junk behind the counter to fill four industrial-sized garbage bags. One I crammed full of empty Windex squirt bottles. What on earth could Jasper have wanted them for? Obviously not for cleaning.

Another anomaly. What possible use would he have for a thousand copies of the same phone book? Slight exaggeration, but it felt like an endless chore as I flipped through the thin pages looking for any marked notations. Didn't find any, but several books had pages ripped out. Why?

I cross-referenced a few, as in, studied the contents of the missing pages using an intact phone book. There was no obvious pattern.

"Huuumph," came the growl of a smoker's cough from the front of the store.

A Charley horse sprinted up under my ribcage when I twisted to get a look. Couldn't anyone in Sedona read a *CLOSED* sign? Pressing my hand into the cramp, I straightened and stretched it out.

An older, street-worn man staggered through the door under the weight of a stained gunnysack on his shoulder. He had long, string-dreaded hair. I couldn't really tell the color because who knows when it was last washed? His clothes looked equally gritty. A whiff of stale whiskey, old sweat, and musk preceded him.

I started breathing through my mouth and hoped I didn't inhale anything contagious.

He swung the sack down. It landed on the floor hard enough to rattle the glass shelves.

"I've got rocks for you." He swayed, reached out and planted his hand on the counter to steady himself.

"I'm sorry, but I don't need any more rocks," I said.

"Jasper said he'd take a hundred pounds."

"Ralph, quit bothering the lady," T.J. said, coming in from the store-room. "You heard her. She doesn't need your rocks."

"But Jasper said he needed them."

"Jasper is dead. This lady has the store now and she don't want your junk."

"I need twenty bucks," Ralph said. "Jasper said he'd give me a twenty for them."

"More like a ten spot," T.J. said. He set a box of doorknobs on the counter and smiled at me. "You want to keep these? You might be able to use them later."

"No. Feel free to take them if you want. Otherwise, I'll just throw them away."

Ralph shifted his gaze to me, leaned forward, and belched. "Okay, pretty lady, you can have them for ten dollars."

"What kind of rocks are they?" I asked, thinking I'd have to honor Jasper's contract with the man if only to get rid of him.

"Top quality alabaster."

Ralph rolled back the top of the sack to reveal three chunks of grainy cream-colored boulders. For my namesake, it looked a little disappoint-ing. Nothing at all like the carved pieces I'd been shown as a kid.

He grabbed the smallest chunk, spit on it and then spread his saliva over the rock's surface with his thumb. It transformed the cream color into a rich, almost translucent- orange. He held it out to me.

"Pretty," I said, not wanting to touch the germ-slime. "I always thought alabaster was white."

"Some is. Some isn't. This here is sixty pounds of the finest orange alabaster you can find." His words slurred. "You can't have the sack. Where do you want them?"

I pointed outside. Maybe it would rain and wash off his biohazard contribution. I divided sixty pounds by twenty dollars and came up with three bucks a pound. It sounded reasonable. Wait. I had it backward. Twenty should be divided by sixty. I grabbed the calculator. 33.3333333 cents. Wow. I could sell it for seventy-five cents a pound and make a good profit.

"My money?" He held out his hand.

Luckily, I'd stuffed some cash in my pocket that morning. I handed him a ten, a five, and five ones.

He squinted at the bills for a full thirty seconds. "You sure this is ten dollars?"

"Twenty," I said. "It's what Jasper promised you."

His mouth spread into a wide grin that revealed more gums than teeth. "You're all right, alabaster-lady. I'll bring you more rocks next week."

"No, don't. I don't need any more rocks."

"But—"

"You heard the lady," T.J. said. "She don't need any more rocks, so don't you be bothering her."

Ralph shot T.J. a dirty look. "I'll just dump these on THE ALABASTER pile. Outside." He leaned in close and whispered, "Watch out for the sky ghosts. They're the ones who got Jasper."

The comment caught me by surprise. Before I could react, he'd staggered out the front door. I scooted from behind the counter and followed. I was still inside the store when a series of thumps hit the building. By the time I got outside, he was carefully folding the burlap bag into a neat square.

"Ralph," I said. "Do you know who killed my uncle?"

He flinched and shoved the sack into a green duffle he must have stashed before going inside. "No. I don't know nothin'."

"Ralph." I spoke softer. "If you know something, you have to tell me. Jasper deserves justice."

His face blanched. "No time to chat." Blotchy pink spatters spread in a Rorschach design across his jaundiced skin. "Gotta go."

"Wait. Please?"

He hitched the duffle up onto his shoulder and turned. "I've got things to do. Important things."

I reached out a hand but stopped short of touching him. Keeping my voice low like talking to a skittish horse, I repeated his name again in an effort to gain his trust and calm him. "Ralph. Who are the sky ghosts? What did they do to Jasper?"

"It's not safe." His furtive eyes scanned the lot, his words low and gravelly. "I warned Jasper. He wouldn't listen. Didn't believe me. Now he's dead."

"Who are they?"

"Better not to know. You don't want to end up like Jasper."

"What about Colin?"

"Colin was a fool. But you? Jasper said you were smart. Leave it alone. Stick to the rocks. You don't want to be abducted."

"Abducted. By who?"

The whites of his eyes grew huge and he pointed skyward with both index fingers. "Aliens."

His face muscles began to twitch and he started to hyperventilate.

Okay. My crazy-person-whisperer act had failed. Ralph wasn't even close to calm or rational. Total disappointment. I doubted he lacked the focus to provide any reliable information about either murder.

Each of his next words came out as single gasps, like we'd been transported to 20,000 feet and the air was too thin. "They've come for me a couple of times. I fooled them. They think I'm harmless." He spun in a circle, arms spread wide, and keened like a hungry kitten. Then he grabbed me and we were both going round and round. I tried to pull free, but his grip was surprisingly strong. The stench of his alcohol and garlic- drenched breath overwhelming.

"Ralph!" I shouted, all pretense of calmness abandoned. "Let me go."

He did. I stumbled back and managed not to topple into THE ALABASTER pile. He stopped, stood tall and announced, "The tiger let me keep my brain." After this piece of stunning revelation, he headed toward the road, suddenly spry. Maybe talking about aliens and wild animals had invigorated him. I know my heart was beating a little faster.

I found T.J. in the storage room. He was almost finished rekeying the locks.

"Has Ralph always been. . ." I let my words trail off. I couldn't think of a polite word for crazy. "Is he dangerous?"

T.J. shook his head. "No. He's harmless. But it's a damn shame. When he was young he had a bright future. Then he shipped out to Vietnam and came back damaged."

"What happened to him?"

T.J. shrugged. "Hard to say. A lot of young men went to serve flag and country, but they returned as shadows of themselves. Sometimes, I think the lucky ones were the ones that didn't come home."

His last words made me think of my uncle Flint. Would he have turned out like Ralph? Or more like Doc and Carl? "I take it you're not a vet?"

"My number never came up."

I heard someone call my name from the front of the store.

When was I going to learn to lock the front door? Hopefully, real customers would be just as eager to come in once I had things sorted out and cleaned up.

CHAPTER TWENTY-THREE

"What happened?" Jacob asked.

I still hadn't finished cleaning what was left of the display case last night's intruder had knocked over. I'd swept up the broken glass and had gathered a couple of the rocks that had been knocked onto the floor before I'd been distracted by Tamara's phone call and Ralph's visit. I stared at the monumental amount of garbage in the sales room, thinking it would take forever to get it in shape.

The boy picked up a crystal from the floor and set it on one of the phone book stacks on the counter. "You have an earthquake? Or did the Tasmanian devil come shopping?"

I smiled. So when away from mom and sister, the boy wasn't totally shy. Plus, he had a sense of humor.

"You know how it is," I said. "Whenever you clean a mess, you end up making a bigger one." There was no need to tell him about my late night visitor. He might tell his mom. Who knew where it'd go from there?

"You want me to put these away?" Jacob asked, indicating the stacks of phone books. "After, I'll drag this deconstructed case to the back room."

"I plan on tossing the books," I said.

He shook his head. "Once you get open, you'll wish you hadn't."

"Because?"

"They're great for wrapping the small stuff and not so messy."

I looked at the spaces I hadn't cleaned yet and laughed. "Didn't think Jasper cared about the mess."

"He didn't, but he liked that the phone books are free. It was my idea." He moved behind the counter. "Let me put them back."

I made a faux crying sound. "I spent an hour cleaning them out." And then I thought of my other afternoon efforts. "I suppose you're going to tell me that those old plastic spray bottles have value, too."

He laughed and nodded. "What do you do with them?"

I pointed to the pile of trash bags.

"You probably only need a half dozen at a time. But don't toss them. Otherwise, you'll be scrambling to get more in a few months."

"And I need them, why?"

"For the rough rock."

I felt like I was playing twenty questions and losing. Big time. I gestured for him to keep talking and said, "What rough rock? And for what purpose?"

He rolled his eyes like I was mentally impaired. "The rough rock is outside. It's unfinished. As in, not polished. To see what it looks like polished, you have to get it wet."

"I see. So we fill the bottles with H_2O and let the customers have water wars with the rocks."

"You got it," he said. "Otherwise some collectors spit on the rocks and gross-out the other customers who won't want to buy anything if they think it could be covered in dried people-slime."

The old miner spitting on THE ALABASTER replayed itself in my head and I shuddered just thinking about it. "Don't tell me the old equipment catalogs, bottle tops and candy wrappers are useful, too."

"No. They're junk."

"That's a relief."

Jacob started replacing the phone books under the counter.

T.J. came in. "All done. Here's your keys. Brass ones open the inside locks. Silver colored, the outside."

"Great," I said. "How much do I owe you? I have a debit card."

"I'll send a bill. I prefer checks." By the time he left, Jacob had almost finished his phone book job.

"I need to be in Cottonwood by five," I said. "Thanks for the help."

"I can stay and do some more cleaning," he said. "Mom's taking inventory or something and won't be done for a couple of hours. I'd rather work with rocks than Bibles."

"I'm not sure when I'll get back."

"No problem. I'll lock up. Jasper gave me a key."

"T.J. just changed the locks."

"Oh." Disappointment oozed from that one little word like a trickle of cyanide into a gas chamber.

And I felt guilty like I had somehow ruined his life, which was a ridiculous reaction even for me. I hardly knew the kid. For all I knew, he could have lent his key to last night's intruder. That seemed equally ridiculous.

"This is a gigantic mess for one person to clean," he said.

He was right. Besides, Jasper had trusted the boy. That was good enough for me. I set one of the front door keys on the counter.

"Tell you what. I should be back in a couple of hours if you want to keep working and if it's okay with your mom. You can give the key back tomorrow."

"Thanks," he said like I'd given him a jailhouse reprieve. "I'll be right back."

"Make it quick. I need to leave A.S.A.P."

He took off like he was running for his life. He was back in less than three minutes. I gave him a list of things I'd liked done first and asked him to keep an eye out for Tamara's missing paperweight.

Five minutes later I was heading west on the 89ALT in my Escort. It was four-ten. Barely time to get to the UPS store before it closed.

Driving one handed, I rubbed the mailbox key between my thumb and index finger. Was this a wild chicken race? Or would the contents of the box provide answers to Jasper's past?

Or to his murder?

I drove past the fire station, headed uphill and was gaining altitude when red lights started to flash behind me.

"Crap." I glanced the speedometer. I hadn't been speeding and hadn't run any red lights. Had I missed a speed trap? Maybe it was my California license plate, but that didn't make sense. Sedona was supposed to embrace tourists, not harass them.

Hopefully, it wouldn't take long.

I steered to the side of the road and slipped the mailbox key into my pocket. Then I positioned my hands on the steering wheel at the ten and two o'clock marks so that when the cop approached the car he'd see them. There's no point in making a patrol cop nervous wondering if you have a gun pointed in his or her direction.

In the rear

view mirror I watched the officer get out of the patrol car.

"You've got to be kidding." My frown creased into wrinkles. "Stone."

He reached the front passenger side and motioned for me to roll down my window.

"This is harassment," I said before he could ask for my license, registration and proof of insurance.

He looked in the back seat.

"Pop your trunk."

"Why? You don't have probable cause."

"You're a person of interest in a murder investigation," he said and smiled. "And," pause, "are fleeing town."

I couldn't help it. I snorted. "You're kidding. I'm just going to Cottonwood to shop."

"We have stores in Sedona."

"Not a Best Buy. I'm computer shopping."

He grinned and crinkle lines appeared around his eyes. "Nice try, but you just drove past Staples."

"They don't sell Mac's. And I'm a Mac kind of girl."

"And here I thought you went for an Alex. Now pop your trunk."

"I don't think so," I said, winding up for a speech. "You're just harassing me. You don't care about finding the real killer. You just want a quick solve. Besides, I'd say you have a better motive than me to want Colin dead."

"What are you nattering about?"

"Colin dumped your sister in high school and I know it pushed her into the drug scene." His confused frown was most satisfying.

"That's ridiculous. I'd laugh if she wasn't in rehab for the fifth time in as many years."

"Like I said, you have a strong motive to wish him dead."

"I didn't threaten to kill him. You're not the crack investigative lawyer you pretend to be."

"What does that mean?"

"She discarded him. Her drug problem had—has nothing to do with Colin. She was an addict from her first hit."

"Then why did I hear Colin broke her heart?"

"Because I started that rumor. Colin was my best friend. He was devastated. And embarrassed. Dumped by a loser chick, my little sister, who preferred getting high to spending time with him. I owed him that much."

"She's still your sister. It's not nice to talk about her that way and to make it seem like Colin turned her into a drug addict. Some best friend."

"Yeah, well, that's none of your business. Now open the trunk."

We stared at each other for a long moment.

"I don't think so," I said. "Get a court order. I really have to get going."

"You should have checked-in before leaving town."

"What are you? My mother?" I mentally jerked my leash. What was it about this man that made me react like an immature schoolgirl? *He's a professional. You're a professional. Act like one.*

I took a deep breath, let it out through my nose, and gave him my professional smile. "This may be Arizona, but the U.S. Constitution over-rides the peccadilloes of local governments and police departments." I paused to let that sink in. "In case you didn't get the memo, I have not been charged with any crime. Therefore, you cannot restrict my move-ments. If I want to go back to California, I can. If I want to go to Utah, I can. Heck, I can even take a trip to Washington D.C. if I want. And you have no right to treat me like a criminal."

His smiled faded like road-kill left too long in the sun. "All I'm asking for is a little courtesy here." The glint in his eyes sharpened and his voice turned stone cold. "I don't know you from Eve. What I do know is that you have profited from the death of two men who were murdered in my jurisdiction. Men who were long-time, personal friends. And at this moment, you're the best suspect I have. So if you like, I can arrest you here and now."

"That would be a total waste of both our time." I decided to throw him a bone. "I realize you're under pressure to solve both murders, but how do you think I feel? The two previous owners of THE ALABASTER are dead. It doesn't take much stretch of the imagination to realize that I could be next. Then you'd have another beneficiary to investigate."

"So the estate is tied up?"

"For two years. During that time, I'll receive a salary and a percentage of the profits over a hundred thousand. But if I fail to run the business for that length of time, then everything goes to the Sedona Foundation."

He didn't comment.

"Maybe someone connected with the foundation wants the property," I said.

A raindrop splattered on his hat.

"It could explain why an intruder broke into the shop last night."

That took him by surprise. "What? Why didn't you report it?"

"Because I wasn't ready for another all-nighter with the police. Once I threatened to shoot off their kneecaps, they bolted. This afternoon I had the locks changed."

I noticed a subtle shift in his attitude. He leaned down to eye-level. "Murder isn't a game. If what you say is true, you could be in danger. Maybe you should reconsider Alex's offer for temporary accommodations."

"Not possible. The will is very specific about my on-site residency. Don't worry. I'm taking precautions."

He straightened, all business again. "Do you have an Arizona permit to carry a gun?"

"No. Because I don't own a gun."

"But you threatened to shoot the intruder."

"A bluff, but they didn't know that."

"I don't like it. You shouldn't take chances. If it happens again, you dial 9-1-1 and stay put." He rubbed his forehead. "Maybe you should get a gun."

"I don't like guns. I'll be fine." He was being so solicitous I was tempted to tell him about the key. Tempted, but not that stupid. "Hey, I'd really like to get to Cottonwood before all the stores close. I don't want to be out late."

"Okay. But I'm not liking it. Drive safely." He returned to his squad car, flipped a u-turn and headed back toward West Sedona.

I raced the seventeen miles to Cottonwood and hoped I'd make it in time. If I didn't get lost, I should have five minutes to spare.

Red rock and pines flew by as the road wound through the rolling hills. Looked pretty. Maybe my next trip would feel a little less rushed and I'd appreciate the scenery. I crested a hill and got my first daylight view of the Verde Valley. As far as the eye could see, everything looked sage green and white-gray, leaving behind the dramatic red rocks in my rear view mirror.

The dashboard clock read nine minutes to five. I pushed on the gas pedal, thinking that the odds of being stopped by two cops in less than a half hour were pretty slim. A chance I'd take.

Once I entered Cottonwood, the 89A morphed into South Main. I scanned street numbers as I cruised past modern buildings and into the older section of town. I almost missed the place, because it didn't look like the typical UPS store nestled in a mini strip mall. The store sat alone on the left, just past the stoplight.

"Wahoo." I had three minutes to spare.

The tired sand-colored flagstone building stretched back from the road with just a small storefront street side. Its high front windows were plastered with UPS logos under the shadow of a rust-red awning. The entrance was a single solid door.

I swung into the dirt parking lot alongside the building, locked my car and raced inside.

CHAPTER TWENTY-FOUR

The clerk made a point to glance at the clock on the wall. He gave me a weak smile. He looked to be in his eighties and probably should have retired ten years earlier.

"I won't be a second," I said, holding up the little brass key.

"No rush, honey." He'd already put on his outdoor jacket but was too polite to tell me he was closing.

Using my body to block his view, I opened box 88. The little door swung open. Stuffed inside was a large manila folder, bent double to fit the space. Squeezing it so it wouldn't catch and tear, I slid it out, snapped the box shut, and smiled at the clerk who now waited at the door, keys in hand. Ready to lock up.

"So you're taking it out?" he said.

"What?"

"Taking the envelope. My boss was about to cancel the box because the young feller seemed to be using it for a safe deposit box. Not a mailbox."

Young feller? Did he mean Colin? To an octogenarian, someone forty-something probably would seem young.

All along I had assumed the box was Jasper's and Colin had found the key. This changed things. How long had he had the box? Would the clerk tell me?

I glanced down at the envelope and saw it was addressed to Colin. "You must mean my partner," I said, "The guy that rented the box?"

"Yeah. A good-looking fellow, like a movie star."

"Well, we're going to be closing out the box anyway," I said. "Can I get a final accounting? Our tax man will want a copy."

He gave me a funny a look. "We rent by the month. It's all paid up. I'll make a note not to renew,"

"You young people have too much disposable cash. Why open a box for two months to store a few papers? Speaking of which, you tell your partner the next time he needs a safe deposit box, get one at the bank."

I hustled to the car and quickly tore open the envelope. Inside was a packet of letters with an APO return address held together by a wide red rubber band. All addressed to Jasper. What was Colin doing with letters addressed to Jasper?

In addition, there were at least a dozen old yellowed news articles from the sixties. Someone had handled them a lot, judging by the smudged print and felt-like quality of the paper. Tucked between them and a handwritten list of dates with foreign, as in Vietnamese sounding names, was a pink envelope addressed to Jasper. Hmmmm. An old romantic flame? It seemed out of place. The Vietnam War was over by the eighties. Resisting the urge to read it first, I disciplined my curiosity and proceeded in a logical, practical perusal.

It was getting dark, but not too dark to read.

I quickly shuffled the envelopes into chronological order based on their postal cancellation stamps. Six letters in all. Five from Flint sent to Jasper in 1967. The pink one had been sent in 1985, sixteen years after the others. I started with Flint's first letter.

June 17, 1967

    Greetings from BOOT CAMP

    Hey Jasper,

    First String! Way to go. Don't let coach run your butt off this summer.

    Sorry I didn't write sooner, but the first couple of weeks were grueling. Up at
4 am for a 10k run before breakfast, then all day classes, weapons training, drills

and more P.T. until midnight. I think our Army's trying to kill us before the enemy does. I lost ten pounds the first week.

Sure miss Mom's cooking. Eat an extra slice of apple pie for me.

The other guys here are pretty cool. But the drill sergeant gives new meaning to the word asshole. Don't let mom read this.

Two weeks left to go.

I put in my paperwork to be a paratrooper. Should find out this week if I'm accepted.

Hang loose and don't let Mom & Dad talk you into joining up as soon as you graduate. You've got the brains of the family and shouldn't let 'em go to waste. Get your degree first and then you can join as an officer. More prestige. More pay.

Flint

I set the letter on the passenger seat and eagerly read the next like I was gulping down a huge pile of curly fries at the end of Lent after giving up junk food. Flint and Jasper were coming to life. I so wished I could have grown up knowing both uncles.

August 10, 1967

Greetings from JUMP SCHOOL

Hi Jasper,

Thanks for writing. It's good to hear the real news from home. All Mom writes about is the weather, how much she misses me, and how much better I mow the lawn than you do.

Made my first jump from a plane today. You can't believe the adrenal rush. I'm addicted. Captain says I'd be a good candidate for the 1/327th Battalion Recon Platoon of the 101st Airborne Division. It's an elite group of soldiers and is the highest decorated unit for its size in the entire army.

I hope I make it. Keep your fingers crossed for me. It'd be an honor to serve my country in that way.

So far I'm ranked #2 in the training unit and I'm shooting for the number 1 spot. ½ the guys didn't make it past the second week. Most were sent back to infantry units and are in the jungles of Nam fighting the Vietcong.

It's lights out. I'll finish tomorrow.

2 weeks later. A lot has happened since I started this letter. I've earned my

parachutist badge and got my orders this morning. I'm assigned to the 1ˢᵗ Brigade and ship out next week so I won't make it home before I go.

Something else I wanted to tell you, I met a girl and she's the one. As soon as I get leave we're going to get married. Her name is Mariana. You'll love her and I'm sure Mom & Dad will too, once they get to know her. She's beautiful and everything I could want in a wife. Here's her picture and address. Write her a letter and welcome her to the family for me, okay?

Flint

I shuffled through the papers three times. There wasn't a picture. I was so intent that I almost jumped out of my skin when something banged on my window. Letters exploded from my hand like a New York ticker-parade. At the side of the car stood the UPS clerk. His lips and arms moved in tandem, but I didn't have a clue what he was trying to tell me.

I rolled down the window, hoping my car wasn't on fire.

"Sorry, ma'am. I need to lock the gate." He pointed to the exit.

"I didn't realize," I said, glancing at the papers on the floor. I grabbed what I could reach and placed them on the seat.

"That's okay, missy. It's just that I have to lock the lot. Otherwise, the snowbirds sneak in and park overnight."

"Oh," I said, wondering why a tourist on vacation would want to spend the night in a dingy parking lot.

"It's crazy," he said. "They can afford a two hundred thousand mobile home but are too cheap to spring for a camping space. Don't make sense."

"Sounds par for the course," I said and started the car. "I'm a new owner of a business in Sedona. It explains the gate across the entrance to my parking lot. I'll have to remember to close it."

"That'd be a smart move. You wouldn't believe the mess people leave. And I'm not just talking about the trash in our recycling bin. You'd think they'd be smart enough to know this wasn't a dog park."

"Thanks for the info." I started the car. "Sorry to have held you up."

"No problem." He gave me a cheery wave as I exited the lot.

I was dying to read the next letter and not just to further my murder investigation. The two letters I'd read already had given me a greater insight into the personalities of my uncles than the stories I'd been told. It was obvious they were close. Trusted the other completely like true brothers. I wondered where my mom fit into their lives. Would one of the next letters reveal why she'd been so angry at the mention of Jasper's name after so many years had passed?

Seemed tragic that Flint wasn't the only casualty of the Vietnam War. He died and Jasper disowned. Both lost to the family. And for what?

CHAPTER TWENTY-FIVE

I mpatience dictated my next decision. There'd been a chain restaurant on the outskirts of Cottonwood. I'd stop for coffee and pie and read the rest of the letters. There was no way I could stave my curiosity for the mere thirty minutes it'd take to drive back to Sedona.

I pulled into the spacious and almost empty lot and parked near the front door. Good. The fewer customers the better. It lowered the chance of running into someone who'd recognize me. Of course, an empty parking lot usually signals poor food, but that was okay. I wasn't stopping for a great meal—just a place to read. A bigger plus is that it meant with few customers, it wasn't likely they'd be hustling me on before I'd read every slip of paper in the envelope.

I found a booth near the back and settled in. The waitress came over chewing a wad of gum and obviously bored with life in general. She dropped a menu on the table and tapped out a hurry-up-and-place-your-order rhythm with her pen on a small pad. Maybe her goal in life was to get laid off so she could collect unemployment.

"I'll have coffee and a large order of fries," I said, having decided against the pie. Fries cooked at a high temperature—ergo, hopefully killing any nefarious germs lurking on the premises. Alone for the moment, I pulled out the sheaf of letters and read the next one.

September 10, 1967

Greetings from BIEN HOA, VIETNAM

Hi Jasper,

Just a short note. Nam is everything I expected and nothing like I thought it'd be. Nothing can prepare you for the heat and humidity or the smells. All I do is sweat.

I should be here for about a month of additional training with the 90th before joining-up with my unit.

Thanks for writing Mariana. It meant a lot to her and to me. Keep up your studies. Maybe by the time your number comes up, the draft will be abolished.

And thanks for the offer to introduce my girl to the folks. But hold off. You know how they get sometimes. Better to wait until I break the news to them myself.

Flint

I was hooked. Who was Mariana? No one in the family had ever mentioned her. What happened to her? Did she break Flint's heart? Or did my family run her off after he died? It was obvious Flint had some concerns about letting Jasper introduce her. I quickly returned the letter to its envelope before moving on to the next. The front door opened, letting in a stream of cool air that reached back to my booth. I glanced up, relieved that it wasn't anyone I knew.

September 30, 1967

Greetings from THE JUNGLE

Hi Jasper,

Things move fast over here. I flew to Camp Eagle, spent one night there with the other unit replacements, and the next day we were choppered to a hilltop to join the recon brigade. Cool, tough guys.

Altogether, there are about 45 of us. Pretty much all we do is hump up and down mountains looking for the enemy. Every day's the same. We're up before daybreak, pack up our gear, hump through the jungle to the next high spot, and set up a night perimeter.

Got a new uniform—French camo fatigues, a boonie hat and beret. We don't wear any insignias on our uniforms other than our jump wings and Mekong scout badges. Not our names, rank, or country. It's kind of cool. The other troops call us the Ghost Warriors.

To answer your question, no I haven't killed a Vietcong yet.

Mariana says she can't wait to meet you in person. Thanks for writing her. Now that I'm in the field, I'm not sure how often my letters will get through.

You may think I've got it made hiking and camping every day, but humping a rucksack full of c-rations and chasing Charlie is no picnic.

The tropical storms are the worst. Everything's wet. And if you can find a patch of dry ground you have to share it with the snakes, rats, and mice that are trying to stay dry, too. Before you go to bed tonight, imagine what it's like trying to sleep with rats crawling over and under your poncho liner all night.

I don't know when I'll get a chance to send this, but I'll get it out. Even though it's not easy being here, I'm proud to be an American fighting for the freedom and democracy of not just our country, but for the world.

Flint

It was obvious and a little sad that Flint's boyish enthusiasm had faded. I couldn't quite put my finger on what had changed. It was like he'd shifted from youthful optimism into an adult mindset. He sounded young. Pumped up on patriotism and doing his part to keep the world safe. Still idealistic, but all the trappings of boyhood had dissipated. Was it just the long hours, the danger and the settling reality of combat that had transformed him? Or had he witnessed something so evil he couldn't bring himself to shatter the dreams of his younger brother?

Okay. Maybe my interpretation was a little over dramatic. Adding emotions to his words that weren't there. Letting the filter of what historians said about the war influence me. That our county's involvement in Vietnam had been a mistake and resulted in the unnecessary loss of lives, including the zombie vets that survived the war, but not its nightmares.

Maybe what I'd read so far had nothing to do with either murder. But then why had Colin kept them secreted in a private postbox? It brought me back to a nagging question. How had they come into Colin's possession?

Pieces were coming together. Was it possible that someone's past was wrapped up in the present? Someone involved with Jasper. Is that why he was killed? Or was I being melodramatic? And why had Colin hidden these in the next town instead of leaving them at THE ALABASTER? It would explain my nighttime intruder. Were these letters what they were searching for? Was it smart keeping them on my person?

But how would personal letters lead not to just one, but two murders? I didn't know yet, but I'd find out.

Sickly ooze clawed its way into my stomach. My lips suddenly felt dry and I licked them. I'd met several vets since I'd arrived, and hated to think it could be one of them. All Jasper's friends and presumably Flint's as well. Men I'd come to like. It couldn't be one of them. They couldn't be the only vets in Verde Valley. The place was teaming with old retired guys. If I remembered right, there was a group of them that played cards once a month with Carl and Doc.

I'd have to add the veteran's membership files from the various communities within a fifty-mile radius. However, not until after I'd studied the contents of the mailbox.

Until now my view of the war was all talk, history and Hollywood gloss. As I held Flint's letter, I realized I was seeing first hand how it'd transformed the innocence of a generation. Still, half the puzzle was missing. I wished I'd had Jasper's letters, too. Was there a possibility his letters had been returned in Flint's things? A long shot, but I'd check with Mom. I resisted the urge to call her right then. Too late in the day to get a civil answer. I'd put it on my mental to-do list.

The front door opened again. I recognized the new customers to my dismay. Not because I didn't like them, but I didn't want to be interrupted.

Becca spotted me right away and waved. Smiling, she and Tamara headed straight for my booth.

Quickly I tucked the letters back into the envelope. Even if I now suspected the murders were linked to Vietnam and the past, I didn't want to be like Stone and leave other possible leads buried. I'd pursue every one until I had proof-positive I had the killer.

This gave me a chance to ask Becca about her mom's business arrangement with Jasper. Kids were a lot smarter and more observant than most adults gave them credit for.

"Allie," Becca said. She looked so much like her mother Sarah. "Didn't expect to see you here."

"Me, neither," Tamara said, half glaring at me with her slightly almond shaped eyes . "Thought you had errands."

I didn't have to answer because the waitress butted between the two girls with my fries and coffee and did a quick retreat.

"We've been to the movies," Becca said and started to tell me all the details of the romance comedy they'd seen. And how dreamy-hot the lead kid had been, like I'd be interested in a post-pubescent teen heartthrob.

"You may as well join me," I said, half-hoping they'd refuse.

"If you're not too busy," Tamara said, tossing her long dark hair and sliding in next to Becca, who'd already made herself comfortable.

"I finished up my errands and decided to get a snack before driving back." I pushed the plate of fries to the center of the table. "Help yourself."

"I'll pass," Tamara said, making a face.

Becca added in a low stage-whisper, "Their food's not so great. We came in for ice cream."

There wasn't any cream or sugar on the table so I braved a swallow of coffee and pushed the cup away. Bitter and had the worse aftertaste, like someone had thrown in a cigarette butt. To get the taste out my mouth, I sampled a fry and immediately wished I hadn't. It must have been fried in two-month-old grease after cooking up a school of toxic herring.

"You're right about the fries," I said. "You should have warned me."

Becca said, "They're not as bad with ketchup."

"If you don't mind a disgusting aftertaste," Tamara said and handed over a breath mint. "This should help."

"Thanks," I said. "But if the food is always this bad, why do you come here?"

"For the killer hot fudge sundaes," the girls said in unison and burst out laughing.

The waitress came back and eyed the girls with a frown. "Are you two ordering?"

"Hot fudge sundae," Becca said.

"Me, too," said Tamara.

"Make that three," I said. "You can take away the fries and coffee."

"You'll have to pay for them," the waitress said, popping her gum to make her point. "And the coffee."

"That's fine," I said. "But you and the cook should try a fry before you toss them. That way you'll know why we didn't eat them and warn other customers not to order them."

She rolled her eyes and went to get our sundaes.

"I hope your mom's not too stressed," I said to Becca. "With how Colin treated her."

"It turned her into a total crabby-witch, with a B." Her face colored. "Don't tell her I said that."

"I won't." I lowered my voice. "FYI, it won't get any better. Your mom will always think she knows what's best for you. Even when she's dead wrong."

Both girls laughed.

Becca grinned. "Yeah. For all her faith, she called Colin that same night. He was too busy to talk so they planned to meet over coffee the next morning."

That surprised me. "I told your mom not to worry," I said. "Colin couldn't make her move without my agreeing."

"Yeah, but she said Colin had a way of getting what he wanted."

I wondered if Sara mentioned to Stone that she and Colin had a meeting set up for the morning he was murdered. Or why she hadn't at least told me. The fact that she hadn't said anything seemed a little suspicious. Had she already discovered his body earlier and waited for someone else to make his death official?

Patsy had filled the bill and lived up to her name at the same time. Maybe Sara could be a little more devious than I'd assumed. Of course, her reticence could stem purely from self-preservation and the mother-tiger instinct. She had two kids to support and raise. She couldn't do that from jail.

I hoped these speculations were totally off base for Becca and Jacob's sake. They were awesome kids.

"So, your mom still treats you like a kid?" Becca said, frowning.

I nodded. "Even after I got my law degree."

"So unfair." Becca turned to Tamara. "You're so lucky. Your mom's cool. She doesn't boss you around all the time."

Tamara smiled. "That's because one, she's busy. And two, she doesn't believe in public displays."

"I haven't met your mom," I said. "What's she do?"

"Sure you have. She runs the Sedona Charitable Trust."

I felt totally stupid. How had I missed that? "And Carl Morton is your grandfather? The one you "borrowed" the paperweight from."

"Yep."

"He seems pretty understanding. Why don't you just tell him?"

"He may be, but Mom would be furious. Becca's never seen her with her dragon claws unsheathed."

"I don't believe you," Becca said. "Your mom's sweet."

"No she isn't," Tamara said and winked. "Uncle Alex is sweet. Sweet on Allie." She giggled.

What had I said about kids being way too observant? Thankfully the Miss Congeniality waitress arrived with the sundaes.

The girls were right. The hot fudge sundaes were killer. Rich creamy vanilla ice cream, drizzled in just the right amount of rich hot fudge, blanketed in a dollop of whipped cream, sprinkled with slivered almonds and topped with a mouthwatering maraschino cherry. Literally, it was a burst of heaven on the tongue, and every bite worth putting up with the cranky waitress.

Over their protests, I treated the girls. "Consider it your ice cream finder fee," I said. "And speaking of finding things, Tamara, I'll seriously look for that paperweight. I haven't forgotten."

"Thanks," she said and we left together. I would have stayed a little longer, but I'd had enough of the waitress's evil eye for one evening. That and I didn't want to chance running into someone else I knew.

Back in the car, I remembered I had a flashlight stowed under the seat and fished it out. The battery-god must like me because although it hadn't been turned on for at least six months, its beam was strong and bright.

I slipped the next letter from its envelope.

CHAPTER TWENTY-SIX

October 22, 1967

Greetings from HELL

Jasper, if you're reading this, it means it got past the censors.

Little brother, one thing you have to promise me is that if your draft number comes up near the top, and you don't get a student deferment, you'll head for Canada. There's nothing noble about this war. It's one day of hell, followed by another and another.

Some of the guys in this unit are certifiable monsters. There's a reason this unit has such a high kill rate. They've killed over a hundred unarmed civilians in the last month—old people, women and children. Peacemaker's the worst. Not his real name, but what the other guys call him. He's started to wear necklaces made of his victim's ears. Some of the other guys are doing it, too.

Makes me ashamed to call myself an American.

I didn't sign up for this.

I tried to talk to the captain, but he blew me off and just kept whittling the unit's insignia onto a white rock he found in the ravine. He told me that unfortunate casualties are one of the realities of war. And, that I needed to do my job and look the other way. That's not so easy when

Peacemaker is raping ten-year-old girls and taking sick pleasure in killing babies and beheading them.

I've put in for a transfer. I'm not sure if it will come soon enough.

Whatever it takes, don't end up here.

Miss you. I hope and pray Mariana will still want to be my wife when I get back. I'm not the same guy she fell in love with, but my love for her is even stronger than before. If something happens to me, make sure she knows that.

Flint

The ice cream in my stomach curdled as bile rose into my throat. My eyes teared and burned at the same time. I blinked, squeezing tiny of puddles into the outer corners of my eyes.

It was all so heartrending, like a Shakespeare drama. Everyone operating with false assumptions that ended in tragedy.

Flint's hopes, dreams and pride of country dashed. Jasper becomes a draft-dodger and is disowned. What I couldn't understand is why didn't Jasper show this letter to the family? To my mother. To my grandparents. To make them understand why he couldn't follow his brother into the army. For the second time this evening I was tempted to call her. But it would be futile. I'd call her first thing in the morning. And I didn't care how busy she was, she would listen to this letter. Even if I had to read it to her on her answering machine.

Getting emotional was clouding my judgment. I reviewed it again, this time as a prosecutor, knowing that man has the capacity to perpetrate evil. There are certain individuals that have no regard for human life. They are the bad guys. Our government is supposed to represent the good guys.

A battle of emotions waged in my heart, vying for attention.

In war, men are forced to kill. I got that, knowing I couldn't do it, but raping children? Killing babies? All for country? That I could not understand. How could our government take young idealistic men and turn them into monsters?

The only comfort the letters revealed, is to know my uncles were good men. Both lost to senseless violence. The fact that Colin had hidden the letters meant that they had to somehow be linked to the murders.

How or why? I didn't know yet, but I felt it in my gut. It was a good possibility someone had killed to keep them secret. Twice. If he'd had no problem raping girls or killing babies, he'd have no problem killing me.

Who was Peacemaker? I hoped I hadn't met him. What if he was someone I knew? What if I liked him? I wasn't exactly a pro first impressions. Take Alex. I'd thought he was a cold, paper-pushing lawyer—perhaps a little dangerous. Then he'd taken the pizzas out to feed the homeless. That's when I realized he was one of the good guys. Too bad he ruined it by trying to micro-manage me. Which was not going to happen. But I was getting off track. This wasn't about Alex and me living happily ever after.

Just thinking about him had clouded my concentration. Why had Tamara brought him up?

I still had one last letter of Flint's to read, but it had grown cold. The temperature must have dropped twenty degrees in the last fifteen minutes. I didn't have enough gas in the tank to just sit there with the car and heater running. It was time to head home. I started the car, backed up and headed for the exit to the street. A derelict figure half-ran, half-stumbled in front of the car. I slammed on the brakes and just missed running into him by a thin whisker of air.

The figure planted both hands on the hood of the car and I realized it was a man with long stringy hair flying in the wind. The features of his face seemed distorted in the weird lighting from the headlights. Like when someone puts a flashlight under their chin to tell scary stories in the dark during a camp-out. Was he trying to appear crazy to run a scam on me? Why else had he darted in front of my car and risked his life? I'd read about a series of car heists in LA that started with one man blocking a car's path, while another person rushed the driver's side with a gun in hand.

I quickly scanned for a possible accomplice. Didn't see anyone. The lot seemed deserted, except for two cars I assumed belonged to the cook and waitress.

Who'd want car-jack this vehicle? No sane crook. Maybe the guy was just drunk and confused. And needed help.

I put the car in park and rolled down the window a few inches. Cold air crept in like a thief.

"You have to move!" I shouted. Even if he was harmless, I didn't want to get out and confront him.

"Help me!" the man called out. His voice sounded vaguely familiar. He crumpled on the front of my beat-up Escort spread eagle and scrabbled in vain for purchase. As if in slow motion, gravity pulled at him and he slid down the front bumper leaving dark streaks on the hood. Just before he slipped from view his face was caught in full light and I recognized him.

I jumped out and rushed to the front of the car, fog-bursts from my mouth rising like a trail of smoke as I rushed to help. He lay sprawled up against the right wheel. His ragged breathing hummed in unison to the car's motor. This was good. He was alive, but his eyes were locked in a fixed stare.

I reached down and gently touched his shoulder. "Ralph! Are you okay? What's happened?"

His blank gaze swiveled to meet mine. There was a gash on his forehead that needed stitches. And his hands were scraped like he'd been in a fight with an angry armadillo and lost.

"Ralph?"

He blinked, his eyes focused and he recognized me. "Jasper's alabaster girl."

"You're hurt. I'm going to call an ambulance to take you to the hospital."

"No! They're in league with the men from the sky." He waggled his finger for me to lean closer.

I bent down and to my surprise, didn't smell fresh alcohol in the unwashed aroma permeating from his clothes. Whatever he was on, it didn't have an odor.

"They came for me." His chest heaved in and out in a sudden coughing fit. I was afraid he was about to die, but then he grabbed my wrist with the strength of a younger man. "When they come for you, you gotta pretend you're stupid. Promise?"

"Who?"

"Promise me, Alabaster. You don't know anything. I didn't tell you anything. It's the only way you'll be safe."

"Okay, I promise. Who did this to you?"

"You can't know. Jasper found out and he's dead. Same with the boy-man."

"You mean, Colin?"

"Yeah, him."

"Listen to me, Ralph." I kept my words soft so as not to excite him any further. "I'll call the police. They'll protect you. And have the people who did this to you arrested."

"Noooooo." His arms and legs went into motion as he tried to get to his feet, but he was too beaten up and weak. All he managed was to sit, leaned up against the front of the car. "I used to be a ghost. Now I'm just a dead man."

"I can't leave you here like this. Let me get you to the hospital" My heart was slamming. I was in a panic. He looked bad. "You need a doctor," I said.

"No, take me to Doc. I can trust him."

"You mean Doc Shore?"

"Yep. At the clinic."

"Where's that?"

"Sedona."

"Oh," I said and I realized he was talking about the place I'd given my blood. "Are you sure you want to drive that far? The sooner you get treatment, the better." Which was true, plus I didn't want him to die in my car.

His eyes narrowed and he shook his head, his dreads quivering like a nest of snakes ready to attack. "Don't want to go there."

"Okay," I said, but I didn't feel good about it. "Let me get something to staunch your bleeding." I fished some unused napkins out of a takeout bag in the back seat.

"Here," I said. "Hold these on your wound. Apply pressure. But not too hard."

His legs scuttled on the pavement like an out-of-control marionette missing a string. I reached down to help him get up. He ignored my offered hand and managed to stand using the car as a crutch.

"Wait there and keep the pressure on." I rushed to open the passenger door. I returned, got my shoulder under his arm. Between his weak effort, the car to stabilize his balance and my shoulder, I got him into the passenger seat. It took all the energy he had.

He slumped back barely conscious, but in a daze. I had to buckle him and wished I hadn't promised to take him all the way to Sedona. He needed medical treatment ASAP, but I was afraid of what he might do if I broke my word and took him to a closer hospital.

"I'd feel better taking you to a doctor here in town," I said.

"Let me out." He fumbled with the door handle. "I don't want to go to no stranger-doctor."

"I said I'd take you to the clinic, I just don't feel good about it."

He relaxed and started on a disjointed rambling monologue. None of it made sense. About halfway back to town, he ran out of steam and slumped into unconsciousness.

Oh God, don't let him die on me. Suddenly I felt guilty I hadn't insisted on taking him to the hospital in Cottonwood. It had been stupid to let this mentally impaired man convince me otherwise.

Driving with one hand, I reached over and felt for a pulse in his neck. It was there. I gulped in a deep breath and pushed my foot down on the gas pedal. If a cop stopped me, the odds were that I'd get a police escort to the clinic.

Ralph was still out when we arrived. I left him in the car and raced inside. A young man in a white jacket grabbed a wheelchair and brought it out. He opened the car door and startled Ralph. The old desert rat rose up like a cobra ready to strike. When he saw the guy he smiled.

"Doctor Freddy," Ralph said. "The tiger got me. Call sawbones. I need stitches."

"You're going to be just fine." The young doctor helped Ralph into the chair. "But you'll have to put up with my care tonight. Doc's in Flagstaff."

"Okay, I trust you, Dr. Freddy."

"Thanks for bringing him. You're Jasper's niece, aren't you?"

"Yeah."

"I accompanied Doc to the crime scene to examine the body. Saw you." He talked as he pushed Ralph into the clinic. "Doc's training me. I'm hoping to take over as county coroner when he retires."

I followed him into the clinic. He appeared to be in his mid-forties, looking more like a teddy bear than a doctor.

"Nice to meet you officially," I said.

He laughed. "Now, tell me what happened to Ralph here."

"Not sure. I found him like this in Cottonwood. I tried to take him to the hospital there, but he insisted I bring him here."

A nurse appeared from behind a green-curtained partition. "Room's ready."

"Take him back," he said to her. To Ralph he said. "I'll be right with you, but first Martha's going to swab your wounds."

As soon as they were behind the curtain, Dr. Freddy lowered his voice and said, "You did the right thing bringing him here. Less traumatic for everyone involved."

"Is he going to be okay?" I asked.

"Except for his forehead, most of his wounds look superficial. Head wounds have a way of bleeding. I won't know for sure until I examine him." He smiled and looked a little abashed. "Could you wait till I fix him up and give him a ride home?"

"I guess so," I said, while my mind was screaming noooooo. "I'm not family."

"Doesn't matter. It's more important he stays calm. I could keep him here for the night and take him home after my shift, but . . ."

"I'll wait."

"Great. If it turns out his injuries warrant his spending the night, we'll keep him. It's just that sometimes institutional settings agitate him and he has to be sedated. I'd rather not do that if it can be avoided."

I sat in the same green vinyl and stainless steel chair I'd occupied while waiting for my blood test. The cold seeped through my jeans and I shivered, thinking this was not how I'd planned to spend my evening. Belatedly I remembered I'd forgotten to lock the car doors and Flint's letters were just laying on the back seat.

Talk about stupid.

I went out, got them, locked the car and came back inside. Whatever heat my posterior had transferred to the chair had dissipated in my short absence.

Alone in the waiting room with just the muffled mutters from behind the examining curtain, I pulled out Flint's last letter in the packet. It had a brown stain.

November 3, 1967

Jasper,

Maybe you won't get this. Sawbones the medic, promised to send it. I trust him. I'm hurt. Bad. He's helping me hold on. Medivac chopper's on the way.

Last night orders came down the pipe to recon a suspected VC stronghold a few clicks east.

It was an ambush.

Heavy machine gunfire. The worst. Captain got hit. A bullet in his hip.

Next thing the VC pulled back. We went into retreat. Another machine gun burst and a bullet slammed into my back. Sawbones dragged me to cover and performed surgery on the spot. Good man. He swore when he removed the bullet. A slug from AK47.

Someone yelled at him to leave me behind.

I have a feeling I might not be coming home. Love you.

Don't let them draft you. And Mariana. See that she has a good life. Don't let me down, little brother.

Flint

I held the letter realizing these must be Flint's final deathbed words to Jasper. It brought it all home to me. He was stuck in the middle of a battle for a cause he no longer believed in. Hurt and in anguish while dodging a barrage of bullets, knowing he might not make it home.

I closed my eyes and let the emotions of the letter wash over me. Raw rivulets of tears burst from my eyes and snot dripped onto my upper lip. I tried to stop the flow of both with the back of my hands, wiping the wetness onto my jeans. Agony squeezed my heart. I'd only felt this intense grief once before. When my father died.

Was how I felt merely transference? Or was it simply emotional exhaustion?

Before Alex tracked me to LA, I'd been operating in a safe emotional limbo. Going through the motions, but void of hope, trust or a sense of purpose. I'd been afraid to feel because I didn't want to deal with the abandonment of my ex-husband, my profession and my mom. Or my own self-rejection. Jasper had changed that. He'd restored my faith in myself. I was not a victim. And I was going to make it in the rock business or die trying.

Purged, I smiled. I owed it to Jasper to restore Mom's faith in him. I pulled tissues from my purse, blew my nose and mopped my face. I looked down at the letter again, not to read it. Just to think about its impact.

How would Mom feel? What regrets would these letters bring? How she'd lost two brothers. One to war and the other to the family's stupid pride. Tomorrow I'd call to warn her they were coming before I faxed them to her.

My emotions in check, the reality of Flint's final words slapped my gray cells into action. I knew why Jasper was killed. He'd figured out Flint's death didn't align with the final official military report. I wondered if it was possible to get a copy of the official incident report? Or is it was buried under a slew of bureaucratic red tape.

Somehow Colin figured it out and I suspected had used the information to blackmail the killer. Thus he'd signed his own death warrant.

If Colin could ferret the truth from the contents of the manila envelope he'd hidden, then so could I. But I'd be smarter. I wouldn't paint a big bulls-eye on myself.

I'd discover the truth and turn it over to the police.

The green curtain snapped open.

"He's good to go," Doctor Freddy said. "Closed his head-wound with a kind of medical Superglue. Cleaned his other scrapes. He could use a shower. And see that he takes two of these." He handed me a bottle of pills.

"He jammed me with a needle," Ralph said. "I don't like needles."

CHAPTER TWENTY-SEVEN

I opened the door to my little apartment and flipped on the lights. It looked exactly as I'd left it. The recliner, the little table, the desk drawers closed and Jasper's dog-headed cane were all in their place.

Ralph followed on my heels, closer than a shadow. He shut and locked the door before I had a chance to take the next breath. Out of self-preservation, I breathed through my mouth. Once the adrenaline had faded from my blood, I'd become hyper-aware of his nauseating body odor.

Now that he'd been stitched up and had calmed down, it was hard to recognize the disoriented guy I'd taken to the hospital. He was one tough old buzzard—a hundred percent better.

"Don't let the ghost men in," he said. "Keep it locked. I'll stay here tonight to confuse their probes."

Okay. His one hundred percent wasn't exactly normal, but he seemed lucid enough considering his obvious P.T.S.D.

"Sounds good," I said. I didn't want to upset him, but I didn't think I'd last the night. "How about a shower? There's plenty of hot water."

"You're stuffed up. You weren't before," he said as squinted at me. "Did they get to you? Plant little microbes in your nose?"

"No, I'm fine. Just a little chilly." Mentally I added that I'd breathe normally once he'd had a proper bath and his filthy clothes disposed of outside in the dumpster.

"I'd like a shower. Jasper used to let me use his whenever I wanted."

"And you still can. Let me get you a towel."

"I know where the towels are," he said and preceded me into the bedroom.

I had a sudden thought. "Jasper had a lot of clothes I'm going to have to get rid of. Would you like them? I think they'd fit you."

A wide grin appeared on his face. "I'd like that. Kind of like taking Jasper with me wherever I go."

"Great." I pulled open Jasper's sock-and-underwear drawer and flung open the closet. "Help yourself. Take whatever you want. You can leave your old clothes in the hamper." I'd toss them later.

While Ralph showered I opened a couple cans of chili and set them to heat on the stove. Not a great dinner, but warm and filling. I pulled out a box of crackers, set out bowls and silverware and then sat at the desk to plan my next steps.

First thing in the morning I'd give Doc Shore a call to see if we could get together for coffee. I'd read the writing on the wall and realized he had to be the medic Flint had mentioned in his final letter. Flint had trusted him, and so would I. Unofficially, he should be able to confirm the possibility that Flint had been murdered by someone in their unit.

After I took Ralph home, my next thought was to give Mom a call and put an end to the ridiculous family feud she'd waged against Jasper. I owed it to both of them to clear his name and memory. I'd send her copies of Flint's letters. Or should I? I chewed on the end of my thumb-nail and when I realized what I was doing I made a fist, tucking my thumb inside curled fingers.

Deep down I felt the need to restore Mom's faith in him, but this wasn't the right time.

Or the smart time.

How stupid would it be to discuss the letters with anyone? Especially when the odds were high that they were the catalyst to Jasper and Colin's murders. I wasn't ready to hand them over to Stone. He could still be involved. But keeping them on the premises was dangerous. I jumped up and looked for a place to hide the manila envelope. Not a lot of great choices. I settled on cramming them into a discarded cereal box from the storeroom and put it in a cupboard in the kitchen.

Change of plans—before taking Ralph home I'd go to the bank, get a safety deposit box and stash the original copies of anything that could be used as evidence in a court of law. Until then, pray that no one knew I had the letters. It suddenly felt good to have Ralph there. He was a survivor.

I gathered Jasper's notes, thinking I should probably make copies. My eyes began to swim. Was it emotional exhaustion? Information overload? The altitude? I just couldn't think. Nothing was making sense. In the end, I realized it didn't matter. What I needed was food and the scent-tendrils of the chili made my mouth water.

I heard the shower shut off.

Ralph could use the bedroom. The sheets hadn't been changed, but I doubted he would care. As soon as Ralph settled for the night, I'd finish going over everything Colin had squirreled away in the mailbox. At the same time, I'd list all the unknowns and do some research on-line.

Looking things up on my phone would give me a massive headache and use too much data. This meant another trip to the library. Which reminded me that I needed to call the local cable company and get WIFI installed. And buy a new computer.

I went to stir the chili. Suddenly it didn't look like enough, so I opened another couple of cans. If any was leftover I could finish it later. I returned to the living area just as Ralph came out of the bedroom. He had on a clean pair of jeans that fit pretty well and a white, sleeveless ribbed undershirt. His arms were thin, almost emaciated with age.

"You didn't find a shirt?" I said.

"I like the air on my skin. Keeps it healthy." He sniffed. "Something smells good."

That's when I noticed a tattoo on his shoulder. My hand flew to my mouth to keep myself from gasping. The design matched one of the drawings Tamara had made of THE ALABASTER paperweight; the one of the upside-down ice cream cone with wings. Only now, I recognized it for what it was. A military insignia.

"What's your tattoo mean?"

Ralph's eyes went wide. He slapped his hand over the ink-art. "It's from when I was a ghost tiger."

"What do you mean? Ghost tiger?"

"I don't want to talk about it."

"Please?" I rushed to the desk and found the pictures Tamara had drawn and showed them to him. "What's the tiger represent?"

His eyes flared like he was a caged animal about to be tasered. "I'm tired. I want to go to bed."

"Aren't you hungry?" I said. "I heated up some chili. You said it smelled good."

"Not hungry anymore."

"Are you sure?"

He turned his back to me and shuffled toward the bedroom.

"Wait. You need to take your pills."

He stopped, turned and held out a hand. I put two little yellow capsules from the bottle Dr. Freddy had given me into Ralph's hand. He dry-swallowed them.

"I'm tired," he said and went into the bedroom.

I felt guilty about his going to bed without dinner, but what could I do? I had four cans of chili simmering on the stove so I had a bowl and a handful of crackers.

Loud snores came from the bedroom. I looked in. Ralph lay face-down and fully dressed on top of the bed. I remembered an extra blanket in the wall cabinet, got it and covered him. He didn't even flinch. It sounded like Ralph was out for the count. Time to finish reading the contents of the manila envelope.

The next item in the packet was a telegram to inform my grandparents that their son Flint David Marlon had been killed in action. Jasper must have taken it with him when he left home and I wondered about that. Had he carried around these letters, re-reading them and re-experiencing Flint's death, for the last fifty years? And how had Colin gotten hold of them? Had Jasper given them to him or had he found them here at THE ALABASTER?

I was left with the pink envelope and the list of Vietnamese words. On closer inspection, I realized the list had been written in Jasper's neat printing. I'd check the words out at the library. I was betting they were locations or battles. Not having a computer seriously hampered my investigation. Like I'd been caught in an early 80's time warp. At least I wasn't sitting here in leg warmers and big hair.

I brought the last envelope to my nose and sniffed. After more than thirty years, I still caught the slightest hint of rose scent. Must have been a powerful potion.

Large flowing script filled three pages of the pink rose-embossed stationary. I flipped to the end to see who'd written the letter. It was signed, Mariana. Flint's girlfriend.

May 3, 1983

Dear Jasper,

You're a hard man to track down.

I'm sorry I didn't respond to your letters after Flint died. It may sound trite, but I want you to know that I truly appreciated all you tried to do for me back then. It was selfish to wait this long to tell you.

I ask for your forgiveness and for your help. I know I don't deserve it. My only excuse is that I was young and afraid of what people would think if they found out I was an unwed mother-to-be. In the eyes of my Kansas Bible Belt community, I'd be no different than a street walking slut.

If Flint had come home, it would have been different. But he didn't. And when he died, a part of me died with him. All I had was his child growing inside of me. I had to do what was best for our baby. That's when I decided to sever all ties with you and your family.

I moved home and married Randy Phelps. We'd been best friends since kindergarten. The problem was that while I loved him as a friend, he always adored me and wanted to marry me. It became too much and so I left White City and eventually met your brother.

When I returned to White City, I told Randy about Flint and that I was pregnant. He still wanted to marry me. He was a good husband and a good father to Colin. No one ever suspected he was raising another man's son. Six years after we were married Randy crashed his truck in a snowstorm and I was alone again, but respectable.

I hope you can forgive me for keeping Flint's son from you all these years, but I wanted to save him the shame of being called a bastard. And now I need a favor from you for his sake.

I've been diagnosed with cancer. Both Randy and I were only children. His parents are gone. My dad passed last year. Colin's only thirteen. If I die his only other relative will be my mother and she's not in the best health. Could you come and meet Colin? You'd be surprised how much he looks like Flint.

Maybe he could even visit you in the summer. Then if I don't make it until he's eighteen, he won't be alone.

I'm sorry to drop this on you out of the blue, but if you're the brother Flint said you were, I know I can count on you. Please call me. Soon.

Sincerely,

Mariana

P.S. I have one last favor to ask. Colin can't know about his real father until after my mother's gone. It'd kill her to know the truth.

Whoa! Colin and I were cousins? That explained why we both had the same rare blood type. And why Jasper had made us his co-heirs. Colin must have inherited his obstinate stubbornness from our side of the family. Maybe if I'd taken the time to know him we could have been friends and he wouldn't have seemed such a jerk. And it explained why he hadn't really hit on me. I'd thought it was because of Alex.

Or was I having a *blood is thicker than water* reaction? Excusing his behavior because we were family. I wondered. Had Jasper overlooked his nephew's shortcomings because he was his brother's child? Is that why he'd overlooked mine? I'd like to think that I had it more together than Colin, but if I didn't, I'd make sure to in future. I'd make Jasper's legacy proud.

I toyed with showing Mariana's letter to Stone, to burst his rare-blood-type-evidence against me. But then I'd have to explain how I'd gotten the key to the mailbox. That might be premature. He'd find out soon enough once he got the results of DNA tests that Colin and I were related. And I wouldn't tell my mom. Not until the murder was solved.

The snoring stopped. I tiptoed over to the bedroom door and peeked in. Ralph had rolled onto his side, but still looked sound asleep. I eased back and shut the door.

My mind swirling like a Greek whirlpool of doom, I had a second bowl of chili. Regretting the pig-out session, I cleaned up the kitchen, making sure Flint's letters were still secure in the cereal box. Chewing a couple of mint-flavored Rolaids, I settled in the recliner for the night. Not sure of how Ralph might react if he woke at four a.m. and didn't remember where he was; I didn't bother changing into my P.J.'s.

Exhaustion crept over me like a silencing hand, smothering my fears and doubts. I slept like the dead and awoke to someone pounding and shouting my name.

"Miss Renault? Allie?"

"Ralph!" I sprung up. My blankets slithered to the floor. I raced to the bedroom, expecting to see my guest in the throes of a post-traumatic fit. I blinked hard. Was I still asleep? Was this the beginning of a nightmare?

The room was empty. So was the bathroom.

More pounding.

"Allie! Are you in there?"

I recognized the voice. It wasn't Ralph. And the pounding wasn't coming from this room. I spun around, raced to the apartment door and flung it open.

"Jacob! What's happened?" I said, remembering I'd given him a key.

He breathed loud; his eyes popping like he'd just escaped being eaten by a tiger. Panting, he said, "I didn't know what to do."

"You okay?" I asked, suddenly afraid. Had Ralph done something totally crazy?

"I'm fine," he swallowed. Pink blotches appeared on his pale face. "I don't know how they got in? I know I locked the doors."

They? Had someone broken in again? Or was THE ALABASTER the scene of a third murder?

I grabbed the dog cane for a weapon. "You stay here," I said. "Call the police."

CHAPTER TWENTY-EIGHT

"The police?" Jacob said, repeating my words. His expression changed from near panic to total confusion. "You don't need them."

"Then what's going on?"

"The ladies got in." He sounded frustrated. "I don't know how and I told them you were closed, but they wouldn't listen."

"Ladies, as in . . .?" I relaxed my grip on Jasper's cane.

"You know. The old ones. Dorcus and her sister."

"Just one sister?" I said.

"Yep. They brought something for you."

"What?"

He shrugged. "Don't know. But they each got a box. I told them I'd give them to you, but they insisted on seeing you. Personally."

"Okay."

"And Dorcus said . . ." His voiced morphed into a pretty good imitation. "Not to dawdle. They had places to go. And people to see."

Now that he'd passed the proverbial message, the tension lines around his eyes relaxed. The ball had been lobbed into my court.

I sighed. It wasn't his fault. "Tell them I'll be out in ten minutes. If they can't wait, they can come back later."

"They won't like it." A frown creased his forehead. He held up an index finger and shook it at me, his voice morphing once more. "When you get older, you'll regret all the time you've wasted dillydallying."

"And the Oscar goes to Jacob," I said, laughing. "For your sake, I'll hurry. Promise."

"Please do." He sounded like I'd sent him to entertain a horde of hungry baboons and he was the dessert.

As soon as he left, I shut the apartment door and locked it. Before I splashed water on my face I had something more important to do. In the kitchen, I checked the pantry and gasped. "Noooooooooo."

Crap. Like Ralph, the cereal box had disappeared. A scribbled note on a used napkin lay in its place. The pen used to write the message had torn through the layers of the soiled tissue. Only half of the scrawled words were legible. I half-guessed the message as best I could.

I think it read: *You're out of cereal. Don't like chili for breakfast. Went to Mel's. I'll catch a ride home. P.S. t@#$& D@&*

Only one person could have written the note. Now all I had to do was figure out what he'd done with the cereal box. Had he found the letters and absconded with them on purpose? I wanted to kick myself. Putting them in the cereal box and leaving it in plain sight had been stupid. The contents of the manila envelope were the only hard evidence that linked Colin and Jasper's murders.

And I had lost them.

I read Ralph's note again, squinting until I was almost cross-eyed and my forehead ached as I tried to make out the postscript. Truth say? Tree bay? Wait. Were the last words, *trash day*?

I checked the garbage can under the sink. Empty. It'd been almost overflowing when I'd gone to bed.

Had taking out my trash been Ralph's way of saying thank you?

Where had he taken it? I didn't remember a trashcan outside and my dumpster hadn't arrived. Thankful I'd slept in my clothes, I quickly finger combed my hair and pulled on tennis shoes. Outside, I scanned the parking lot. No cans. From behind the building came the wheeze of airbrakes and a series of clunks and clinks.

I sprinted to the dirt alley behind the apartment. A shiny white diesel behemoth with a spindly yellow metal arm clutched a black garbage can in its grip. The side-loader Mac truck's engine growled, its headlights stared me down, daring me. A short man in blue coveralls patted the side of the truck as if to urge the mechanical monster into motion. It responded like a circus elephant center ring. The can quivered as it was lifted in slow motion off the ground. One foot. Two. Three.

I ran forward, screaming. "Stop. Wait! Don't!"

Neither the driver nor the man on the ground operating the dumping mechanism heard me. Or if they had, they'd ignored my shouts.

My arms whirled like an out-of-control windmill. The man on the ground finally noticed me when I grabbed his arm. The can now hung six feet overhead.

"Bring it down," I said. "Please."

The man brushed my hand from his arm and I realized he had a big wad of chewing tobacco tucked between his gums and lower lip. "Lady, we have a schedule to meet." He spit on the ground.

"You don't understand. Something got put in the can by mistake. I need to retrieve it."

"Something valuable?" The man's weasel eyes lit up, his tongue adjusting the position of his tobacco.

"To me," I said, my stomach churning.

The can inched up another foot and stopped. The man touched the middle button in a little box on the side of the truck. The can started to tip.

"I can pay you." The words burst from my mouth and I crossed my toes.

His hand hit the little control panel and the can froze at an awkward angle, its contents threatening to spill. "How much?"

"Twenty bucks?"

He laughed. "Not worth it."

"How much then?"

"Fifty." His eyes narrowed. "And another twenty-five for the driver."

"That's ridiculous. I could report you." I knew it was an empty threat because I had to get the letters back at any cost.

He shrugged. "And you could spend the rest of your day at the dump sifting through the town's garbage. What's it going to be? Like I said. We don't got all day."

"Can I write you a check? Or give you a gift certificate from *THE ALABASTER*?"

He spit, just missing my foot this time. "Seventy-five bucks. Cash."

"I don't have it on me," I said, trying to think where I could scrape it up. "I'll have to go get it."

"Be quick about it." He spat again, spittle dribbling down his chin. "You have five minutes max. Or we're out of here."

Five minutes to come up with seventy-five dollars. At the corner of the building, I glanced back and saw him tap the truck's keypad. The can straightened without losing any contents and began its descent. At least he was keeping his end of the bargain for the next five minutes.

I raced to the apartment. I had at least forty-five dollars left in my purse. I grabbed it and sprinted to the Bible bookstore. Sara was dusting an already clean-looking shelf.

Breathless, I said, "I need to borrow some cash. It's an emergency. I'll pay you back later today."

"I don't have very much in my cash register and I kind of need it for change," she said, sounding apologetic. "I have fifteen in my purse, plus some coins."

"I'll take it," I said. When I left, I had a total of seventy-four dollars and five cents, fifteen of it in change. It would have to do.

Weasel man wasn't happy about the change, but he took it. I wondered if he'd count it and be back for the ninety-five cents I stiffed him?

As soon as the garbage truck had moved on, I started picking through the trash. Panic rising when I didn't see the plastic bag with the cereal box on top. I tipped the can and frantically pawed through a miasma of rotten food, empty cartons and a pile of lumpy little doggy-poop bags. I stepped on one. It squirted a thin wavy line, like a cake decorator's piping bag.

"Crap" I swore. "Crap. Crap. Crap. Crap." Trepidation spread like cancer and, where my heart should have been, it felt hollow.

My eyes watered in frustration as I put everything back in the can and wiped my hands on my pants. Money and hope both wasted. If Flint's letters were lost forever, Mom would never forgive Jasper. And worse, if they were in the clutches of the killer my life would become a nightmare of watching my back. I only could hope Ralph had stashed them somewhere safe. I had to find him.

I needed a hot shower. Clean clothes. Coffee. In that order. Then maybe I could come up with a new plan. I was halfway across the parking lot when I heard a loud strident voice.

"Oooooooo-hoooooo. There you are. Didn't the boy tell you Rose and I were here to see you?"

Dorcus strode toward me. Her sister trailed a few paces behind like she was being dragged along against her will. Each carried medium-sized cardboard boxes. Rose's looked to be twice as heavy as she struggled to lug it.

"Sorry," I said, thinking whatever they wanted, it could wait. "I don't have time to visit."

"We didn't come to visit," Dorcus said and turned to her sister. "Did we, Rose?"

Rose looked at her feet and mumbled a weak sounding, "No."

"Give Allie the box," Dorcus ordered.

"Can't we do this inside?" Rose whispered. She sounded as pitiful as I felt.

"I suppose so." Dorcus actually huffed the concession and started marching for the front of the store.

My legs betrayed me and followed her of their own volition.

"Jasper's spirit is pleased that you've made progress inside the store."

Great. She still thought she could communicate with Jasper's ghost and I wondered what kind of opiate she slipped into her cup of tea.

"But I'm sure he'd not be so happy you're using the rock bins for garbage." She pointed to the pile of alabaster Ralph had brought me.

"What?" is all I managed to squeak when I spotted the bulging white plastic bag tucked under a chunk of the pale grainy rock.

"Trash makes the place look . . . well, trashy," Dorcus said. "It negatively affects the store's aura. And you don't want that."

I bit back a conditioned *yes ma'am* and rushed to grab the bag. Ignoring her I yanked it open and let out a huge sigh. The cereal box was on top and a quick peek inside revealed the manila envelope. I wanted to cheer. My victory felt short lived.

"Come along," Dorcus ordered.

I trailed along behind them like a chastened schoolgirl, clutching the cereal box and afraid to trust it out of my sight. Once inside the store, I set it behind the counter, out of reach of Rose. She was the kleptomaniac of the sisters, not that I could imagine her taking a smashed, ratty old box when she could lift something more valuable like the bright specimen of quartz she was eyeing on the shelf I'd cleaned and organized.

As if orchestrated, both women set their cartons on the glass jewelry counter. Jacob had managed to disappear. The boy was smart.

"Early to bed and early to rise keeps a man healthy, wealthy and wise," Dorcus said. "In spite of the progress you've made, you won't make a go of this business if you're not up with the robins."

I looked at the clock and pretended to smile like I appreciated her advice. It was still morning by a good five minutes.

"So, what have you brought me?" I asked. I really needed to get them out of there so I could go to the bank. Plus I wanted to talk to Doc and ask him what he knew about Flint's death.

"Rose, you're on." Before Rose had a chance to speak, Dorcus started another lecture. "Rose has been overly tired lately, but the doctor says there's nothing wrong. So, at my insistence Rose consulted a karma coach. Which has proved enlightening. We know why she's exhausted all the time and how to reverse it. Go ahead, Rose. Tell Allie what you've been up to."

One look at Rose confirmed that she'd been bullied into coming and that she would be happier anywhere but here. Even though she was in her sixties or maybe seventies, the expression on her face resembled a five-year-old who'd been forced to admit they'd broken their mother's favorite vase.

From her little girl pouted lips she whispered so low I had to lean closer to catch her words. "I've been bad."

"Speak up," Dorcus barked and roughly patted her sister's shoulder. "Go ahead. The sooner you get this over, the sooner your positive karma will be restored."

Rose hiccuped. "I took those things from the store." Her eyes downcast, she pointed to the cardboard box she'd brought me. It was sealed with tape. "I didn't pay for them."

Dorcus looked smug. "Very good, Rose." To me, she said, "She's been stealing things from THE ALABASTER since we discovered Jasper's treasure trove of spiritually powerful stones. It explains why she hasn't been well."

Talk about awkward. "Thanks for returning them."

"I'll understand if you feel the need to prosecute, but . . ." Dorcus left the words hanging.

Rose's face blanched to the color of past-dated cottage cheese.

"No," I said. "That won't be necessary. No real harm done."

"Rose. Say thank you."

"Thank you," she mumbled.

"And?" Dorcus sounded even more impatient.

"And I promise not to take anything ever again."

"Let's just forget about it," I said in a rush, thankful for the first time that I didn't have siblings. "I hate to hurry you, but I need to get to the bank."

"Very well. One last thing. Jasper is worried about you. Now that Colin's gone, he's afraid you'll be lonely. So I've brought you a special present." She smiled. "Two presents."

"That wasn't necessary," I said and noticed Rose had wandered closer to the exit, her part now played.

"Nonsense." Dorcus put her hand on the second box. "Open it."

The side flaps of this box had been tucked under each other to form a temporary lid. I peaked inside to see two long-haired kittens nestled in one corner. One orange and the other coal black.

"Oh," escaped my lips. "They're so cute."

"They should help with the rat problem."

I scooped both kittens from the box, cradled them to my chest and caressed their soft fur. They purred and I felt my heart melt even though I'd never been fond of cats. "They're too little to catch rats."

"They'll grow. Mind you, they've had their first set of shots. They'll need another round next month. The vet needed monikers so I consulted Jasper's spirit and we've named them Onyx and Carnelian."

"Which is which?" I asked.

Dorcus straightened her back and looked down her nose at me like I'd disappointed her. "Isn't it obvious?"

When I didn't answer, she said, "You need to learn your rocks if you want this to remain a successful business." She fanned her face as a blush of red crawled up from her collar. "I can't imagine why Jasper insists you're the perfect person to run the store."

She shivered, stared blankly into the air and started to keen like a bad ghostly soundtrack for a low budget horror film. Was she having a stroke? Or another vision? Either, or, she seriously needed help.

I glanced at Rose. She'd stopped in front of a display of pink colored quartz. Rose watched her sister's back, the expression on her face unreadable. Her upper teeth bit down on her lower lip for a moment before sliding into a sly smile. She reached out and her fingers caressed a smooth polished piece of what I remembered Jacob had called rose quartz. How fitting.

Then she caught my eye and jerked back her hand back as if it'd been scorched by corrosive acid. She blushed and hurried out the front door.

Dorcus had stopped her warble and looked like she was having a silent argument with the air, or perhaps her spirit guide. Her eyes narrowed. Went wide. Rolled. And with a final shake of her head, she said, "The black one is Onyx."

Not sure what that was all about. I held up the kittens to my face. "Hello, Onyx. Hello, Carnelian." Onyx licked my nose. It tickled.

I gently put them back in the box. "I'll find a better bed for you little guys, but for now this will have to do." The two kittens curled into a black and orange ball and went to sleep.

"Mind you, they're box-trained. You'll need to get them food, a scratching post, kitty litter and the rest."

"Thank you so much for the kittens," I said and meant it, but as much as I'd appreciate the cats, I needed to get to the bank. I headed for the door, hoping she'd take the hint and leave. Impulsively I picked the polished piece of rose quartz that had captured Rose's attention. "Give this to your sister."

Dorcus beamed. "It's working. The karma coach was right. Already my Rose's luck is changing."

She left and I went in search of Jacob, taking the cereal box with me. I wasn't letting it out of my sight until it was stowed in a lockbox at the bank. The kittens were asleep. I heard motors running and tracked him to the workroom that housed the rock equipment. He sat on a stool wearing a dark blue oilcloth apron over his clothes and a pair of safety glasses. He held a rock to a spinning grinding wheel and didn't hear me come in.

"Jacob!"

He shut off the machine and slipped off the glasses. "Just making a cab out of Ralph's alabaster to see how it'd look while you visited with the ladies." He held up a creamy white stone shaped into a dome-topped oval with a flat back.

"That's a cab? I thought it was alabaster."

"It's both. Cab is short for cabochon and describes the type of shape. Not the rock. Cabs are for setting in jewelry."

"It's a good thing I hired you," I said, smiling. "Or I'd be totally lost. As soon as I can afford it, you'll be getting a raise and I'd like to hire you to teach me everything you know about the rocks."

He beamed. "Here are some polished chunks of alabaster. After I saw how you put the quartz together in one place, I thought you might like a section for just alabaster since it's the name of the store."

"Awesome idea. In fact, I think it's a great way to organize the whole store. By rock types and it'll help me sort out what's what."

He took off the apron.

"I have to run some errands," I said. "And I need you to keep an eye on Onyx and Carnelian. They're the store's new night guards, compliments of Dorcus."

He looked in the box and reached in to scratch both kittens behind their ears. Carnelian opened one eye and batted his hand. "Sharp claws."

"Good for catching rats when they get a little bigger. Hope you don't mind cat sitting until I get back. Make sure they don't slip outside until they know this is home."

"No problem." Jacob dangled a strip of shredded paper over the box. The orange kitten attacked, leaping up and swatting at the new toy. He tumbled back onto Onyx and soon both kittens were tumbling in mock battle. Jacob looked at me and winked. "I think I can manage the stress."

"If they nap," I said. "Think you could start sorting out the rocks by type?"

"Sure."

"We can start arranging them on the shelves when I get back. We'll keep the more expensive ones near the cash register where we can keep an eye on them. Who knows, maybe we'll be open for business by the end of next week."

That is if I can solve the murders, I thought.

Back in the apartment I showered and put on fresh clothes. I took the cereal box into the bathroom with me. Once my shopping list was complete, I settled down to read Flint's letters one last time. I wanted to memorize the details before putting them in a safety deposit box at the bank.

After what had happened to Jasper and Colin, it wasn't a stretch to conclude that Flint had been murdered by one of his comrades during the war. Why? Probably because Flint threatened to blow the whistle and expose the atrocities his unit had committed. Obviously, Jasper and Colin had both figured out whom, from the letters. If they could, so would I. But I'd hedge my bet and not confront the killer. I'd gather the evidence and when I had an ironclad case, I'd hand it over to Stone.

First I'd try to identify the players: *Sawbones, the Sergeant Major, the captain and Peacemaker.* I'd already surmised Doc Shore was the medic. The only man in the unit Flint could trust. I'd give him a call and use the excuse I was trying to piece together my family history because no one in my family would talk about my uncles.

I pulled out my cell and punched in his number.

CHAPTER TWENTY-NINE

My errands took longer than expected. I'd stopped at the library for a quick research session on Flint's unit and didn't get back to the store until almost two-thirty. My mind was reeling with what I'd found out. The military insignia carved into THE ALABASTER paperweight matched the one assigned to an elite unit called Tiger Force that carried out missions in the Quang Ngai province of Vietnam. Like Flint's letter had intimated, it operated under the radar and committed the longest series of atrocities of the war—seven months of *murder, rape, and mutilation.*

I read several first-hand accounts that described the unit as ghost soldiers. They'd appear and disappear *like the mist.* They didn't wear dog tags and the only insignias on their uniforms were *jump wings and Mekong scout badges.* No names, no rank, no country affiliation. They had the highest VC kill rate of the war because they killed unarmed civilians, the elderly and children. To disguise their crimes they'd often arrange the bodies in a circle with the heads in the center and explode a grenade to cover-up what they'd done. Then they'd plant weapons near the corpses and move on to another village.

It was strange that I'd never heard about any of it. Every high school student in America has studied the Vietnam War and about the Mai Lai

Massacre in which American soldiers were court-martialed for war crimes. It was shocking to learn that Mai Lai wasn't the isolated incident I'd been taught. That in reality, it was just the proverbial tip and the truth was hidden under the endless casualty counts of American soldiers.

The heinous crimes of the eighteen members of the Tiger Force went unreported. Why? In hindsight, it's obvious. Their actions were ordered, sanctioned and deemed necessary by our government. Making them political ghosts who'd never be prosecuted.

So why would a member of that elite force kill to keep their participation a secret? It didn't make sense. I'd found one website that listed names. It's not like their identities were truly secret. Unless, it was Flint's death that put them in jeopardy.

I tried to fit the pieces together as I looked at what Jacob had accomplished in my absence.

All in all, the store looked great. Most of the clutter had disappeared into a pile of big plastic bags in the storage area. He'd wiped down the majority of shelves and dusted the merchandise. The rocks still needed to be organized, but the store looked like it had potential to become a money-maker.

The kittens were on a rest break, curled on a bottom shelf in a heap of dust rags. I reached down and gave them a tickle, expecting them to be happy to see me. Onyx stretched and Carnelian opened one lazy eye before closing it again with feline indifference. I felt a pang.

"I have kitty treats and toys," I said to coax them. Like they cared.

"What did you bring for me?" Jacob said, laughing.

I handed him a form. "You're officially on the payroll. You need to fill this out for the accountant."

His face lit up.

"Minimum wage to start. If business improves we can talk about a raise in six months. Okay?"

"Sure."

"Did I get any calls?" I was disappointed Doc hadn't called back on my cell and I was hoping he'd tried the landline.

"Nope."

I tried his number again and left a message to call me. While running around I'd decided it'd be smarter to wait until I talked to him before I stirred any potential vipers' nest. I didn't want to end up like Jasper and Colin. Plus I wanted their killer brought to justice. I'd hold off on further investigation until I had a chance to question Doc about Flint's death. I needed facts before jumping to the wrong conclusions.

And the store needed my attention.

I felt a little guilty that Jacob had done the lion's share of the work and it was my business.

"Why don't you take a break?" I told him.

"If you don't mind," he said. "I'd like to cut and polish some more alabaster. It works up really fast."

"Go for it. I'll finish up out here."

He went back to the cutting workshop.

I grabbed some cleaning supplies and set to work on the last aisle. It took almost an hour, but I was pleased when I wiped down the last shelf. Some of the stones were gorgeous minus the thick coating of grime. You didn't even have to like rocks to appreciate their beauty. One piece in particular I loved. It was a dark gray polished piece the size of a flattened lemon. When you moved it under the light, a flash of blue danced on its smoothed surface.

Jacob came back into the store.

"Good timing. What's this?" I asked, holding it up.

"Labradorite. You have more over there. Want me to put it with the other pieces?

"That's okay. I'll take care of it."

It dawned on me that if I was going to run a successful rock business, I'd have to become legit and start my own collection. I set the Labradorite piece behind the counter.

"How about I sweep before I leave?" he said.

"Sounds good, and I'll tackle the windows."

"I'll get you a ladder."

Jacob was turning out to be the real gem of the store. Once I figured out the cash flow of the place, I'd move up his raise.

The store had tall ceilings, at least twelve feet high. The windows were about eight feet high, ten feet wide. Six of them. They ran across the front wall and would let in a lot more light once they were cleaned. I swept down cobwebs, humming as I worked.

Jacob asked, "You want me to unpack Rose's box?"

"Sure. Just put the stuff on the counter."

The kittens came alive. Their nap had supercharged them, transforming them from sweet innocent kittens into covert attack cats. A sharp race of needle-like pricks shot up the back of my leg.

"Ooow!" I yelped and stepped down from the ladder.

Soft warm fur tickled my neck and I felt a nip on my earlobe.

"You little toot," I said and pulled Onyx from my shoulder. His nails snagged my T-shirt. I tried to cradle him like a baby to sooth him, but he was having none of it. He was in fight mode and attacked my hand like it was the enemy.

I carried him to the front counter and set him on the glass. Carnelian was at my feet engaged in batting a slip of paper. She abandoned the receipt and launched into action. With the heart of a lightning bolt, she scaled my leg, jumped onto the counter to face her brother. Standing on her hind feet like a super ninja and her front paws spread wide she struck. The two rolled tail-over-tail and plowed into a little carved dinosaur. It toppled on its side.

"No playing on the merchandise," I said, scooping up the kittens and setting them on the floor before they broke something. I shook my finger at them. "If you're going to be in the store you, have to behave."

Inwardly I shuddered. I sounded like Dorcus.

Speaking of which, I looked at the items on the counter. "Is this the stuff Rose brought back?"

Jacob walked over. "Yeah. She didn't take anything too valuable."

I picked up the little dinosaur and set it on its feet next to a petite cluster of quartz crystals, feeling pleased with myself because I could identify the specimen. There was a piece of Labradorite similar the one I'd decided to keep, only smaller.

"Looks better in the sun," he said.

I walked over to the window. The sky had grown darker. Inside the room had, too. I flipped on the overhead lights.

"Mine's nicer," I said and went back to looking at the items.

That's when I spotted Tamara's missing carved paperweight. My first impulse was to call her to tell her I'd found it, and then I remembered. It wasn't hers, but her grandfather's. I picked it up. THE ALABASTER felt cold in my hand. I ran a finger over the fierce-tiger carving relief. It was attractive but at the same time primitive. I could see why the girl had thought it might be a valuable relic.

How old was it? Who had carved it? A warrior? Or a witch doctor, to ward off evil? That was ridiculous when I considered the second carving on the bottom. The one Tamara had thought was an ice cream cone with wings. The same design I'd seen tattooed on Ralph's shoulder. The one he'd been so protective of. A shiver ran down my spine. My heart started to speed up and I flipped the paperweight.

As I examined the winged military insignia carved into the bottom I had the strange feeling that this was the key to the murders.

Was this what the intruder had been searching for? Along with the letters? Was I holding the one solid piece of evidence that lead to Jasper's murderer?

It hit me. Suddenly everything made sense. I knew why Jasper was killed. Why Colin's blackmail attempt had backfired and why he too was murdered. Why my uncle Flint had died at the hands of a comrade. All three men sacrificed to keep another man's deadly secret.

And I knew, who's secret it was. My heart felt the punch of betrayal.

"Allie, are you okay?" Jacob asked. "You don't look so good."

I didn't feel good. A sick dread washed over me at the thought of what I had to do. I berated myself for being so gullible. I was supposed to be sharper than that. And I felt sad because I truly liked the man I had to expose.

A weak "no" escaped my lips. I still didn't want to believe the truth, but the evidence stared me straight in the face. For the first time, I realized what it was like to be personally involved in a murder investigation. All my experience as a prosecutor didn't prepare me for this. I understood now why family and friends were reluctant to give evidence. It wasn't because they wanted to lie to the police. They just couldn't believe the truth.

I wished I'd been jumping to conclusions, but I knew I wasn't.

"Thanks for all your help. Let's call it day." I pointed to a calendar hanging next to the filing cabinet. "This is your time card. Just write your hours down at the end of each day."

As soon as Jacob left, I went back to the apartment clutching the carved alabaster orb in my hand. This is what Tamara had been looking for. The kittens rode on my shoulders. I showed them their litter box and fed them. After they settled down for a nap on my lap while I tried to decide the best course of action. I still hadn't identified Peacemaker and now that I had the paperweight I wasn't sure it mattered. I knew the identity of the captain.

If I could just talk to Doc.

As Flint's only real friend, he'd have to tell me the truth about what happened in Vietnam. It was one thing to keep silent about what Carl had done during the war. I wasn't naive. I realized things happened in combat. The stress of the battlefield. Snap judgments of life and death. Regrettable mistakes made. All that. But Jasper and Colin's deaths didn't fit the category. They were cold-blooded murders.

I knew what I had to do. I'd try Doc one last time.

He still didn't answer. This time I left a longer message. "Doc, I really need to talk to you. I think I know who killed Jasper and Colin. I need your input before I lay I it out to Stone. Please call me A.S.A.P."

I started pacing. My stomach growled, but I was too agitated to eat. I'd wait five more minutes and go on to Plan B. Just in case I was repeating family history I pulled out a sheet of paper and wrote a detailed report of my suspicions and what I was about to do. I found an envelope and addressed it to *From Here to Eternity* and penned a short note to Sara to deliver it to Stone if I disappeared or was murdered. I found a stamp and went out to mail it.

The phone was ringing when I came back. I rushed to answer it.

"Hello?"

"You called?" It was Doc's voice. The sound of an engine roared in the background.

"Yeah," I said, breathing a sigh of relief. "You're kind of breaking up."

"That's 'cause I'm calling from twenty thousand feet. I'm flying over Tucson as we speak. Not sure of how long the connection will last."

"Then I'll make it quick. I read Flint's letters. Who was Peacemaker?"

"He died three months after Flint. Stepped on a landmine."

"And the captain was?" I wanted confirmation.

"Carl. Later he was promoted to colonel."

"He killed Jasper," I said. "I have the evidence."

"Don't confront . . . might be dangerous. . . " He was breaking up. I didn't catch what he said next.

The connection died.

It was enough and there was no point in delaying what I had to do. Wanted to do. Confront Carl face-to-face and ask how he could kill a friend in cold blood. After, I'd call Stone and deliver the suspect.

Carl wouldn't kill me. There'd be no point. I had insurance. Doc already knew my suspicions. That I'd written a letter to be opened in the case of my untimely death. That I had Flint's letters.

I picked up the landline.

I didn't want to make this next call, but I had to.

CHAPTER THIRTY

I clutched THE ALABASTER paperweight. It felt heavy in my hand as I waited for Alex to pick up. If our last conversation had seemed awkward, this one would require a new adjective. Knowing how he worshiped his uncle, he'd never be able to forgive me for exposing the ugly truth. It saddened me. While I didn't want to jump into a relationship with him, a secret part of me had been hoping it might be possible in the future. Once I was truly on my feet and he realized I wasn't a helpless female and could take care of myself.

"Allie?" he said when he answered. His voice caressed my name. "Change your mind about another dinner date?"

I was tempted to lie to him, but I knew firsthand how lies destroyed faith.

"Actually . . ." I couldn't think of a tactful way to say it, so I went into my fallback lawyer-mode. "It's more serious than that. I'm sorry. I think your uncle murdered my uncle. And Colin. "

"What? Are you crazy?" His voice was no longer in caress-mode.

"No. I wish I were, but I have evidence. I wanted to tell you first before I confronted him."

"Where is this nonsense coming from?"

I did a quick rundown of what I knew and what I had guessed. I told him everything. About the letters. About the paperweight. About how the two linked Carl to Tiger Force and the atrocities that were committed under his command.

"You're sure?" His voice sounded resigned. "Absolutely, positively sure?"

"I'm sorry. What this will do to you. To Ming and Tamara. I feel bad. I like him, but it doesn't change the truth. Or what he's done."

"Let me talk to him first. Please? He won't lie to me. I promise to call Stone."

"No. I need to do this. To know why after all these years he killed an old friend."

Silence.

"Alex?"

"I can't let you," he finally said. "I owe him so much. He's been a father to me. Let me talk to him first."

"Why? So you can warn him of his right to remain silent?"

"Damn it, Allie. He knows his rights."

The connection cut.

"Shit!" I was in such a hurry that I grabbed my keys and was backing my car out of its parking space when I realized I didn't have a clue where Carl lived. Double, double, toil and trouble shit.

Sara hadn't left even though it was after closing time. The sky had turned dusky. And in my agitation, I noticed the red cliffs above town were now a darkish brown like dried blood.

I jumped out of the car and raced to her door. She was locking up and coming out.

"Do you know where Carl Morton lives?" I asked.

"Up in the Coffee Pot Subdivision," she said and pointed over the rooftop toward the cliffs. "It's named for the Coffee Pot Rock. See it? "

There it stood, over two thousand feet high. A monolith shaped like a percolator style coffee pot complete with a spout overlooking west Sedona. Grayish white rock resembled a lid and the orange-red sand-stone served as the pot. To complete the illusion, a wispy white cloud hovered over the spout. I couldn't believe I'd totally missed seeing it earlier. But then I'd only been in town a short while and I'd been consumed with my inheritance, my new partner, Alex and the murders.

"His house is just beyond the intersection of Coffee Pot Drive and Maxwell House. You can't miss it. It's huge. A red stucco split-level home with a fabulous cacti garden and a huge Hopi sculpture made of copper, brass and turquoise colored tiles. The place has a great view."

"How do I get there?"

"Take a left at the second light and drive to the top."

Alex's BMW was parked out front. He'd beat me there, but then he didn't have to stop for directions.

I made my way up the winding walk to the front door. The window was open and I could hear Carl and Alex arguing. Actually, it was more like Alex using courtroom tactics and Carl trying to dial his nephew down a notch.

"What were you thinking?" Alex said. "Keeping a war trophy that exposes your part in the war."

"It's not a trophy. It's a reminder. I regret the part I played for Uncle Sam, but I'd been conditioned to take and give orders for the greater good. If I had to do it all over again, I'd have holed up in Jerome on the hill."

"You don't mean that. You were a decorated soldier. A colonel and a war hero for God's sake."

"God had no part in that war." Carl coughed. "In Nuremberg, lesser men were tried as war criminals for following orders."

An awkward silence followed his words.

I had the creeping realization that I was about to hear solid evidence that Stone couldn't ignore. I pulled out my cell and dialed THE ALABASTER. Jasper's recorded voice sounded like a sage's omen. "If you bite the bullet, you'll pass lead." I waited for the proverbial beep. Thank god the answering machine wouldn't cut off until the tape did. Stepping off the walk and crouching low, I sidled up to the open window and set the phone on the sill.

Carl coughed again.

"I can't believe you tortured and killed innocent civilians," Alex said.

"I didn't, but I stood by while my men did. I'm not proud of it. Only one soldier was horrified about what was going on."

"Jasper's brother?"

"How did you know that?" Carl said.

"Allie called me. She says she has Flint's letters. He wrote he was about to blow the whistle on the unit. Then he died. She thinks a soldier in the unit murdered him."

"That's not what happened. We walked into an ambush. We were both shot-up. In spite of Doc's efforts, Flint didn't make it home."

"That's not what she thinks. She thinks it was an American bullet that killed him. She suspects that Jasper came to you for the truth about Flint's death."

"What are you suggesting? That I killed Jasper to keep my war years a secret?"

"She wants answers. She won't give up until she has the truth."

He was right. I wouldn't.

"Did you say Allie has the paperweight?" Carl asked.

"You're missing the point. She thinks you're responsible for Jasper's death."

"I didn't kill him. I'll call her. She's reasonable. Tell her I'd like the paperweight returned."

"Why?" The disbelief in Alex's voice was palpable. He sounded like he was as rattled as I was.

Carl sighed. "It reminds me of the potential for evil in every man." Pause. "And I played a part. I looked the other way while my soldiers committed atrocities."

"It wasn't your fault."

"That's what I told myself. Because at the time I wanted to believe our unit's covert activities would save American lives. Would win the war."

My mouth went dry. If Carl hadn't killed Flint, then why murder Jasper? Or Colin? I'd been so sure the paperweight had been the catalyst. It was time for my entrance. I reached for the doorknob with one hand, the doorbell with the other.

"Oh God," said Alex. The two short words sounded like they'd been ripped from his soul.

I froze, my fingers becoming one with the warm brass orb in my hand.

"I've made a terrible mistake." Pure anguish. "It was an accident."

"What do you mean?" Carl asked.

I craned closer, tense and confused.

"Don't move," a voice whispered.

Something round, cold and metal pressed into the back of my neck. A gun barrel? I froze. A man's hand snaked around my waist.

He pushed me forward.

"Time to join the party," he said.

CHAPTER THIRTY-ONE

The man behind me kept the gun pressed into the back of my neck. The strong Old Spice aftershave left little mystery as to his identity. Its cloying scent almost anesthetized me and filled me with equal parts of shock, nausea and disappointment.

Now I knew the identity of the bastard who'd taken Jasper's life, Colin's and probably countless others.

It wasn't Carl.

It wasn't a random thief in the night.

It was the one man Flint had trusted. A killing-chameleon disguised as a human being. The good army medic who'd had his back.

The gun shifted to just under my jaw.

Doc roughly reached around me for the front door knob. It swung open on well-oiled hinges. He jerked me close and his heartbeat thudded into my back. Mine tried to leap out of my chest locked in a race of life and death.-He shoved the gun harder into the soft tissue under my jaw, his hot breath searing my ear. If I survived, I'd have my own distorted purple-heart bruise for bragging rights.

"Move." Clutching me even tighter, he duck-walked me over the threshold.

I stumbled, my hope clattering onto the beige tiles. Crunched under his size eleven Nikes.

We paused in the open entry hall. Carl's and Alex's heated discussion drifted through the wide arch leading to the front room.

Doc pushed the door shut with a backward kick of his foot.

"Are you going to behave yourself?" he asked.

I nodded.

"See that you do. I'd hate to splatter blood and gore all over Carl's nice home." He released his grip. The gun barrel traced a path to the center of my back, leaving a prickling memory-path in its wake.

I shivered.

He took a small step back. I no longer felt the barrel pressed into my skin, but knew it still hovered close enough to leave powder burns. Close enough, even with a small caliber bullet, to kill.

Doc tapped my shoulder. "Time to make our entrance."

My stomach flip-flopped. Maybe Carl could talk some sense into his old friend. Or perhaps Alex, a generation younger, could get the drop on Doc. I had no choice at the moment. I did what Doc ordered and forced my leaden feet to work.

We moved through the arched doorway and stepped down into the sunken room. Part of me noted the unique Asian décor, but I was too jittery to appreciate the ambiance. Neither Alex nor Carl noticed our entrance.

Carl sat at his dark walnut and abalone inlaid desk. He leaned forward, his head in his hand as if he could somehow massage away the memories.

His skin had taken on a grayish pallor and he sounded exhausted. "Alex, it's all a matter of public record if one knows where to look."

"Doc said if it came out, you'd go to jail for the rest of your life."

"For a smart lawyer, Doc sure played you."

"What do mean, he played me?"

"The government would never charge us. Because it would force them to reveal their own dirty little secrets."

"But that could ruin your reputation."

Carl shook his head. "No. It'd just be some bad press until the next scandal came along."

"But Doc said—"

"Ahhhhemmm," Doc said, grabbing the two men's attention. "Hope you don't mind Allie and I dropped in for a confab."

"Allie, I told you not to come," Alex said. "That I'd take care of everything."

Carl eyes lit up when he saw me. "Did you bring my paperweight?" Then he frowned when he saw the gun in Doc's hand.

"Doc?" Carl said, disbelief crawling up his paling face. "What are you doing?"

Doc kept the gun trained on my chest and motioned for me to move next to Carl and Alex. I couldn't stop myself from glancing at the window and instantly regretted it. Please, don't let him spot my phone on the sill.

"It's my show," Doc said. "Allie was nice enough to let me know she was coming here with the paperweight. Where is it? I want it." The click of the trigger seemed to echo in the closed room. "Now."

Carl stood, stumbled and abruptly plopped back in his desk chair. It rolled back a few inches. "It's not yours to take, Doc."

"Like hell it isn't," Doc said. The gun alternated its aim between Carl and me. "If I'd known it existed, I'd have gotten rid of it years ago. It exposes us." Doc nodded to me. "You have a choice, Allie. Hand it over. Or?"

Or what? Was he threatening to shoot Carl and Alex as well as me? I couldn't let that happen.

"It's here," I said, holding up my purse. To my chagrin, my voice quivered. "It's in my bag."

"Alex. Retrieve it from her purse."

Alex took my bag, and pulled out the infamous war relic. A white tiger head carved on an alabaster orb. He set it on the desk in front of Carl.

"Bring it to me." Doc pulled a handful of black plastic zip ties from his front pocket. "Restrain her, hands and feet."

"He'll do nothing of the kind," Carl said. His voice sounded strong and I could imagine him leading a troop of men into battle.

"He will. He's already in too deep to pull out now."

Carl groaned and grabbed his left arm. "Ohhh. What did you do, Alex?"

Alex and Doc spoke at the same time, their words tripping over each others.

"It was an accident," Alex said.

"He stabbed Jasper to save your sorry ass," Doc said.

My mouth went dry. No. Not Alex. I stared at him disbelieving. His eyes looked anguished, brimming with regret.

Carl's face blanched as he cast a disillusioned glance at his nephew. His hand jerked to his chest and he panted out the words. "Alex. Tell me he's lying."

Alex's words spilled out in a guilty rush like a man in a confessional. "Doc said Jasper had the paperweight and Flint's letters. Together they'd prove a case against you and that there's no statute of limitations on war crimes. I couldn't let you be sent to jail for the rest of your life. Not after all you've done for me." He gulped a ragged breath. "Jasper was off on a rock hunting adventure. It was the perfect opportunity to retrieve the damning evidence."

"Why would you think a paperweight I carved would lead to my incarceration?"

"Because of one of Flint's letter. It identified you. Carving it."

Carl shook his head, slumping even lower. "Why didn't you come to me? Why listen to Doc's lies?"

"Because I owe you everything," Alex said. "You've been a father to me. Educated me. Took me in as a partner. This was something I could do for you."

Carl's breath became more labored. Couldn't Doc see that his old friend needed medical attention?

"Call an ambulance. He's having a heart attack," I said.

All three men ignored me. I had to do something. Grabbing the landline on Carl's desk would be suicide. That left my phone on the window ledge only a few feet away from where I stood. Could I get it and punch in 9-1-1? I eased a centimeter to my right.

"Jasper wasn't supposed to be there," Alex went on. "He came in with a knife and startled me. I didn't recognize him. I thought an intruder had broken in. We grappled. I fought back." His voice choked. "It was an accident, I didn't mean to kill him. I called Doc to see if he could save him. He came, but it was too late. Jasper was already dead. I'd killed him. I should have called Stone, but then it would have all come out."

"How touchingly naïve." Doc chuckled. "My boy, he was still alive when I got there. Why do you think I sent you away?"

"What?" Alex cried.

"Jasper's death was a convenient necessity. Like his big brother Flint's, I helped both men move on to eternity. Do you have any idea how it feels to be a god? To hold a man's life in your hands? To decide who lives and who dies? I do it every day."

I stared at him, my mouth open.

He turned his smile on me, but didn't seem to notice that I had made steady progress toward the window.

"I'm afraid Jasper's little niece is next."

"For god's sake . . ." Carl wheezed, coughed. A splotch of blood dribbled onto his lower lip, its bright red color in sharp contrast to his pallor. "Stop this nonsense. Enough innocents have died." He slumped into his chair.

I grabbed for the phone, but Doc was faster. He snatched it, striking out like the snake he'd become.

"You won't be needing this, Missy," he said and pocketed it.

"Carl needs help," I said. "He needs to get to a hospital."

"Too late for that now. My old friend has become a liability."

"I don't know why I listened to you. You're a monster." Alex lunged at Doc and at the same time yelled, "Allie, run!"

I hesitated. I wanted to stay and help Carl, but what could I do? I went for the phone on the desk. At the same moment, Alex slammed into Doc's side and the two went down taking the phone with them, ripping its connection from the wall.

"Get out of here." Alex's voice was muffled, but the message clear.

There had to be another phone in the house. Where? The kitchen? The master bedroom? Adrenalin pushed me down the hall, stopping at every doorway, scanning each room for a phone. Seeing none. Moving on.

Crashes came from the front room followed by a loud gunshot.

Silence.

Then a voice called out. "Allie, I'm coming to get you. Don't run. It'll only prolong the agony."

I risked a glance back. The hall was still empty.

Flinging open the last door along the long hallway, I slipped inside. Instead of a room, I found myself at the top of a steep stairway that led down to a black darkness. There was no option but to descend.

Would I find an escape to freedom?

Or would I be snared like a rat in a dank dark maze with no exit?

CHAPTER THIRTY-TWO

I had to decide. Quick. Hide in the dark, or turn on the light for a speedy run down the stairs? Speed won, and I flipped on the light switch at the top. Taking two steps at a time, I reached the little landing where the stairs switched-back for the final decent.

Overhead I could hear doors slamming at intervals and Doc's muttered curses.

It sounded like he'd proceeded about halfway down the hall. Halfway to my door? I gulped in cold air and tried to still my audible panting. Breathe deep. Breathe slow. Breathe silence.

He took his time to search each room before moving on to the next. Awarding me precious time to hide. Every second of my freedom meant a greater chance of Carl's survival and possibly Alex's. That is if Doc hadn't fired a fatal shot. But then again, maybe his methodical search meant the other Carl and Alex were already dead.

Bile rose in my throat and I pushed it down. Swallowing hard, I pressed on. At the bottom of the steps I spotted another set of light switches and flipped both. The upper stairway went dark, and the room was illuminated. I speed inventoried my escape options. They weren't great.

I didn't see another exit. The only windows were a row of narrow six-inch rectangular-shaped panes running the length of one wall. The room had a pool table. Dartboard. A bar stocked with liquor. A full wine rack. A refrigerator. A round card-table surrounded by chairs. An over-stuffed leather couch lounged in front of a giant wide screen TV.

I was trapped in a man cave with no credible hiding place or escape route, except to return up the stairs into the arms of a killer. I grabbed three darts from the bulls-eye and a pool stick from a rack on the wall. Then running around like a crazed woman, I started smashing lights. One by one until the room was plunged into darkness.

The door opened overhead, and I scrambled under the pool table clutching my pathetic MacGyver weapons.

The light came on above the stairwell landing. It didn't light up the room but instead cast eerie shadows.

Slow, deliberate footfalls descended the stairs. His voice preceded him. "I know you're down here, Allie. I can smell your fear. It's intoxicating."

I hunched into a tight ball under the table, facing the stairs. I willed myself to stop breathing. Pulled the cue back.

"I didn't want to have to kill you. I thought you might be different. But no, you're just like the rest of your family. Never letting go. You all had to find the truth. The whole truth. And expose it, regardless of the people you'd destroy. You. Flint. Jasper. Colin. You're all cut from the same cloth. But you're proving to be the most difficult to kill."

Doc knew Colin was Flint's son?

He reached the bottom of the stairs, his feet fully visible from the knees down. I inched back into the protective shadow of the table.

"A crazy genetic trait. You all contacted me with your suspicions. I have to admit Colin's blackmail demand fooled me at first until I realized he was Flint's son. Then it all slipped into place."

How did he find out? Did Colin tell him?

"I have my own version of the truth. I wasn't about to let him destroy my good reputation. I'm curious. What did you do with the gun?" He stepped into the room, using his phone for a flashlight."

My heart hammered even harder.

"I gave that gun to Ralph, thinking it as a kind of insurance. When he told me he'd given it to Jasper, I was furious. Upped his meds. But then .

. ." His feet crunched on a patch of broken glass. "It made you the perfect patsy to frame for Colin's murder. Your public threat to kill him sealed the deal." He coughed. "I really am curious. What did you do with it? Stone should have found it in the glove box. He's a competent officer."

A shiver of terror prickled my skin. The fact he was telling me all, confessing everything, made one thing crystal clear. He didn't plan to let me live.

"I want the letters." He moved closer to my hiding place. "Now where would I try to hide if I were you?"

I gripped the pool stick tighter, my fingertips numb. I prayed the heartbeats thudding in my chest didn't give away my location. In horror, I watched his feet approach and then walk past to the bar. It was my only chance. I swiveled on deadened knees to face his position. Wait. Don't be in too much of a hurry. Hang on until he steps closer.

And then he was there. I lashed out with the pool stick while he was still in motion. Thrust the stick between his feet and used the momentum of my pent-up adrenaline to knock him off balance.

He stumbled and lost his footing. Fell to the floor. I heard the gun smash on the tile. I grabbed a dart and back-scrambled from under the pool table, then ran for the stairs. But he was fast, surprisingly agile for a man in his sixties. He slammed into my side. We both went down.

I kicked free and scuttled up the stairs on my hands and knees. Just short of the landing, he grabbed my right ankle. I still had the dart. Reaching back I stabbed flesh. He howled and let go.

I didn't hesitate. Didn't look back to see where the dart had struck. I flew to my feet and up the last flight of stairs like a phoenix returning to life. I flung open the door. Raced out. Slammed it shut. Locked the dead-bolt from the outside. Breathed a sigh of relief. Doc couldn't get out until the police arrived. And then I smelled the acrid scent of smoke. Its haze billowed in the hall. Was the place on fire?

I had to get to Carl and Alex to see if they were okay. Call the authorities and get them out of the house—if they were still alive.

I sprinted to the front room.

"Crap. Crap. Crap."

Flames danced on the interior wall. Smoke hung thick in the air. I coughed. Carl was slumped at his desk, his face a pasty gray. Alex sprawled on the floor at an awkward angle. He moaned. I checked his pulse. It beat strong. Carl's was faint and irregular. He was in the greatest danger. Thankfully the chair he sat in had wheels.

Leaning over his body and holding him in place, I scooted the chair toward the front door, stopping only to maneuver up the two steps to ground level. Outside it was dark with only a waning moon and street-lights. A few elderly neighbors had come out to gawk. I spotted a familiar face emerging from the gloom.

"Sara! Call 9-1-1."

She ran to me. "It's done. They're on their way."

"Help me get Carl out of the chair."

"What's happened? What caused the fire?" she asked as we lifted his dead weight.

"I don't know," I said. "Stay with him. I need to go back inside for Alex."

I raced back inside pushing the chair. The smoke was thicker. I could hear gunshots from the hall, but I knew Doc's little six-shooter didn't have enough bullets to take out the dead bolt. I imagined him balanced on the top step unable to get a run at the reinforced door. Desperate to force his way out. I felt a little sick.

I coughed and pulled the neck edge of my T-shirt over my mouth. Alex was semi-conscious.

"Allie," he mumbled, his voice laced with pain. "Doc started the fire. Is Carl okay?"

"Let's just get you out of here." It was like I was helping a total stranger. Someone I didn't know. Someone I had no feelings for, but a fellow human being. I don't know how I got him into the chair, but I did. Somehow got him out to safety.

"I loved you," he said. "I'm sorry."

I had nothing to say to him other than, "You're safe. The ambulance will be here soon." I sprinted back to the house.

"Allie!" Sara yelled. "You can't go back in there."

"Doc's still inside," I called over my shoulder.

"Wait for the firemen. They have the right equipment."

"There isn't time." I plunged back into Dante's hell. Hot. Smoke black air. Crackling flames. Doc was a cold-blooded murderer. He killed three members of my family and who knew how many countless others. Still he didn't deserve to die at the stake.

A wall collapsed with a whooshing roar. I dropped to my knees, suddenly and totally disoriented. Was I headed into the house? Or out? Someone grabbed my arm, dragged me. Had Doc escaped? Was he pulling me into his personal hell? I struggled to free myself, sucked in a gasp of heavy smoke and collapsed. My chest hurt and it felt like I was about to drift off to sleep.

My assailant hoisted me onto a shoulder and carried me like a rag doll. I wanted to protest, but couldn't resist his brute strength. The last vestige of my energy had been spent. We burst from the inferno and I gulped in air.

"Relax, you're safe now." I didn't recognize the deep voice, but it sounded comforting. "A shot of oxygen and you'll feel right as rain."

The fireman carried me to the ambulance with the flashing lights in the dark and left me with a paramedic.

"Are Doc and Alex okay?" I asked when I could speak.

"On the way to the hospital. Now it's time to get you fixed up."

I relaxed.

He hooked me up to oxygen and began asking a series of yes-no questions. It would be hours before I felt normal—at least physically. Mentally, I wasn't sure if I'd ever feel normal. Stone chose that moment to arrive on the scene.

"At the center of things again, I see," he said. "Are you okay?"

I nodded.

"Good. You're lucky. What were you thinking going back into a burning building?"

"Doc's still inside."

Stone's jaw tightened. "What went down here tonight?"

The medic interrupted, "She needs another twenty minutes on the oxygen and then should go to the clinic for a total check up."

"I don't want to go to the hospital," I said. "I'll be fine."

"At least finish the breathing treatment," he said.

"No. I want this off my chest now." I pulled the plastic tubing from my face.

"Can we have a little privacy?" Stone said.

The medic reluctantly stepped away.

I launched through the events of the evening. Once I started talking, I couldn't stop myself. I spilled it all. Everything. All about Flint's letters. The significance of the paperweight. How Carl had carved it during the war. How it linked the unit to war atrocities. Which in turned indirectly connected Doc to Tiger Force. Something he desperately wanted kept secret. I told Stone about Colin's blackmail attempt and our being cousins. Doc's treachery. The only thing I left out was the gun in the wall at the Eagle Inn. This was Stone I was dealing with. There was a limit to my confession.

He scowled at me. "This does not sound like the Doc I've known all my life."

"I know it all seems unbelievable, but it's true."

He shook his head, his lips pinched. "You have proof of these allegations?"

I nodded.

He looked doubtful. "Evidence that will stand up in a court of law?"

"Yes."

At that moment a wall of the house exploded and my red Escort took the brunt of the rubble. Irreverently I thought it's a good thing Jasper left me a car in his will.

"Take me to *THE ALABASTER*," I said, "and you'll have all the evidence you'll need."

Five minutes later I played him the tape on Jasper's ancient answering machine, again thankful that my uncle hadn't upgraded to a modern device that only allowed for thirty-second messages. Not every word was clear and crisp, but there was enough to confirm my story. There was more than enough evidence to put Doc away for the rest of his life. And Alex for a ten-to-twenty year sentence.

What surprised me the most is that the tape only ran for twenty-five minutes. It had felt like a lifetime. It ended with what sounded like a simultaneous explosion and Doc's agonized shriek of pain and what could only be horror. Another loud blast and then nothing. I knew Doc's final moments would haunt my dreams forever.

Stone's cell rang. "Stone here." He listened, his face grave. His blue eyes stared at an invisible space in the air. "Thanks for the update."

The phone went back in his pocket. He turned to me. "Carl didn't make it."

A hollow weight pressed at my heart and my eyes watered. I blinked. "And Alex?"

"They medevac'd him to Phoenix. He'll live, but has a severed spinal column. He'll spend the rest of his life as a quadriplegic." He let me digest that before going on. "There's no sign of Doc. Trapped the basement, odds are low he survived. They'll search for his remains as soon as the site is safe."

We sat there in silence for a long while. So much had happened in such a short time. A few weeks ago I'd been given a new lease on life. New friends. The possibility of a meaningful relationship once I'd got myself established. How could Alex have flirted with my feelings after what he'd done? Or had it all been an act? At this point, it didn't matter. We didn't have a future together and never would.

"So," Stone said, shaking me from my reverie.

"I guess you'll want the tape."

He took no move to eject it from the machine. "You know, there are a lot of families that will be ripped apart by Doc's actions."

"What do you mean?"

"Doc was the country coroner. He testified in countless murder trials. Families will be forced to relive their loved one's murders all over again when the cases are retried."

"Why?" I asked and realized the answer before he explained.

"You know every convicted criminal will petition the court for a mistrial." He rubbed his forehead. "Doc's testimony in each will be questioned. I don't mind the extra work, but to drag all those families through it again after they've found peace seems beyond cruel. Do they deserve that? Does it serve justice?"

I thought back to some of my own cases as a prosecutor. The havoc murder brought to the victim's families. Marriages destroyed. Distraught husbands and wives descending into addiction. Displaced children. Abandoned hopes and dreams.

If this all came out, he would continue to destroy lives from the grave.

Stone nodded at the answering machine. "That's the only real hard evidence to convict Doc."

"What are you suggesting?" I asked. Stone's attitude surprised me. I'd assumed he was a by-the-book, straight-arrow kind of cop. "I thought you took an oath to preserve justice. We both did."

"I think perhaps justice has already been served?"

"Do you?"

"After hearing the tape. Its obvious Doc didn't make it." Pause. "Alex will serve a lifetime sentence in a bed or strapped in a wheelchair unable to even perform the minutest task. Death would have been kinder."

As horrible as it was to think of Alex, or any man, trapped in a living-death sentence, it didn't change what he'd done. "He stabbed Jasper," I said.

"In self-defense."

"He left him for dead. That's what I can't forgive."

"But he didn't. He called Doc. Doc killed Jasper. The most the courts would convict him of is aggravated assault during a robbery. Given his condition, I doubt he'd serve a day. They'd commute his sentence."

"And he'd be disbarred."

"You think he's going to practice law now?" He stood and held out his hand. "Just forget I said anything. Give me the tape."

"No. Let me think a minute."

I sat there and weighed the pros and cons. My mind was a jumble of thoughts. I pictured the families affected if this all came out. I thought of Carl. Of Ming and Tamara. What good would come of making every-thing public? Painting Cal as a war criminal?

It all came back to Doc. The monstrous pain he'd cause if those convicted murderers were allowed to appeal based on Doc's association with their cases. Especially when the evidence, minus Doc's testimony, proved their guilt beyond a reasonable doubt. No mother or father, brother or sister, son or daughter should have to relive the horror of a second murder trial.

It was up me to stop Doc's legacy of suffering. He couldn't commit murder ever again, and I wouldn't let him destroy more lives from the grave. Not on my watch. Justice was in my court.

Stone licked his lips.

"The law is the law," I said. "And justice is the law."

"But is this justice?"

Yes. I was confident I'd made the right decision. The players in Flint's, Jasper's and Colin's deaths had come to justice.

I leaned over the answering machine to push the delete button and stopped. Instead, I ejected the tape and slid it into my pocket.

"What are you going to do with that?" he asked.

"With what? I don't know what you're talking about?" I said, thinking I had the insurance I'd need if anybody ever decided to prosecute me for Colin's murder.

There's no statute of limitations on murder!

CHAPTER THIRTY-THREE

I sat in the apartment drinking a cup of coffee. Onyx and Carnelian romped at my feet, attacking my toes. The phone rang. It was the mortuary. Colin's funeral was tomorrow. Mom would arrive in the morning.

"Is there anything special you want him to wear?" the man asked.

"Does it matter?" I said. "It's going to be a closed casket."

"True, but sometimes there's a token, a favorite shirt or something special for the departed to take to eternity."

"I know just the thing," I said.

I went to the bedroom. I still hadn't removed Colin's stuff. I opened the drawer filled with his boxers. I pulled them out and piled them on the dresser top to select the perfect pair—black silk imprinted with shiny red lips. I put them into a nondescript brown paper bag and smiled, thinking he'd like the gesture. It would be my parting gift to him.

Once the boxers were bagged, I headed for the garage out back. My Escort had found a new purpose at the local junkyard. It was time to take Jasper's Javelin for a spin. I drove into the alley. Leaving the engine running, I got out and closed the garage door. Note to self: buy garage door remote.

"Now that's a classic. If you ever want to sell—"

I recognized the voice and turned. "Chief Stone."

He wore his cowboy uniform and tipped his Stetson once he'd caught my eye.

"Just stopped by to let you know it's official. Forensic tests prove that Doc's remains were the ones in Carl's basement."

"Thanks. Then it's officially over?"

He nodded. "I have to ask. Just a matter of curiosity. What made you suspect him as the killer?"

Should I tell him that until the very end the clues all led to Carl? Or should I let him think my detective skills were brilliant? Or just tell him what I'd discovered and let him fill in his own blanks?

"It started with Tamara," I said. "And her fascination with *Pawn Stars*. That was the catalyst."

"I don't see it," he said.

"Let me explain and then you can comment." I fisted my right hand, held it up and popped up my thumb. "One. Tamara thought Carl's paperweight might be a valuable relic and worth gobs of money. So she took it to Jasper."

"Why?"

"To find out what its value so she could surprise her grandfather. Quit interrupting or this is going to take all day. I have things to do."

He gestured with his hand that he was zipping his lips.

"Two." Up went my index finger. "When Jasper saw the paperweight, it triggered an old suspicion about how his brother Flint died in Vietnam. It's possible Flint might have been killed by a fellow soldier. The paperweight provided a new piece to an old painful puzzle. I'm betting he pulled out Flint's letters from the war to see if he could make a connection."

Stone nodded to show he was following me but didn't interrupt again.

"Three. One of the letters focused on the unit's captain that carved on some white rock and looked the other way while his men committed atrocities. Because the paperweight belonged to Carl, Jasper suspected he was the captain from Flint's letters. I don't think Jasper wanted to believe it. Four—"

"Wait."

I held up my hand. "Let me finish. Four. Jasper took his concerns to the one guy his brother Flint had trusted during the war: Doc. Now, this is where it get's muddy. I'm guessing Doc thought he'd convinced my uncle that his suspicions about Flint's death were unfounded— along with Carl's part and the unit's war crimes."

"That's a big assumption leap."

I resisted rolling my eyes at him. "My *assumption* is based on the fact that Doc didn't kill Jasper sooner. Instead, he manipulated Alex into retrieving the letters and the paperweight. If they disappeared, the evidence would disappear, too along with any chance of a belated public scandal. I'm not sure Jasper bought it."

"Because?"

"I think he was looking into Tiger Force. I found a paper written in Jasper's handwriting that listed the unit. His computer disappeared and I'd bet money that a hacker would find Tiger Force in its search history. Then there's the fact he hid the letters so neither Doc nor Alex could find them."

"Along with the paperweight," Stone added, tapping his forefinger to his lips.

I laughed. "No. That was Edna."

Stone frowned. "Edna Kincaid? What does she have to do with this?"

"Nothing, really. It's just that she shoplifted the paperweight from Jasper. That's why no one could find it. The more Doc looked, the more paranoid he became. Five. Doc killed Jasper. Six. Colin found the letters. You know the rest."

He nodded. "Colin couldn't resist trying a little blackmail."

"What's not totally clear or rational is why Doc would kill to preserve his image. The information about Tiger Force is on the web."

"I can answer that one," Stone said. "I did a little digging. He was raised in rural Georgia—one of those places where everyone knows everyone. No record of a father. His mother was the local prostitute. His school files indicated he had it pretty hard. Neglect. Bullying. Fights. At sixteen he joined the army and did well for the first time. When he got out he became a doctor, then county coroner and local philanthropist. Maybe that explains why the community's respect was so important to him and he was afraid to lose it."

I didn't speak for a minute. Instead, I remembered Doc justifying his actions when he'd made me his prisoner. "Or maybe killing made him feel superior—to hold a man's life in his hands. To decide who lived and who died, like he was some God." I shuddered.

"Yeah, well." Stone took off his hat and fiddled with the brim. "He won't hurt anyone ever again. One last thing. I stopped in on Alex. He'd like to see you. To try to explain."

"Okay," I said, making my voice neutral. I knew I'd have to see Alex at some point, but I wasn't ready yet. I needed time to process all that had happened. Time to try and understand his actions. Time to forgive him for the part he'd played in Jasper's death. Time to grieve for all that might have been if Doc hadn't played God.

CHAPTER THIRTY-FOUR

M om and I stood at the gravesite. In the distance, Bell Rock watched like a majestic red sentinel overseeing Colin's interment. The cloudless sky glowed a bright blue. It was early afternoon, but the breeze felt cool in spite of the sunny day. He would be sleeping for all eternity next to Jasper's grave.

"My, Colin had a lot of women friends," Mom whispered, her eyes darting over the gaggle of tear-and-mascara-streaked faces.

"Shhhh, Mom. It's a funeral."

"Don't shush me."

The minister didn't miss a beat, but raised an eyebrow and gave us a sharp look as he finished his final litany. "Ashes to ashes and dust to dust. May Colin Flint Phelps rest in peace."

One by one, mourners moved forward to say their final farewell. Some dropped a handful of dirt on the casket. Others, mostly women who were strangers to me, said their tearful goodbye with a single long-stemmed, blood-red rose.

Patsy came next. She stepped close and clutched my arm. "His aura is fading." She looked at Mom. "You know in spirit we are family. He'd want us to stay connected."

Mom looked uncomfortable, and I was thankful she'd restrained from responding.

"Thanks for coming," I said.

"I'll stop by next week to talk about my space at THE ALABASTER."

Dorcus, Rose and Edna came next, decked in black from their shoes and stockings up to their identical little pillbox hats. Dorcus took charge and grabbed my mother's hand. "Don't worry, Jade. I've been in communication with Jasper. Rest assured he's in a better place. He says he forgives you. Our condolences."

"I—um." It was the first time I'd seen my mother speechless.

"I know what you're thinking. That I'm a crazy old lady. That this is Colin's funeral and I'm confused." Dorcus sniffed. "I'm not. Colin's spirit has already gone to the beyond, but Jasper needs to make peace with you before he can go." She patted Mom's arm. "He says he kept his word. It wasn't him that blabbed. He never told anyone about that night he helped you sneak back in the house when you were fifteen."

Mom's face blanched. "I don't know what you're talking about," she squeaked. I had the feeling that she was lying. Maybe Dorcus did have a connection to the dead.

The three sisters left.

Mom's hand flew to her face and her shoulders began to shake. I thought she was crying and reached to comfort her. To my surprise, she wasn't crying but laughing. She pulled an orange gladiola from the floral spray she had delivered for Colin's funeral and walked to Jasper's grave. She kneeled at the headstone and placed the flower tenderly on the ground.

I felt my eyes prick with tears. Beth appeared at my side, her face a mixture of grief and radiant joy. She embraced me in a tight hug. "It's a boy," she whispered. "A son to carry on Colin's name."

Tears rolled down my cheek.

I STOOD behind the counter and surveyed my store. THE ALABASTER had been open for two weeks and thankfully I was done with the mystery business. For good. I may have solved the crime, but I was no detective.

If I ever came across another dead body in the future, I'd leave it to Stone.

I needed to focus on selling rocks.

Studying the register receipts, it was clear that I wasn't going to get rich quick, but if sales continued on the same path, it would provide a comfortable living.

The bell over the door tinkled and I looked up.

"Hi Ralph."

"Where do you want me to put this here alabaster?" he asked, hefting a large sack.

"On the pile," I said. "When you're done, come back in. I made a batch of chocolate cookies this morning that need eating."

"Roger Wilco." He gave me a grin and went out the door. His sack almost knocked into a man coming in. "'Scuse me."

"Hi," I said, eyeing the man's charcoal gray suit and matching tie. "Can I help you?"

"Are you Alabaster Renault?"

"Yes," I said, experiencing a moment of déjà vu.

He held out his hand. "I'm Harold Marcum, president of the Sedona Chamber of Commerce. I'm sorry I didn't come to see you earlier, but I've been out of town."

"Nice to meet you," I said.

"I'd officially like to invite you to join us."

I smiled.

It was nice to be asked, but I wouldn't accept.

Alex had one thing right. Family loyalty was important and I wasn't about to go against my uncle's wishes to join the Chamber when it promoted what he'd felt was a bunch of New Age mumble jumble. Jasper might not be around to protest, but if I joined, I knew for certain he would disown me from the grave.

ABOUT THE AUTHOR

S. D. Brown lives in Northern California where she and her husband own a rock shop and a gem and mineral museum. She spends her time selling rocks, collecting rocks, traveling and writes when she can find the time.

ACKNOWLEDGMENTS

Thanks to Sue Wyshynski, Jen Sowle, Georgia Salmon, Martha Long-shore and Christine Sackey for all their comments, critiques and encouragement.

A big thank you to B.J. Basset who was there at the beginning

And thanks to my husband who supports my efforts.

97239450R00162

Made in the USA
Columbia, SC
15 June 2018